JONA
BOOK 1

PRINCE OF DREAMS

BY A. CORRIN

All rights reserved. No part of this publication may be reproduced, stored or transmitted in any form or by any means, electronic, mechanical, photocopying, recording, scanning, or otherwise without written permission from the publisher. It is illegal to copy this book, post it to a website, or distribute it by any other means without permission.

This novel is entirely a work of fiction. The names, characters and incidents portrayed in it are the work of the author's imagination. Any resemblance to actual persons, living or dead, events or localities is entirely coincidental.

Credits:
Cover illustration by Eva Soulu–www.evasoulu.com
Interior Illustration by Katie Hofgard
Map by Rengin Tumer–rengintumer.com

Contents

Chapter One: Instant Hero — 1
Chapter Two: I Almost Beat Up a Bully — 15
Chapter Three: The Second Dream — 25
Chapter Four: The Final Dream — 44
Chapter Five: Moving Shadows — 55
Chapter Six: Rankers — 77
Chapter Seven: Fighting Garrett — 85
Chapter Eight: I Meet a Gaggle of Griffins — 105
Chapter Nine: I Make Out with a Monster — 124
Chapter Ten: Meanwhile, Back in Reality — 143
Chapter Eleven: Tree Spirits — 147
Chapter Twelve: I Find Out My Wings Work — 162
Chapter Thirteen: Meanwhile, Back in Reality — 177
Chapter Fourteen: The Worst Vacation Destination Ever — 183
Chapter Fifteen: Peter's Secrets — 196
Chapter Sixteen: I Almost Get Stoned — 212
Chapter Seventeen: Meanwhile, Back in Reality — 227
Chapter Eighteen: Bar Fights are Intense — 234
Chapter Nineteen: A Father-Son Talk — 248
Chapter Twenty: Meanwhile, in the House Next Door — 253
Chapter Twenty-One: Werewolves and Gargoyles — 257
Chapter Twenty-Two: Meanwhile, Back in Reality — 274
Chapter Twenty-Three: I'm an Unlucky Boi — 278
Chapter Twenty-Four: Meanwhile, Back in Reality — 295
Chapter Twenty-Five: Victorious — 301
Chapter Twenty-Six: Bonding Time with Kayle — 318
Epilogue — 329
About the Author — 331

To all of my students with their wide-eyed wonder.
Persevere and one day you, too, will find your wings.

And to all of the friends and family who never stopped
encouraging and believing in me: let's go on an adventure
in the Land of Dreams.

CHAPTER ONE:
INSTANT HERO

At first I thought I was playing football. I was standing on a grassy field holding something football-shaped in the crook of my arm, cradled against my chest. There were people running toward me roaring aggressively–just like the opposition does in the heat of a game when I'm gearing to bolt for a touchdown and they want nothing more than to take down the quarterback.

But when I looked down, I realized that it wasn't a football I held–at least, not anymore–but rather a silver helmet reeking of metal oil. The kind of helmet that knights used to wear. And the guys sprinting at me turned into random people emerging from gray clouds of ash and smoke, their faces stretched in horror, their eyes stark in their dirty faces. They ran right past me like I didn't exist. I could have sworn that there had been a goalpost behind me, forking up into the sky, but now it was the ashy remains of a fire-blackened village. More smoke chugged from straw huts. Cattle and pigs roamed free, trotting in circles all confused while women jogged briskly around them screaming for their children.

When I looked down again, I saw that my football jersey had been replaced with a full suit of armor that glistened in the sunlight shining brown through the smoke clouds of ruin. In my other hand I held a sword. I didn't feel confused at the turn my dream had taken. If anything, I felt a weird kind of anticipation.

Then I saw the reason for the panic–a gigantic dragon materialized through the smoke in front of me, its scales the color of mud, its eyes round and savage like a snake's. It saw me, the only tasty morsel standing between it and a feast of innocent people and roared its fury down at my face. I felt heat wash through my blood and stuffed the helmet over my head, throwing open my arms and bellowing back at it, "Show me what you got! Come at me!"

And it did—but in the instant that its jaws darted down and my sword rose to meet it, everything became slow motion. I saw myself and the beast about to lock in combat as if I were watching a movie, and I started to get that weird, foggy feeling you get when you're about to wake up. Damn, I look badass; I thought vaguely as the smoke started to obscure my view of what was happening.

In the final few moments before I returned to reality, I saw a flash of white in my periphery, like a huge horse or something had jumped by to aid my dream-self in combat. I saw someone in a black cloak and hood watching from the fringes of the demolished town and heard a voice say, "He's almost ready."

Then a patch of icy snow slid down my back.

"Oh!" I leaped to my feet, pinching my coat at the collar and shaking it until a clump of melted snow fell out the bottom and hit the floor with a splat.

My friends laughed their heads off and my best friend, Tyson, backed out of reach of any immediate retaliation, shaking water off of his fingers, tears of mirth streaming from his eyes.

"Oh, you jerk!" I laughed weakly, the shock of having been yanked from my daydream by the sudden cold leaving me dizzy.

"What were you thinking about?" asked my friend Kitty in that gentle voice of hers. "You were staring off into space for a good minute or two."

"Minute and a half," said Ben, cradling Kitty's head against his shoulder, combing his fingers through her long, dark curls, and waving his phone at me to show that he had a timer going.

I scowled at them. My friends and I had decided to spend the day up on the Coloradan slopes fifty miles west of our hometown of Firestone. The conditions were excellent–a fresh layer of powder had come in overnight. The sky was a crisp robin's-egg-blue, and the sun still had a bit of latent summer warmth, despite it being the end of September.

The trouble was, I couldn't help dwelling on the dream I'd been having off and on for the past few weeks. I'd had it again last night, and it was getting annoying. I didn't want to tell my friends about it and have them make fun, so I stood there like an idiot, floundering for an excuse, when the greatest girl in the world came to my rescue.

"What's going on?" Nikki, braiding her long, chocolate-colored hair, came over to us from where she'd just purchased her lift ticket for the day. When I started walking toward her, she looked up and smiled warmly, her hazel eyes twinkling.

"I was daydreaming about my wonderful girlfriend," I said, swooping in to kiss her cheek.

Nikki wrinkled her nose at me while Ben pretended to vomit and Tyson made a dramatic sound of adoration, like someone watching baby bunnies play.

"Go get your rental," Nikki said, dropping her braid over her shoulder and swatting me with her lift ticket.

"Yes, ma'am," I said, and imitated tipping my hat.

It bothered me a little that I was the only one of my friends who couldn't afford my own snowboard. Well, actually, I probably could afford one if I didn't have to pay Dad's bills and if my lame part-time job wasn't working with Tyson at the lumber and soil farm. I was so low on the food chain of employees that Tyson was my boss.

I slipped past other skiers and snowboarders shutting their purses and sneakers into lockers or sitting on benches to lace up their snow boots and exchanged smiles with the woman at the rental counter.

"Hey, Jon," she greeted, bumping my fist with her own. "The usual?"

"*Por favor*, Sandy," I replied and perched on a bench to untie my wet tennies.

Sandra came around the desk lugging a pair of boots and a snowboard. I laced up the boots first, making sure they were snug, and then measured the board against my chin to make sure it was still the correct height.

As I twisted to pick up my beanie and put my phone back in my pocket a bark of pain slashed across my hip and I sucked in a breath. I lifted my coat, studying the giant bruise splashed across my hipbone and just beginning to turn yellow.

"How'd that happen?"

Tyson had found me. He looked stonily from the bruise and then into my eyes.

I tried to smile, but all my mouth would do was twitch. "Don't worry about it, man." I let my coat drop and made to shuffle past Tyson, but he caught my arm.

Lowering his voice, he murmured, "Your dad again? What'd you do this time, sneeze too loudly?"

I snorted. "Talked back. He pushed me into the counter."

Tyson chewed on his lip, shaking his head. I could tell he was furious but trying not to show it for my sake. "Sorry, man," he said, after a bit. "Give me a call next time. I can come pick you up and you can stay the night, okay?"

"Sure," I said, and this time I did manage a genuine smile. He trailed me back out into the commons area and I dragged my battered and scratched rented snowboard alongside me, thinking bitterly of my dream. Me? A knight in shining armor? As if. I heaved a sigh. As if I'd be anything more than *this*... A small-town jock with a homelife that would drive even the most successful psychiatrist to hang up their Rorschach blots and retire.

The others were chatting, waiting for us, occasionally glancing at the tv set above the lodge's giant fireplace which was tuned to some news station.

"You hear this?" Ben asked us, flicking his head at the flat screen. I frowned up at it, slipping my arms around Nikki's waist and giving her a squeeze.

The news story's scrolling headline caught my eye: "Country's Defense System Unable to Defend Against Mass Mayhem Nationwide."

The reporter spoke gravely, and the video footage she was discussing about some political meeting flashed instead to a map of the United States. Red dots were scattered all over the place.

Ben swore softly.

I felt a weird tingle of fear run up my spine. It was an almost wild and inexplicable type of fear, like something big was happening that I couldn't comprehend. I'd tuned in a little late to the story, but I leaned forward, straining to hear.

"Swings of violence have, in recent days, soared in occurrence, as you can see on this map, eliciting concern in our nation's capital. It seems that gangs have abandoned secrecy and struck out in mass movements across the world. States that were relatively shy of violence before now face kidnappings and murders in the shadows of the night. But the government hasn't called any gangs to accountability, claiming to have no evidence."

The camera cut to some cranky white-haired guy from the FBI who was saying, "Gangs aren't involved in spying on the affairs of the government. And we must remember that America isn't the only one suffering from these attacks. Israel and Africa and Russia...they're all taking it with us. These aren't gangsters, and this isn't a cult; these are terrorists." He dodged a dozen microphones and ducked inside a shiny black car.

The reporter returned and concluded her story, her voice grim. "Many wonder whether or not these are indications of the threat of war. But the question on everyone's mind nationwide is: a war with whom? This is Teresa Sullivan, the nine o'clock news."

The story went to the newsroom where the facts turned to some violent, mysterious robbery in Wisconsin.

"Crazy times, eh?" Ben said, shaking his head. We all nodded in agreement, wandering outside and toward the lifts that would carry us up the slope. Tyson was chatting with Kitty and Nikki about the flight he would be taking to his sister's wedding on Wednesday, and Ben was filling me in on something he'd recently learned in his fire cadets program. He suddenly tapped my arm with the back of his hand and pointed off to the side.

"Is that Garrett?"

I squinted toward a group of guys clustered by a stand of pine trees. I recognized the guy in front instantly by his spiked-up black hair and the stud in his ear.

"Yep," I said, feeling a hot spurt of dislike burn in my insides.

Garrett was talking to a kid maybe a few years younger than us, pointing at the lift we all moved toward as if giving directions. He and his friends laughed about something and the kid laughed too, a little delayed.

"What, so they're picking on kids now?" Ben growled.

"Par for the course," I grumbled back. "He won't do anything out in public like this, though. It's not his MO."

Garrett was a lost cause. As far back as I could remember, he'd always been the town "bad boy," all angst and backtalk. He was the kind of guy who sassed teachers, smoked behind the school, and started fights with other kids. But he liked to give me special attention. There had always been a sticky vendetta between Garrett and me since elementary school, and it had festered early in the ninth grade. He had publicly embarrassed Nikki just to get to me, rumor had it. I would have taken him apart that day–or any day since–if Nikki hadn't begged me not to. So I usually tried to avoid him.

I tried to keep an eye on him through the crowd, but as people paired off in line to grab a seat on the chair lift and go up the slope, I realized that he'd disappeared.

We took the lift uphill and once everyone had made it to the peak, we pointed nose down and took off. Immediately, I felt icy air on my barely exposed cheeks, and the bumps of curdled snow threatened to tip me over, but I found my level of balance and concentrated on my speed. I didn't want to go too fast; there was a batch of fun trick obstacles coming up, and I needed the challenge.

We rounded a bend, and I saw the grinding rail. Bending lower so my butt almost touched the snow, I pushed off and spun sideways, hitting the rail perpendicular. Sliding off with a spin, I kept my knees coiled to absorb landing impact and rejoined my friends, swerving aimlessly through some orange cones set in a straight line. Tyson gave me a high five and veered to try a backflip, a trick only he had mastered.

I led the way down a side path, and for a while, we chased each other past the beautiful mountain scenery. We were currently the only group on the trail, and it felt like we were, I don't know, like, *part* of the surroundings. As if the hill belonged to us. *This* was what I'd needed. *This* was freedom. Just me and friends, not a care in the world, no responsibilities, no stress, no wacky dreams, and no deadbeat dads.

I was racing a tiny red cardinal flying beside me through the trees when a high, squealing kind of sound caught my ears, making my skin crawl before I'd even really comprehended what the sound meant. I flipped my board around ninety degrees and dug the back into the snow, skidding to a stop. Snow flew in a powdery wave around me. My friends halted behind me.

"Did you hear that?" I asked, pulling my face gaiter down to expose my ears to sound better.

Tyson and Nikki exchanged cocked eyebrows.

"Hear what?" Ben asked, his penetrating eyes framed like a ninja's between his hat and scarf.

I slowly inched closer to the trees and tilted my head. "Somebody's screaming," I mumbled. I slipped into the fringe of trees and heard it again, long, plaintive, and agonized.

"I'm going after them," I decided with finality and freed my board from the snow, vanishing into the trunks.

Nikki yelled after me, "Jonathan, no! *You're going to get yourself killed!*"

I hardly heard her—worst-case scenarios raced through my head. What would I find? Was someone hurt? Dying?

I almost hit a tree and reeled back, slowing down to lean against another's trunk. As far as I knew, I faced at least two dangers besides crushing myself against a trunk. One was that a large amount of snow could collapse on top of me, deposited by overweight branches. Another was that I could sink into a tree well, the piled-up snow around the trees, and suffocate in six-foot drifts.

The scream rang out again, and I headed toward it, finding a deep and crooked trail. I followed it and came to an area choked with brambles that were badly broken and bent, as if someone had struggled to clear a path...or stop themselves.

I kneeled and slid through, thorns grabbing at my white coat. Coming out into an area where the trees were farther apart but thicker, I spotted what I was looking for: a concave bowl of broken-in snow at the base of a tree. Steady moaning and cursing trailed out from inside it, punctuated by yelps of pain and cries for help.

I coasted over and braked, peering into the depression at the crumpled body within. It was the boy I'd seen talking with Garrett. Now that I was up close to him, I guessed that he was maybe twelve or thirteen. He wore a bright-orange coat with black pants and a beanie. His face was chapped and his board bent to one side, his left foot twisted with it.

He saw me and closed his eyes in relief, murmuring hoarsely, "Help me, please. My ankle." He leaned forward, retching in pain.

Wincing, I asked calmly, "What happened?"

The kid fidgeted in an effort to get comfortable and replied a bit guiltily, "I went off the trail...wanted to try something harder. But I hit a tree, and...I think I sprained my ankle."

While he talked, I shifted away some of the snow and made a slanting path down to him. "Preteens," I mumbled.

"Just help me," the kid grumbled.

I got out of my straps and moved down to tenderly hook my hands under the boy's arms. I pulled him out, ignoring his piercing protests, and asked his name.

"Carl," he spat through gritted teeth.

I laid him across my lap while I strapped back in and tugged his board out of the pit, and said lightly, "Well, Carl, now we know not to go down the big-boy paths without some practice, right?"

Carl met my gaze with his sharp gray-green eyes. "What are you, like a year older than me?"

"Try about four, Pips. Now here's what we're going to do." I settled him into the snow by me and attached his board to mine by clipping his foot-holster strap to one of my boot buckles. His board tilted and slid down-hill, just barely pulling at me until I firmly settled my weight in. I helped Carl sit on his board, his injured foot out in front of him and propped up behind the knee by one of his empty, floppy boot buckles. He was weighing us down even more in front, and this time, I let him slowly but surely start to pull us forward. Carl twitched when he tried to tilt his leg to one side and cursed violently.

Checking ahead to try and discern a safe path, I murmured, "Watch your mouth."

"Okay, Mom," Carl snapped.

"Do you want me to leave you here?" I asked.

"No," he said quickly. He twisted to look me in the eye and say something smart but glanced over my shoulder and focused on something behind me instead. Grabbing the sides of his snowboard, he began to throw his weight forward, pulling hard against me. "No, no, no, no, no!"

My arms flew out. "Dude, you're going to push me over, what...?" I turned around and made an inarticulate noise, my innards sinking.

Sitting on a boulder half submerged in the snow, and watching us with beady yellow eyes, was a grizzly bear.

It was huge—it could blanket my entire torso with one of its paws. Power emanated from its ropey muscles, and it held itself with the savage confidence of an apex predator beholding an easy meal. Its nose went up, scenting the air, and I caught a glimpse of its freakishly sharp fangs.

I moved slowly, sliding back and forth, creating a slick patch of snow so that I could unstick myself. What had I heard about surviving grizzly attacks? Play dead? Act tough? Climb a tree? I tried to avoid making eye contact with it while also keeping it in my periphery. Carl's whimpering was not a very reassuring backdrop, and he pawed at me, clawed at the snow.

The bear reared up on its hind legs. Holy shit. It was the biggest animal I'd ever seen. It made a hellish growling sound, and I dismissed "acting tough" from my list of ways to fend it off. Its claws made it look like it was holding ten knives in its ham-size paws. I hoped with desperation that my friends hadn't tried to follow me off the trail and were instead waiting for me at the bottom of the hill. Suddenly, the monster bear roared and started at us, leaping off its rock with a concussion that I felt through the snow and approaching with alarming speed.

"Go!" squealed Carl.

I pushed forward; *he* pushed forward, and we were off.

The air roared against our faces, chilling us. I could hear the bear running after us, breath whuffing and paw steps thudding. I leaned to one side, bellowing at Carl to do the same, and we avoided a tree.

We swerved side to side, zigzagging in wide curves around foliage, Carl paddling at the snow helpfully to maneuver his own turns. Soon, I couldn't tell if the bear was still chasing or not; I couldn't pick up any more sounds from it–just the hissing whisper of boards on snow.

Carl peeked back around my legs long enough to observe, "It's back there a ways watching us. It gave up."

"Thank God." Near-death experiences will really turn you to faith. But another problem came to my attention when I saw level ground through the trees.

"Um, issue coming up," I started.

"What now?" Carl asked, looking side to side as if checking for another bear.

"We have to stop. And we are going...really fast," I explained slowly.

Carl slouched when he, too, realized our predicament. "Great," he said.

We hit level ground so suddenly, it felt like being whacked behind the knees with a baseball bat. We shot into groups of skiers and snowboarders, everyone diving out of our way, and aimed for a steep drop-off straight into the parking lot below.

I desperately dug my board into the snow, feeling shock waves of impact thud in my kneecaps. Everything seemed to be in slow motion. I reached down and unbuckled the cord connecting Carl and me. I stretched out my arm and shoved him over onto his side where he bumped once and lay still, watching me over his shoulder.

There was only one option left. I fell back fully on the ground. Freezing-cold snow shot up the back of my coat, refreshingly cool on my skin. The bruise on my hip throbbed. My momentum slowed almost immediately, and I came to a stop with my board dangling over the edge of the drop.

Arms wrapped around me and pulled me back. Someone removed my board, and I balanced on legs like noodles. My friends crowded around, joined by others clamoring for answers.

Ben supported me, and Nikki was forcing me to look in her eyes.

"Are you alright?" she asked, her voice breaking.

I hugged her tightly and whispered, "I am now."

CHAPTER TWO:
I Almost Beat Up a Bully

A couple of hours later, I was sitting in the back of an ambulance draped in a blanket and sipping hot cocoa. Carl was one ambulance over, lying on a stretcher with an ankle brace.

A news crew was over interviewing his parents. They had already talked to me. I heard the reporter saying, "...according to his friends and the injured youth's parents, Jonathan He'klarr is, indeed, a hero."

I frowned and hunched lower over my drink. Anybody else would have done the same thing. It was only by chance that I had heard Carl's cries for help before he had become that bear's porridge. But still...looking over at Carl lying on his back, pale and exhausted, filled me with a kind of fierce joy and odd protectiveness. He was alive—because of *me*. I felt that I'd struggled my way out of a cocoon of obscurity, nothingness, and darkness to see my own potential. It was a strange, exciting, and frightening new feeling.

People I didn't even know were clapping me on the back as they walked past. Gaggles of girls that I pointedly ignored grouped up nearby to glance over at me flirtatiously, daring each other to get my number. My phone was buzzing as people from school bombarded me with texts, asking me if what they'd just seen on the news was true—had I really just saved someone's life on the mountain? I didn't respond to any of them—just sat there, chewing on my thoughts, trying to make clearer sense of them.

A familiar voice made me look up with a broad smile. "Jonathan Hero He'klarr! Waz up, man? How's life on this side of the tracks?"

"Hey, Ty," I said, scooting over to make room for him to sit. I raised my cup. "Cocoa's good."

He clapped me over the shoulder. "I'll bet it is. You're lucky you're as fast on a board as you are on the gridiron." He gazed around at the crowds, the reporters, his fingers clenched in his lap as he twiddled his thumbs around. Then, like he was acting on impulse, he leaned close and said, "Hey, next time don't go charging away like that on your own, okay?" His tone was sharp.

Surprised, I studied him, my own musings sinking to the back of my brain. Normally, Tyson was the comedian. Nothing could dampen his spirits. But this had bothered him. He was shaken. He spoke again, and I could hear a small quiver weakening his voice.

"I'm your best friend. I've had your back for...years. The next time you run off to fight a bear, just...just maybe bring me along, okay?"

I smiled at him. "Sure thing, Ty. Next time, I'll let you tag along." He bobbed his head like a bird by way of a humorless nod, but then let out a breath like he'd been holding it out of nerves, and stretched out on his back, his arms behind his head. My recurring dream popped back into my head as if to make a point and I thought of my dream-self shaking a sword at a dragon and bellowing a challenge.

My phone buzzed again, like an irritating mosquito, and I lifted it up and looked at it. My friend Vince was calling. I stared at the screen blankly until Vince went to voicemail, and then studied my background image: me holding up my phone and smiling into the camera, my turquoise eyes lit up by the setting sun, and Nikki beside me, running one hand through the waves of my dirty-blond hair. I felt so different from that guy in the picture. I'd just saved a kid's *life*.

Maybe I can be more than what I am after all...

Traditionally, on our drive home from the mountain, we all stopped at a popular restaurant called *Brown Bear Diner*. The irony was not lost on any of us.

When we entered, and the little bell over the door jingled, we were recognized by a few other people who'd also been up playing in the snow and they greeted us cheerfully, raising their drinks.

"Hero He'klarr!" one guy shouted and I bobbed my head and waved, uncomfortable at the attention.

My friends slipped into our favorite booth by the front window where we could watch the sloping pasture across the road and maybe spot a grazing herd of elk passing by, and I went to use the restroom. But when I entered, I saw that it was occupied by a raucous crowd of three or four other guys, playfully shoving each other into stalls and loitering by the sinks. I hesitated, and one of the guys, calmly washing his hands, looked up in the mirror to see who'd entered. His eyes, as green as the mountain trees I'd boarded through to rescue Carl, lit up with malice.

It was Garrett, his poofy black parka still wet from the mountain snow.

"Look who it is," he said snidely, and his friends stopped bouncing off the walls like gorillas at the zoo to sneer at me. "Jonathan 'the hero' He'klarr." They all snickered.

As far as I was concerned, Garrett was the scum of the earth. Your average high school bullies aren't too hard to figure out—oftentimes they just like exercising power over someone, feeling tough and in-control. Not Garrett. He got sadistic pleasure out of every kid he beat up, and his skills of shrewd manipulation would give any certified sociopath a run for their money.

And now I was thinking back to when I'd seen him talking to the kid, Carl, on the mountain.

"Did you make Carl take the black diamond?" I asked.

"Did I make who take the what?" Garrett asked without concern, drying his hands. His friends chortled again.

"The kid who sprained his leg today, who was almost eaten by a bear. Did you make him take the advanced trail?"

"Oh, Jonathan," Garrett simpered, "I didn't *make* anyone do anything." He tossed his paper towel toward the garbage can. It bounced off the rim and hit the floor. He approached me with slow, confident steps, palming his hood back off of his spiky, jet-black hair. "Did I insinuate that he'd be a pussy if he *didn't* take it?" He shrugged. "Perhaps. But he's the one dumb enough to rise to the challenge."

"He's just a kid," I said, shocked. Garrett may have been an asshole, but he could've caused some real harm today. And here he was, completely okay with it.

Garrett blinked as if nonplussed. "...And?" His goons laughed again, but this time I didn't hear it—I took a step forward, grabbed him by the front of his shirt, spun him around, and pinned his back against the wall. The laughter cut off really quick.

"He almost died, Garrett." I snarled into his stoic face. "You almost killed a kid today."

Garrett gave me a slow, crooked smile. "...And?"

I stared at him, appalled. The bathroom door opened, and Tyson came in. He froze when he saw what was happening. I glimpsed Nikki hovering behind him–perhaps they had been drawn to the sound of our raised voices.

"What are you doing?" Nikki cried.

Garrett wrapped his hands around my arms. "Let me go, He'klarr."

I returned my attention to him, my pulse racing. "Or what?"

"Or I'll take you apart." He tilted his head at me. The scarlet gem that studded the gold ring in his ear twinkled at the movement. "But maybe it'll be therapeutic for you. You'll get to stay home, spend some quality time with your drunk-ass dad."

Nikki looked at me meaningfully, raising her eyebrows, tightening her lips, trying to tell me with her gaze not to get uptight. "Don't do it," she mouthed.

The heat rushing through me felt like it had turned into ice. My grip on Garrett's shirt loosened and he shrugged me off. I staggered back away from him. Tyson came up at my shoulder and kept an eye on Garrett's hungry-looking friends. Nikki held the door open, watching nervously.

"Don't talk about my dad, Garrett." I said curtly, my heart beating faster. "This has nothing to do with him."

Garrett smirked. "Does it bother you?"

I should have kept my weaknesses secret, as is man law, but instead I clenched my hands into fists and said, "Yeah, it bothers me, just shut up!"

"Make me," challenged Garrett. He waved his hand at Tyson and Nikki, watching with round, expectant eyes. "Look at your adoring public, He'klarr. Let's give them a show."

My hands shook and my heart raced. Garrett was goading me into stepping over the line of hostile neutrality that had stretched between us for years, tempting me to make a move.

"No, Jonathan," Nikki murmured very gently.

"Yes, Jonathan," Garrett said in a mocking voice that mimicked Nikki's concerned tone. "You have to be getting tired of turning the other cheek." He watched my eyes flicker toward the door and back. Shaking his head, he sank back against the wall and muttered, "Won't even fight back. You are your mother's son."

I lunged at him, fists swinging, shouting profanities. Tyson had felt me tense up, though, and grabbed the back of my coat. Garrett's friends were all shouting, urging us on while Nikki tried in vain to calm me down. Garrett was just laughing, like he was amused, a foot from my eager fists.

"*Let me go! I'm gonna kick his ass!*" I screamed.

"Come on, bro, you'll get thrown off the football team if you get in a fight!" Tyson said over my oaths. "He isn't worth it, man; Jonathan, calm down!" He finally succeeded in getting me in a good grip, and Nikki strode in. She brushed past Garrett, put both of her hands on either side of my face, and said, "Jonathan, listen to me.

Calm down, okay? You're better than this. You're better than him. Don't do this."

The pounding in my ears started to fade away. Adrenaline made me jumpy and tense.

"You're nothin'. Nothin' but trash," I hissed, relaxing slightly to Nikki's touch. She withdrew her fingers and groaned. I almost didn't notice. My skin felt hot enough to sizzle, and all the hatred I'd kept at bay for so long was boiling in my chest like magma.

"You think you're better than me?" I growled. "Crawlin' around in your own shit like the other blowflies? It's time I taught you some respect."

Garrett shrugged. "Maybe. Don't get your hopes up."

"*I'm* not the one who's going to get his ass kicked!" I shouted. Garrett's buds "ooh-ed" on that one, and the encouragement was only tensing me up more. My heart raced at Garrett's insults. I was flushed–feverish, almost.

Garrett watched me, studying me like a hawk watching a mouse scrabbling at the base of its tree. As always, I was chilled by his reptilian apathy, the emptiness in his emerald eyes. I thought about all the times I'd come to school, after Dad had pushed me around a bit or yelled himself hoarse at me for closing the front door too loudly, when Garrett's insults had stung more than usual, as if he'd known when my confidence was lowest, my defense weakest. As if he could read my mind.

Garrett had always been more than cruel, more than mean. He was evil, and it rolled off of him in sick, cloying waves like a mist of poison.

We stood there, evaluating each other, unblinking. I thought I saw a faint crimson twinkle in Garrett's pupils, but when he blinked, it was gone. He straightened his shirt and looked imperiously past me at his friends. In a jaunty, joking tone of voice he said, "I'm hungry." Then, under their laughter and hoots of agreement he said menacingly, "See you later," like a cliché super villain minus the manic laughter. I flicked my head in acknowledgment, watching his retreating back.

After the door had shut behind them, Tyson let me go. "You're crazy, Hero," he said. "What were you going to do, take them all on at once?"

I didn't say anything, going to lean over a sink. As if it would make matters any better, I bent over, plucked up Garrett's paper towel, and threw it in the garbage.

"Go back to Ben and Kitty, Ty," Nikki said softly. "I'll talk to him."

Taking slow, deep breaths, just like Nikki had taught me, I acknowledged my feelings, named them in my mind, *hatred, rage, grief, disgust, shame,* and one by one I buried them back in my subconscious. It was often a very difficult exercise, swallowing the savagely pleasant mental image of me throttling Garrett until his head popped off like a cork from a bottle.

After a moment I felt Nikki slip up beside me. She wrapped her hands around my arm and leaned against me.

"Jonathan, what Garrett said... He was just trying to get under your skin."

I bristled but kept my reply semi-calm. "He pressured that kid to go up the mountain today. Carl was almost eaten alive and he's acting like it was just some big prank. The guy's a maniac."

Nikki nodded silent agreement and I said, "I really don't know why he hates me. But we've always had a tense truce with each other. He didn't have to bring up my parents like that, especially not Mom. Something's changed. This isn't a pissing contest anymore, this isn't him just trying to get a reaction out of me, this is...something else. It's more." I thought of what Garrett had said about my mother and had to force down another spurt of white-hot rage. "He *wants* to fight me, Nikki."

She turned to look at me timidly. "Do *you* want to fight *him*?"

I tried to find a way out of answering that truthfully but couldn't, so I finally replied, "Yes."

Nikki frowned; her hazel eyes gleaming like those of an angry mother wolf. "You're giving in, you know that, right?"

A little too sharply, I shot back, "Just like my mom did." It was kind of a statement-slash-question–a challenge that I hadn't really meant to let slip out.

Instead of appearing hurt, Nikki became stern and her tone was biting, her words coming quick and sharp. "Your mother did things that no other person could. She helped a lot of people. If you fight, you'll be insulting her memory. You'll be acting like your d–" She halted, a concerned look flitting across her face, worried she'd struck a nerve. We both knew that she had been about to say "dad."

That hurt, mostly because I knew she was right. But I tried not to let it show on my face.

"Do you remember what Garrett did to you? The things he said?" I asked in a low voice. "Because I do, word for word."

"It's in the past, Jon," Nikki said, but her voice was tired and I could see that the pain of that experience still haunted her. "Beating Garrett up isn't going to rewrite history." She sighed and asked in a defeated tone, "Is there any way I can convince you not to fight?"

I hugged her with a confident smile. "Nope." I popped the *p*. She smiled a little sadly. "I'm sick of taking crap from that guy," I said, putting a hand on my chest. "I'm sick of *you* having to take crap from him. Next time he opens his mouth, I'm teaching him a lesson."

"You sound so sure that you'll win." Nikki grimaced, starting for the door.

"If I have the heart of my lady, I can win anything," I said, giving her a smug smile.

"You have my heart. Not my favor."

"Ouch," I grunted and wrapped my hands around the hilt of an invisible knife buried in my chest.

Nikki took my hand with a laugh. "Let's go eat."

CHAPTER THREE:
THE SECOND DREAM

When Tyson dropped me off at home that night, I saw that all the lights were off, but Dad's crappy pickup was parked crookedly in the driveway, which told me he was inside, passed-out drunk.

I thanked Ty and started to get out, but he grabbed my arm and murmured, "I'll wait here for a bit. If he gives you any trouble just come back out and I'll take you to my place. My parents won't care."

The pit of anger and depression that had been gnawing at my insides ever since I'd confronted Garrett in the restroom of the diner grew a little wider. I nodded, giving my best friend a tight-lipped smile, and climbed out, shutting the van door quietly behind me.

My steps were soft as I approached the front porch, and I turned the doorknob slowly and carefully. As soon as the door opened, I knew I was in the clear—I could hear Dad snoring from the living room. I shot Tyson the thumbs-up and closed the front door behind me. Pop was slumped in his favorite armchair with a beer can clenched in his fist as if it contained the water of life and he was a dying man. More empty bottles and cans littered the carpet. Dad must've had some friends from work over. *How original*, I thought. I shook my head disgustedly, a sneer curling my lip as I took in his filthy shirt, scraggly stubble, and softening neck muscles where they bulged, his head flopped to one side. Just looking at him brought me an ugly kind of rage—a lot like the rage I had felt in my dream when I'd been about to slay that dragon.

I snuck through the kitchen, grabbing a banana to eat as I went, and picked my way up the staircase. The once polished steps were now creaky and old. Luckily, I knew exactly where all of the loud banshee-wail spots were. Dad had given me a vitriolic lecture for every time I'd forgotten or made an accidental misstep.

Please don't wake up, please don't wake up... I chanted in my mind, my ears pricked for any sound of movement from the living room, but I made it to the upstairs hall without incident.

Everything here looked dusty and old. Dirt had blended into the once red carpet, turning it a worn mahogany brown. It was so ratty I could count the floorboards showing from beneath it. Besides a closet, my dad's room, and a small bathroom, my bedroom was the only other room upstairs. I turned inside it, shut the door behind me, and turned on the light, letting my breath out in relief. I'd gotten pretty good at avoiding confrontations with Dad, but the bruise on my hip was a reminder that luck wasn't always on my side.

I could still hear Ty's van idling out at the end of the driveway through the window I kept cracked for a cool, clean breeze. I sent him a reassuring text, listened to him drive away, and sprawled on my back in bed. Splashed across my entire ceiling was the image of a football player. He was diving over the end zone with the aid of a pair of outstretched wings. It wasn't much yet, but I was proud of it.

All of the day's bumps and aches started making themselves known as I relaxed and I forced my turbulent thoughts away one by one, just focusing on the brushstrokes above me, breathing in the harsh, chemical smell of the paint as it mingled with the crisp autumn breeze slipping in the window. I tried to muster the strength to get up, turn off the light, dress down for bed, and instead wondered what it would be like to have wings like that football player. *Where would I go if I could fly away from here?*

I think that was my last coherent thought before everything changed. The next thing I knew, I was sitting on a cold, wet street. My back had been on a mattress, but now it was pressed against a sopping dumpster. My thoughts had been on Garrett, snowboarding, my dad—now my mind raced and my heart thundered in my chest.

I fought to my feet, struggling as if invisible ropes bound me to the dumpster. The familiarity of where I was made me ache inside. I would've rather had the dragon-fighting dream again—anything but this.

The only light was from a streetlamp at the end of the alley, flickering on and off. I could only move when the light buzzed temporarily on. Without it, I would stumble into the shadows where cold hands would grab me and never let go. Bracing myself, I sprinted toward the alley's mouth. The light flickered. I paused. Hands emerged from the walls, grasping, reaching, bloodstained and claw-tipped, groping blindly for my arms or clothes. I froze and forced myself to remain still until the light came back on, then I bolted again like a hare from its burrow.

When I finally emerged from the alley, I found myself in the middle of the sidewalk on a vacant street. A small car was parked across the road.

A woman was pinned to the open driver's door by a taller man. I tried to run at them, but the ground was too slippery and with each step I took, I only moved inches. But I heard their voices as if their conversation were taking place right beside me. The words had formed over time to match the images that my mind had produced years ago.

Mom's murder as the police reports told me it had played out.

"Give me your keys!" the man growled. He had savage eyes and a hollow face made scruffy with stubble.

The woman, my mother, calmly replied, "Why are you doing this? You don't have to do this."

"I want your damn car!" The man talked loudly over her, holding a gun to her chest. Mom shuddered, hands out, and looked, almost as if for patience, up at the sky. The way the light shone on her golden hair made it look like she had a halo.

The man scoffed and stepped back. "Listen, you bitch, you say all the prayers you want, but I need to get outta here by tomorrow morning, and I'm taking your car, so get the hell out of my way!"

Mom took a step toward her car. "Are you really a killer? Could you really tear apart a family? Take me away from my husband? My little boy?" I lurched forward, pouring every bit of strength I had into trying to move faster. Tears stung my eyes. My jaw was locked against useless sobs, against screams and curses and shouted warnings that would go unheard, wouldn't change anything, wouldn't bring her back.

The carjacker's mouth lifted into a twisted smile, but his eyes were narrowed into slits—all hasty impatience gone and replaced with resolve.

He steadied his arm, said, "You're a mother," with an interested tone, and shot her, hitting her shoulder.

Mom gasped and fell back, her eyes big and her hand swiping at the spreading blood.

The man stepped forward and shot her once more. Mom closed her eyes, pale, her expression twisted in unimaginable agony, and she died. Just as I reached the car.

I turned furiously on the murderer, able to move normally now, and glared into his triumphant black shark eyes with so much hatred that I shook, bracing to waste my strength pounding every inch of him I could until he shot me too.

He opened his mouth, showing me rows of triangular, serrated teeth and rumbled:

"Deceit and lies,
Look in my eyes.
The Prince of Dreams
Must break his ties."

Well, this was a new development. Usually, the guy looked just as I remembered him from when I saw him sitting in court and silently accepting the verdict for the death penalty. Now it was as if he had become a picture of what he was inside, having shed his mask and disguise.

I took a few steps away. And why was he all of a sudden spouting creepy rhymes? I felt like I should have had something just as witty to say, but all I came up with was a half brave, "Yeah?"

The shark-man laughed. "Do you think yourself brave, little griffin?" he asked mockingly. And just as fast as my nightmare had started, it ended, cutting off the monster mid-guffaw.

My eyes blinked open to my bedroom ceiling, the streaks of paint glowing brilliantly in the light of dawn streaming in my window. Covered in sweat, I sighed and forced myself to relax a bit at a time.

That was another dream I experienced on repeat now and again, but it usually wasn't so disturbing. Mom had only been shot once before in previous dreams, and the killer hadn't ever spoken to me directly. The whole incident with Carl and Garrett had really messed with my mind.

I rubbed my face, shivering, and sat up with a groan as stiff muscles reared their ugly heads. The alarm on my phone wouldn't go off for another thirty minutes or so, but I decided to get ready for school anyway. After I'd showered and dressed, I donned my backpack buckling the torso straps, and looked at my phone. Nikki had texted me good morning. My spirits lifted as I texted her back–I needed to tell someone about my dreams. What better person than my awesome girlfriend?

Something clattered loudly downstairs and I heard my dad swear. I flinched automatically at his tone. Now wasn't the time. I shoved my school books into my backpack and headed downstairs, alert and cautious.

Dad was fumbling around the kitchen, making some kind of hangover cure before he left for work. He looked up at me, his eyes bloodshot and bleary, and I nodded by way of greeting, making sure to keep the kitchen island between us.

"You headin' to school?" he asked. His voice was gravelly.

"Mm-hmm," I grunted. I didn't stop walking.

He gave me a vague wave and poured water into a glass.

As soon as the door was shut behind me, I took a deep breath and jogged to the end of my driveway to wait for the bus. The hollow pit in my stomach from the night before opened up again, churning with a mess of emotions–anger foremost among them.

Tyson had found out about Dad's more...violent moments in middle school. I'd shrug off the fact that I didn't have a home lunch because we were out of food at home, or that I didn't dress down in gym because I didn't want kids to see the belt-marks on my back from when I'd smart-mouthed Dad. One day I'd trusted Ty with my secret and told him the truth. He'd known of my mom's death; we lived in a small town, and our mothers had been close, but I had never told him how I felt about it and how it had affected Dad until that day. We had been close friends since infancy practically, but that was when we became *best* friends.

And then Nikki had discovered my secret later on when I'd itched a scab on the side of my head caused by the TV remote being chucked at me when I'd cussed at Dad. It had started to bleed badly, and after Nikki made me let her look at it, she put things together. She also stopped asking to be introduced to my family.

Over the years, I'd learned how to avoid my father when he was drunk. I'd slink into other rooms in the house when I heard him coming and slip out the back door when he came home late from the pubs roaring for me to get my ass downstairs so that he could scream at me, accuse me of doing something else wrong...

Dad wasn't too bad when he was sober; he always apologized, promised not to drink or shout at me, or slap or shove me again, and then gave in and ended up going to some tavern or bar to drink away the pain anyway.

My school bus came trundling down the road toward me and I stuffed my anger and bitterness away. I was about to see my friends again. I was going to school miles away from Dad. It would be like taking a breath of fresh air. Things would be okay.

I always, no matter how much of a bad morning I had, felt pride when I saw my high school. It was the first place in my life where I had found somewhere to belong–a place that accepted me. A cobbled walkway lined by thick and elderly trees led to the foot of some wrap around stairs. The trees formed a canopy of fiery-colored leaves above us, fingers of sun beaming through them to cast shadowy webs on the ground. At the corners of the stairs, great columns stretched up to support an archway, forming a sheltered area below with benches on either side of the double doors.

Having obtained extra money from a bond our school passed, an architect had been hired to construct a unique sculpture of our school mascot for the entrance. The principal had in mind a stone griffin, sitting beside the doors like a sentinel. But the architect had insisted on something more "flavorful."

He had climbed up onto the roof over the archway and, within a few months, made an intimidating stone griffin perched twenty feet tall, squatting back on its lion haunches as if tensing up to leap, and glaring down at those who entered its realm with eagle eyes. Its wings, intricately detailed down to the last secondary feather, were open, and they curled down over the columns as if to say, "This is *my* crib. Only griffins allowed!"

I stopped to stare up at the work of art, trying to calm down by bravely meeting the mythical beast's cold stare. It was painted black with a red underside and yellow irises and wing tips. Our school colors. We're big on pride.

Taped to the brick wall to one side was a black sheet of butcher paper. Red letters said, "Football Game Against the Serenity Grove Minotaurs Fri. the 27th!"

Not to brag, but my football team was one of the best in our school district, maybe even one of the best in Colorado. We had won all three of our games so far, but the upcoming match was looked forward to every year. The Minotaurs were our major rivals; even the freshmen harbored a special loathing for them. Before every game against them, we had a unique assembly just to motivate everyone. As our team's captain, the pressure of leading the griffins to victory weighed heavily on my mind–tantamount to slaying a dragon. Hence, I suspected, my recurring dreams.

Tyson came over, clapped a hand on my shoulder, and laughed, his usual wild grin fixed on his freckled face. "Have you been interrogated about the Great Mountain Rescue yet, Hero?"

I groaned. The kids on my bus had been merciless, begging for a play-by-play account of how I'd rescued Carl the previous day. I knew I'd have to brace myself for a lot of unwanted attention in the coming days.

As our other friends started trickling over Tyson gestured to the football poster on the wall and said, "At least Garrett got you pumped up enough to slay the Minotaurs, right?"

I turned to face him, an eyebrow raised skeptically. "The game isn't until Friday, champ."

Ben, adjusting his fire cadets uniform, waved his hands dismissively. "That ain't a problem. You have a week to make a Garrett voodoo doll and stick little pins in him at random times of the day."

"And what would *that* help?" Nikki asked, a smile playing around her lips. She gave me a quick kiss on the cheek and we all started moseying toward the front doors.

Ben rolled his piercing greenish-gray hawk eyes. "It'll keep him mad and haughty, duh."

"Haughty?" Tyson echoed, puzzled. He shrugged and started to lead us inside, struggling to speak around the huge grin stuck on his face. "That doesn't sound healthy. Can you imagine Jonathan in the locker room before the game?" He adopted a high-pitched yet strict voice, not at all like mine, and pantomimed telling the team a plan. "Okay, guys, the Minotaurs are out there waiting for us. It's time to flash them the red flag and lock horns with the enemy!"

Nikki laughed. It was just the sort of figure of speech I would use.

Tyson went on. "Hold on a minute, guys," he said before turning slightly away, mimicking stabbing a small object in his palm with manic squeals of glee. We all laughed loudly, and I already felt a degree better. Tyson was known for being able to brighten a room.

"Seriously though, did you all notice that Garrett was unusually...loquacious yesterday?" Ben pressed.

"'Loquacious?' Man, what, did you eat a dictionary for breakfast this morning?" Tyson teased.

We stopped by the crowded cafeteria decorated with crimson and ebony sashes and covered with murals, and Ben and Tyson entered to get school-breakfast, still bickering about vocabulary and chatting about me and voodoo dolls. Nikki squeezed past me, brushing my hand with hers.

I stood at the doorway for a bit, looking up at my favorite mural. It showed a football player crouching with one hand clenched over the ball, ready to pass it back. The senior class had done an excellent job with it. Through the helmet, I could see the tense jaw muscles and determined eyes. Because of his bulky mouth guard, his lips were parted awkwardly and his padding gave him the appearance of a brightly colored bear. But just barely, like a golden-colored spirit embodying the kid's force and will, a griffin had been traced in a ghostly way into the player's contours. Its wings were spread, making it look like the human had translucent wings of his own. Its talons were his hands. Its beak was his mouth. Its feathers were his uniform. The griffin and the boy were one and the same. The picture gave me a sense of belonging, like something grand and noble was in me too, just waiting to show itself. Looking at it reminded me of my dream. I wished I could suit up and fight my demons like I'd been about to fight that dragon. I wished I could conceive of a different, brighter future for myself, where I could be more than just a jock with nowhere to go and a short fuse when it came to bullies.

Kitty came in the cafeteria last, giving me a small smile. She walked to the end of the breakfast line, eyes on her shoes as usual, face hidden behind her abundance of curls. I followed and ended up a little behind her with a couple of guys I didn't recognize in line between us. They must have recognized her from class or something because they started talking to her, and my daydreaming about griffins and fighting dragons fizzled when I heard something mocking in their tone.

Tuning in, I realized that they were picking on her, something about an argument she'd had with a teacher in class.

"So I don't believe in the big bang, so what?" Kitty said in a small voice, shrugging. Her face was bright red.

One of the guys, a real charmer reeking of cigarette smoke, showed his yellow teeth as if her discomfort brought him some weird kind of pleasure and he said, "What, do you think the earth is flat, too? You realize there's like, tons of evidence to support the big bang, right?"

"And there's tons of evidence to the contrary as well. I respect your opinion, but I don't have to accept it." Kitty's voice shook a little, like she was about to cry. Other people in line had started listening in as we inched forward and were either expressing pity for Kitty's obvious embarrassment or nodding in agreement with what the other kids were saying.

The second guy, tall, with a long, horse-like face, switched astounded looks with his friend at Kitty's expense and said with appalled disgust, "It's not an opinion, it's scientific truth!"

I got ready to interfere for Kitty's sake—she looked ready to burst into tears—but then something happened that surprised me as much as the two douchebags picking on her.

Kitty's head snapped up and there was a sudden flash of lightning in her eyes that made the two guys switch unsettled expressions, as if Kitty had just picked up a weapon. Though her cheeks were still bright red, Kitty elegantly lifted her chin and said, "So then you're of the opinion that all time, matter, and space came together to create all time, matter, and space?"

The guys stared, floundering for words, as taken aback as I was. One of the guys even looked back at me as if for help and I just blinked cluelessly at him. Kitty kept pushing.

"What about the law of entropy, which implies a beginning to the universe? Or the Teleological argument? The presence of fundamental constants in the so-called laws of nature? The Anthropic principle?"

One of the guys made a sound like a drain being unplugged as he stuttered for words and Kitty flapped her arms in an impatient gesture.

"Come on, you had so much to say just a bit ago. If you want to debate, let's debate."

Finally, shame colored the guys' faces and with muttered oaths and flustered grumbles they left the line. Kitty turned on the spot, covering her mouth in mock surprise and looked at me.

"What? An intelligent Christian?" she gasped.

I laughed, and so did a few of the other kids in line who'd witnessed the verbal smackdown.

I stepped forward, filling in the gap left behind by the two guys, giving Kitty a grin of admiration and putting my arm around her shoulders in a fond, brotherly kind of way.

"Damn, Kitty, where'd that come from?"

She showed her teeth in a sweet little smile, draping her arm around my waist and steering me slowly forward in the breakfast line.

"I don't mind having a discussion, but I won't let them mock me for what I believe," she said in a calm, casual way, as if she had mind-boggling theological debates all the time. Maybe she did.

I studied her as she spooned some canned pears onto her tray and grabbed a bagel, humming very quietly to herself. Of all of my friends, Kitty was the only one Garrett had never messed with. I had always assumed that it was because she was so quiet, she just kind of blended in and stayed out of his way, but now I wondered if it was something else. There was something...oddly *powerful* about Kitty. Something she had that couldn't be touched or taken, something I had never seen before. A unique and solitary kind of–

"Strength," I said.

"What?" Kitty said, handing the cafeteria lady some bills.

I paid for my breakfast too and Kitty waited for me while I grabbed us some napkins.

"I never knew you were so...strong. I never knew a person could *be* strong, like that. With their words."

Kitty gave a high, merry laugh. "It's not my words that give me strength, it's my faith," she said, leading me toward our table. "And everybody believes in something. It's just a matter of how much."

"Well, I don't have that kind of strength," I mumbled.

Kitty adjusted the flowered beret clipped into her dark curls and studied me quietly with a maternal expression. "There are different kinds of strength. Like not doing something when you really want to. Congrats on not pummeling Garrett into a pulp. Nikki's really proud of you."

I chuckled. "It took every ounce of willpower I had."

"He's your foil," Kitty said.

"He's certifiable is what he is," I said, then paused. "What's a foil?"

"He's like...the anti-Jonathan. It's like he exists to test you."

I gave her a puzzled look. "How so?"

She slung her backpack down beside Ben, who was immersed in conversation with Tyson and Nikki, and I waited impatiently while she searched for words. "Well," she said, "whenever he starts causing trouble, you're there to swoop in and stop it. The things he does are terrible but look at what they're turning you into." She gave me another bright smile and shrugged. "A hero!"

As Kitty slid in between Ben and Lia, Tyson's girlfriend, I plopped down next to Tyson and mulled over what Kitty had said.

Kitty seemed to have an answer for everything. An answer for why life sucked so much and why she was so content all the time. But the problem was that these answers required a lot of faith, and that was definitely not my kind of strength. I found it hard to trust something you couldn't see and feel. Ideals, dreams, faith, none of it mattered. None of it belonged in the real world where there were just as many people happy to crush your dreams and mock your ideals as there were people struggling to hold on to them.

I was a bit jealous of her. I admired her courage to so proudly stand up for what she believed in. *I* couldn't do that. Sure, everyone believed something, was willing to put up a fight for something. The problem was, I didn't know *what* I believed in. I pondered that all through breakfast and even after the bell rang to start classes. I knew what I *liked* and what I *didn't* like. I loved spending time with my friends and playing football. I loathed Garrett and the other bullies that idolized him. But was there anything that I was truly willing to fight to the death for? To stand for, even if it meant standing alone?

I had an appointment with my counselor after first period. All of the seniors had to meet with their counselors a few times during the year as part of a graduation requirement to discuss their career or college goals and to discuss steps for life after school. My counselor, Josiah, was a really cool young guy with shoulder-length dark hair that flipped out all over the place and easygoing eyes that were mottled amber and sea-green. When I entered his office, I saw that he was hunched over his desk, peering intently at his phone.

"Bad news?" I asked, shutting the door behind me.

"That depends on what you consider bad," Josiah said distractedly. "I'm almost out of time."

I looked up at him with concern. He sounded a little agitated. Then he held his phone out to me and said, "Can you find the soup spoon?" He was playing some kind of I-spy game.

I rolled my eyes at him, slinging my backpack down by the chair across his desk and plopping down onto the seat while he clicked a few things on his computer. Josiah had a unique fashion sense, like someone from a different time period trying to fit in. Today he had on a pinstripe vest over a white dress-shirt and some nice slacks, as if he'd be going to a speakeasy after work. He leaned back in his leather office chair and folded his arms behind his head.

"Have kids been giving you a hard time about what happened on the mountain?"

"It hasn't been too bad. So long as no one asks for my autograph I think I'll be okay." I held his phone out to him. "The spoon was behind the swing set," I said.

"Much obliged." Josiah set his phone aside and gave me a genuine, fraternal smile, which I returned in kind. Of all of the teachers I knew at the school, Josiah was the most authentic. He loved what he did, and he'd worked patiently with me ever since my freshman year, back when I'd been nothing but a belligerent, short-tempered pain in the ass.

Looking at his computer screen, Josiah said, "So... I see that for your culminating project you're doing a research paper on... mythology? Care to elaborate?"

"It's always interested me," I said somewhat sheepishly. Tyson and Ben had already given me enough flak for choosing something that they labeled "extremely nerdy." Josiah waited, and I added, "I think that creatures of myth say a lot about human nature, I mean. We've created these monsters over time to represent traits that society has deemed 'evil.' Traits like lust, savagery, and greed. And we've used them to teach our children the repercussions of indulging in such traits. These monsters are scary, but not because of their fangs and claws... They're scary because they're *us*."

"Well put," Josiah said, after digesting my words. There was an odd sparkle in his eyes, like he knew something I didn't. "Consider me impressed. Do you have enough sources to cite?"

"Not really," I admitted. "There isn't much in the library about werewolves and goblins."

Josiah held up one finger. "I can help you there." He bent over, rummaged in his satchel, and pulled out three books, setting them in a pile in front of me with a flourish.

All three of the books had bright, shiny leather covers. The one on top especially caught my eye. It had a deep-red cover, rough and bumpy like lizard skin. There were small, downy feathers stuck to it in places, like you'd find in a craft store but more realistic. Some feathers were inky black, some were a silky cream, others were a deep brown, and one cluster above the title was a bright blazing scarlet. It reminded me of someone's scrapbook or journal that they'd take with them traveling or something.

The title wasn't stamped into the book in any modern way, but hand-scribed in swooping arcs of calligraphy. It read:

Magnificent Creature, the Griffin

"Griffins?" I asked, touching one of the feathers in confusion.

"Is that a problem? Griffins are creatures of myth too, aren't they?"

"Well, yeah, but...they're not really *monsters*..."

Josiah pushed the books closer to me and said, "I think it would be interesting if you also explored the other side of the equation. If gremlins and bugbears and what-have-you symbolize unflattering traits of humanity, what do more heroic creatures say about us? What do they say about you?"

I met his eyes at that last, thinking of my dragon-slaying dream, of Kitty's encouraging words from that morning, and Josiah added playfully, "Hero He'klarr?"

I gave him a small, distracted smile and picked the books up carefully, tucking them into my own bag. Griffins were my favorite animal. Researching them could be fun.

"Thank you," I said a little awkwardly. I wasn't used to receiving gifts.

Josiah stood up and reached over his desk to shake my hand to indicate that our meeting was over. "No problem, Jonathan. If you have any questions, I'm here to support you."

CHAPTER FOUR:
THE FINAL DREAM

What with all of the attention I received throughout the day for my adventure on the slopes, and what with the three books Josiah had given me, I completely forgot about telling Nikki about my dream until the end of the day. The books claimed my attention for much of the day. In sixth period, I unzipped my backpack while my economics teacher droned about something or other and pulled out the red griffin book.

The pages were bound with knots of string to the spine. According to the text, a guy named Peter Malone was the author. Illustrated beneath his name was a large and detailed sketch that I was sure symbolized something.

I flipped through and saw an illustration of a thickly sinewed griffin sitting on its lion haunches and airily licking a fore-talon, its sly eyes peering up and behind it. Above it was a fanciful introduction on the "wondrous beast with a knightly heart."

Chuckling at the author's imagination, I closed this book, slipped it back into the bag, and pulled out another book.

This one had a blank yellow cover but for the spiky title:

LOCATIONS

The first page showed a pretty cool tropical beach called Pebble Embark with calm blue waters, warm golden sand, and all manner of flora and fauna. I flipped through other pages, looking at illustrations of cottages built in trees, a street where the cobblestones were interspersed with giant prisms, a small city floating in the sky. This was a little jarring, as my research paper was about mythological beasts, not made-up worlds, but I figured that the books must have belonged in a set and Josiah had to get all three together.

When the bell to end class finally rang, I dodged a few people who wanted to pester me with questions about rescuing Carl, found Nikki, and we went to her house. On the way I told her about the nightmare I'd had about Mom, and about Josiah's gift.

"The man in your dream called you a little griffin?" she asked, her lips pursed.

"Yeah, weird, huh?"

She tilted her head at me. "It *is* weird because...wouldn't that be considered a compliment? Didn't you say that griffins are good?"

"According to most myths and legends, yeah, they're indicative of nobility and bravery."

"Yeah, like unicorns and fairies." Nikki smiled, mischief dancing in her eyes.

"Except tougher," I said, flexing my arms. "More manly."

Nikki just laughed.

Nikki's quaint home was large, paid for by her father, an engineer. Her mother was a stay-at-home mom, and as loco as a Jack Russell on caffeine. The house was rather lacy and warm, stuffed with Victorian furniture inherited from English ancestors.

Nikki's mom was always doing bizarre things to the décor. One day, cute rows of porcelain cats would be lined up on the mantelpiece; the next, photos of deceased relatives. Today, there wasn't anything on the mantel, but gooey ladybug stickers adorned the windows, and a blanket depicting an exotic flower hung on the wall behind an armoire.

"Mom's in the kitchen baking scones," Nikki said, explaining the delicious scent in the air. She fiddled with her hair. "Dad's at work."

I took a deep, relieved breath. Whenever he was home when I came over, he'd take me into the living room and engage me in conversation that reminded me more of a high-stakes interrogation. Probably because he kept glancing pointedly around me whenever I said something less than stellar–toward his open bedroom door where his hunting rifle was propped in full sight. He didn't think I was good enough for his daughter, but in my defense, I don't think anyone would have been up to his standards.

Nikki led me upstairs to her room and sat on her bed. "Okay, show me the books."

I sat cross-legged on the floor and pulled the books out one by one, handing them to her. Nikki touched one of the soft feathers on the griffin book's cover as if it were made of the most delicate lace, then flipped through the old pages, stopping on the illustration of a hatching griffin chick. She smiled tenderly, a finger on her lip. "Sweet," she said.

In the next ten or so minutes, Nikki's mother came in and lay a tray of scones before us, wearing a blue checkered dress like Dorothy from *The Wizard of Oz*. I greeted her, and she fondly ruffled my hair.

"How have you been, honey?" she asked. "Did you pass that algebra test you were worried about? I'm sure it was nothing compared to racing a bear down a mountain?"

"I did pass the test, thank you. I've been"—I shot Nikki a furtive glance—"fine."

Nikki's mom tilted her head at me, and I could see that she knew I wasn't being entirely honest. Her husband probably would have assumed I'd done something improper with Nikki and gutted me right there, but she respected my privacy and gave her daughter a secret smile—the kind that meant she knew I needed Nikki's support at the moment.

She left us, and then Nikki and I lay side by side, alternating between eating and looking through the book, our legs resting against each other's, commenting every now and then on the detailed drawings. Whoever this Peter guy was, he was talented.

Nikki perused the griffin book while I browsed through the book I hadn't looked at yet.

Like the other two, this book was by the same author, Peter Malone. It had a pale-blue cover of similar material and a journalistic theme with small illustrations pasted to the front: glorious mermaids, furious dragons, prowling chimeras, black-cloaked strangers, and a lot more. This time the title was in bold ink and spelled:

CREATURES OF DREAMS AND NIGHTMARES

Oooh. Maybe Garrett was in here.

Having more of a diverse choice of what to read about, I flipped curiously to a random page that displayed a rough but detailed illustration of something called a siren.

Okay, Peter, you've caught my attention...

There was only one picture, and it showed a gorgeous woman floating on her back on the water, her arms extended and her face inviting.

The dreadful siren coaxes all men into her disastrously covetous arms. To them, she is as beautiful as a queen. But it is indeed good luck to have a woman on board in encounters with the siren, for to her, they look like the demons they truly are—with glowing yellow eyes, fleshless skulls, and hollowed-out, emaciated bodies.

The only possible way to defeat them is to cut through them with a sharp water-based tool like a trident or a harpoon, but they must be vanquished swiftly, for their songs, lilting and sweet, entice many sailors to their doom, persuading them overboard into the water and then into the siren's mouth—sailors being their only food source.

"Uugh!" I groaned and flipped way past the page.

"Jon," Nikki said in a marveling tone of voice. She had turned to a page in the griffin book that was all taken up by a collage of faces. Young kids around my age, shadowed and unsmiling. Nikki went to turn the page, but I held it down and raised a finger in a wait gesture. I read silently:

Many youthful hearts, uncorrupted as of yet by the world, are called "griffin-hearted." But only the wise, strong, and courageous can claim the honor of taking on a griffin's form...

I stopped reading and let Nikki go on, reaching for another scone. Those kids' faces had just been so real and forlorn, as if they had somehow aged into early adulthood. I returned to my book, wondering who those kids had been, and saw that when I'd flipped past the section on sirens, I'd landed on a section about creatures called "Rankers."

A large picture showed a tall, thin, hooded and robed guy holding a rapier to his chest. Little was written about him, but what small amount of information there was, was interesting, however morbid.

Rankers are creatures born of nightmares and sinister thoughts, and they are the eternal foe of the griffin. They fight using an arsenal of dark powers; they can vanish into and control darkness, turn invisible, and anything else that will intimidate and cow their foe, for Rankers are essentially spirits that have no moral conscience, appetite, or heart, but a cunning disposition.

Rankers can only be vanquished by brave and determined hearts, but they are hard to find: each has its own "other self," a disguise used to spy on their victims without taking on their mysterious and frightful cloaked form.

"What are those?" Nikki asked with distaste. "They look like grim reapers or something."

"Rankers," I murmured.

"I guess not all creatures are as good as mermaids, huh?" Nikki chortled. Thinking of the sirens I'd read about, I cleared my throat and muttered, "Nope, not all of 'em."

Nikki and I snacked and browsed through the books until we decided to be productive and work on homework. Somewhere in the middle of the essay I was supposed to be writing about *Jane Eyre*, I nodded off and slipped into another world.

The grass was dry and warm. It prickled my face and clothes. The crusty weeds tangled in my eyelashes, and I lifted my head to open my eyes. Everything had that strange, wobbly quality that dreams usually have, like I was seeing things through a filter on my phone, but that sun was uncannily warm on my back and that grass was so realistically poky that for a few moments I was disoriented and dizzy. *What the hell?*

I sat up quick-like and found that I was in the middle of a ring of white flowers. *What the hell?* The ring was in the center of a meadow surrounded by very old-looking conifer trees. The uncannily fresh blue sky was cloudless. I began to sweat as the sun beat down hard on me.

Something moved off to my right, and I looked to see that it was an elderly, dark-skinned man with a long, full white beard and a bald head. He wore a white button-up shirt tucked into some old patchy jeans. His eyes were a wolfy-silver color, and the sun seemed to make them glow. He had been waiting for me to notice his presence, and now he smiled softly.

"Where am I?" I called over to him. When he didn't answer: "Who are you?"

He ignored me and beckoned me over with his hand, still beaming. I stood and stalked closer.

He produced from his pocket a violet-colored pill that looked like a jelly bean and placed it in my palm, closing my fingers around it. He nodded in encouragement, and I gave him a sardonic, *are you serious?* look.

The man laughed. "Every dream needs a focal point," he said, his voice rich and deep and warm. "If you dream about flying you focus on the mechanics of the flight. If you dream about riding horses, the focus is on the feel of the animal beneath you. I want to have a chat and I don't want you drifting away. This will help you focus."

He patted my hand, urging me to eat the bean. I looked around, feeling helpless. There was still no one else around, no buildings or streets that I could see that marked civilization.

"This is a dream, right?" I asked. My voice sounded muffled and distorted. My head was foggy.

"Of course," the man said in a friendly way.

"If this is a roofie or something, I'm gonna kick your ass," I said to the old man, and he guffawed at me. I licked the pill, then swallowed it before I could change my mind. It didn't make me feel any better or worse, and it tasted minty and slightly herbal.

"Good," the man said. "Now keep thinking of that pill, the taste of it, the feel of it in your hand and going down your throat and we can chat for a bit."

Immediately my mind started to clear. It was the strangest feeling—I recognized that I was dreaming, but I didn't wake up. If anything the sensations of that meadow became more real. The air was a tangible element against my skin. Gravity held me firmly to the ground. The vanilla-like scent of the flowers filled my lungs. It felt like I had just stepped from my world into another.

"This is the weirdest dream I've ever had," I remarked faintly, looking around at the trees. Would the dragon from my other dreams come blasting out of the clouds? Would the man who murdered my mom rise up out of the long grass?

"I don't have long," the stranger said to me. "But I want to help prepare you for what's coming." His silver eyes hooked me, and I returned my attention to him. The taste of mint still chilled my mouth.

"What's...what's coming?" I asked.

The man blinked. "Change."

I stumbled a little bit as the ground swayed beneath me, like I was about to faint. The man stuck out a hand and gripped my shoulder.

"Listen, kid. Things are getting bad and they're only gonna get worse. You've been chosen by Michael, one of the Celestials, to take the throne."

"The hell're you talking about? What throne?"

The man didn't appear pleased at my tone. He tightened his grip on my arm.

"*Listen.* You've been chosen because of who you are, and what you're capable of. But there are...*people* out there that don't like who you are and they hate what you may become. They're going to try coming for you, and you need to be ready. You need to take care of yourself until you're ready to come here."

"Come *where?*" I snapped. This guy was really getting on my nerves. The ground shook again. I stumbled but caught myself this time and the stranger let me go. "Is this about the dragon? Where's the dragon? Do I need to fight it again?"

This time the man smiled as if he were proud of me. He gave me a long, searching look and said, "No, son. But you will be ready soon."

"When?"

"When your eyes begin to reflect your heart. This is the sign Michael has granted to let you know that the time has come, and to let the *world* know that someone will sit on the throne again."

"Who are you?" I asked again.

"My name is Peter," the man said. "See you soon, son. It's an honor to finally meet you."

The ground bucked and I woke up on the carpet of Nikki's room with my face on the paper I'd been writing.

The first thing I did was suck in a long, loud breath as if I'd just come up from underwater, and Nikki gave a leap of surprise where she sat reading on her bed.

"Sheez, Jonathan!" She laughed, clutching her heart.

I scrambled up onto my hands and knees, massaging my eyes. "Whoa, what a trip!" I said. Sudden energy zipped through my limbs like an adrenaline rush, and I stood up and started to pace.

Now Nikki looked concerned. She set her pencil down and leaned forward. "Are you okay?"

"Yeah, yeah, I'm fine," I said, breathless. "I just had the most lucid dream." My foot brushed one of the new books and nudged it across the floor. I looked down at them. The red one was open to the title page, and I saw the author's name scrawled neatly beneath the weird symbol: Peter Malone. I laughed at myself. It hadn't been real. It couldn't have been real. It was just the result of a combination of confronting Garrett, reading the books, and dreaming of fighting dragons.

That's what I told myself. I wasn't sure I believed it.

CHAPTER FIVE:
MOVING SHADOWS

I had dinner with Nikki and her parents that evening, which was a somewhat nerve-wracking affair on my part because Nikki's dad questioned me persistently about my career aspirations, my grades, and whether or not I understood the importance of a 401K. Afterwards she offered to drive me home, but I didn't want to chance her seeing Dad, so I declined and started the long walk by myself in the darkness.

I used the time to myself to think about all of the strange things that were happening and tried to figure out why and when they'd started. I'd always had pretty wild, vivid dreams, ever since I was a kid. But the one I'd had at Nikki's was something else. It had felt so *real.*

When I made it to my house, I saw that Dad was already home from work. That was a good thing—it meant he was probably safely passed out in his favorite armchair. I entered with silent steps and poked my head in the living room again to check on him. Sure enough, there he was, snoring like a freight train. The television was stationed to the news and I lingered a moment to listen to the reports. More weird things were happening across the world—and not just crimes but catastrophes too: an earthquake had leveled a town in Texas; floods were obliterating villages in South America; a freak lightning storm had taken out some Russian farmer's entire herd of cattle.

No one had any explanations. The reporters made weak half jokes about it being the end of the world, but most everyone seemed convinced it was global warming, or an indication of shifting tectonic plates or a harsh winter. I wasn't so sure, but there wasn't much I *was* sure about at the moment. A part of me felt like I was missing something–like I was looking too close at a string, not realizing that it was connected to a bunch of others, forming a web.

I took some generic, over-the-counter sleep meds that I found in Dad's bathroom and for the rest of the evening until they kicked in, I read from my new books about dragons, unicorns, the wingspans and types of griffins. The books didn't give me any answers, but they helped to distract me from the strong feeling that, like Peter had said in my dream, big changes were coming.

I felt much better the next day after a night of dreamless sleep. Avoiding Dad, I snuck outside and caught the bus to school, where I met my friends in the cafeteria. I was still the recipient of a lot of unwanted attention and a few underclassmen heralded me as "Hero He'klarr" when I passed their table, but for the most part the popular topic of my snowboarding adventure had transformed into something else: word had finally gotten out about my confrontation with Garrett in the diner and the rumors were spreading like wildfire.

"Did you actually hit him?" one of my classmates asked under her breath in English class. "I heard Jonathan gave him a concussion," I heard someone else tell their friend on my way to algebra. "Jonathan needs to be careful," a junior said sagely to her friends as Tyson and I passed her on our way to PE, "Doesn't Garrett, like, collect knives or something?" I wondered exactly how many kids in the school had anticipated the storm between Garrett and me to break and for someone to put the bully in his place. And what did Garrett think of all of the talk? Although he and I made it a point to try and stay out of each other's way, I doubted he'd approve of all of the unsavory gossip going around on his behalf.

But that was another thing. Garrett had seemed pretty eager for a fight, but I hadn't seen him at all the past couple of days—not even a glimpse. He wasn't a paragon of perfect attendance or anything, and maybe he was just staying home for whatever reason, but after our heart-to-heart in the restroom of the diner I had the feeling that fighting me had become his top priority. Was he scared? Waiting to jump me in between classes?

As I dressed down into my sweats in the locker rooms off the gym, my mind started to overflow with everything that had happened over the past few days. Thoughts circled my mind on a loop: *Garrett wants to fight. I want to fight him. Nikki says that means I'm giving in. Am I? Am I still a hero if I want to get in a fight with someone? What do I believe in? What do I stand for?*

I thought of the books Josiah had given me. Was I a monster? Something angry and violent and sadistic like a...what were they called...Ranker? Or was I a knight in shining armor? A griffin?

When I closed my locker and made to enter the gym, Tyson took my arm and pulled me aside. His face was serious and concerned, which was so out-of-character for Ty that I did a double take around the emptying locker rooms, expecting to see Garrett emerge from a bathroom stall and square up for a brawl.

Instead Tyson asked, "How do you feel?"

"Um. Tired, I guess?" I frowned at him.

He grunted. "Your dad give you another rough morning?"

"No, he was asleep when I woke up. What's with the questions?"

"You seemed a little out of it. I wanted to make sure the rumors weren't getting to you. Wanted to check if your head's in the game." Tyson gave me a wan, supportive smile.

"In the game? Ty," I lowered my voice as the last three guys left the locker rooms, chatting about their web design class. "Garrett doesn't want to play tennis, okay? This isn't pro-wrestling. He wants a full-blown fight."

Tyson waved his hands in the air like I was an over-excited dog that needed shushing and said, "Okay, okay, okay, yes. I know. And I know I stopped you at the diner and I know that Nikki doesn't want you to fight. And Vince *would* kill you if you got kicked off the team. It's just... We all knew this was going to happen sometime, right?"

"Who's we?" I nudged around him and led the way out into the hall. We cut through the gymnasium toward the doors that would lead outside to the track and Tyson gestured broadly at the underclassmen playing basketball.

"*We,* you know...Ben, Vince, Lia, Kitty...everyone in the school. It's about time, too."

I scoffed. "No pressure."

Tyson seemed insistent that I get the point he was trying to make before our shoes hit the track rubber. "Even before what happened with Nikki, Garrett's made it his mission to kick you whenever you're down. And you've gotten in fights for a lot less than the hell he's put you and Nikki through. It's like you've been saving this fight."

I didn't say anything, but I considered his words. Had I been saving this fight? Or avoiding it for Nikki's sake? Neither of those felt right. I didn't want to make Nikki angry or do anything to jeopardize the hard work I'd put into getting on the team and maintaining a positive school record. But my enmity with Garrett went deeper than a petty dislike and a stupid fistfight. I remembered the vacant, crocodilian gleam in his eyes at the diner and felt a prickle of fear crawl along my skin.

"I want to fight him because I hate him," I murmured, and Tyson leaned closer to hear me better. "But that doesn't mean it's the right thing to do."

"What if it's the only thing to do?" Tyson replied just as softly. "You can't reason with someone like Garrett. He almost killed that kid on the slopes for a laugh. Nikki had to see a counselor for a few weeks after the things he said he wanted to do to her."

I lowered my eyes, feeling the heat of old anger creep up my cheeks. Garrett had been forced to go to counseling as well, and somehow he'd ended up convincing his teachers and the school psychologist that his lascivious words had been the result of deep-seated trauma and self-loathing. They'd made him write Nikki a ridiculous apology and signed him off as genuinely repentant.

Tyson elbowed me, watching me think. "Garrett's your Everest," he said. "He's the dragon you have to vanquish."

I looked up sharply. The vision from the past few nights, me gearing up to slay a fire-breathing monster, flashed through my mind. Maybe fighting Garrett *was* the right thing to do. Maybe this *was* my chance to be that knight in shining armor. To not only defeat the dragon and spare *myself* future misery, but to defeat the dragon because it meant sparing others, like Carl and Nikki and anyone else Garrett tormented, as well.

"Huh," I said thoughtfully. "Thanks, Ty. It's a lot to think about."

Tyson clicked his tongue at me. He patted my back and started trotting over to his girlfriend Lia. "No prob. Whatever you decide, just promise me that you won't start anything until I get back from the wedding, okay? I wouldn't miss this brawl for the world!"

The next morning in English class I texted Tyson goodbye and told him to have fun at his sister's wedding, even though he'd already caught the flight and wouldn't get my message until he landed. My teacher, a man who before had harbored a noticeable dislike for me, called my name as "Hero He'klarr" for attendance. He gave me a sly smile, and I worked my facial muscles into what I hoped was a pleasant grin and returned to doodling mean caricatures of him and his horrific ear hair in the margins of my notebook.

Twenty minutes into class the intercom beeped on, and everyone silenced and perked up, hoping for an announcement worthy enough to release them from the torture of trying to understand Shakespeare. The principal's voice was somber and forlorn. He started out by clearing his throat. Bad sign. I anxiously tapped my pencil's eraser on the desktop.

"Staff and students, I have a grave announcement to make. One of our students, Tyson Locklear, has been one of hundreds to suffer life-threatening injuries in the crash of a hijacked plane bound for California."

I didn't hear the rest of the announcement. I felt myself go empty—as if an arctic wind had rushed down my throat and into my lungs.

I stepped out of the classroom, ignoring Mr. William's half-hearted protests, and dialed Rebecca Montral's number—Tyson's sister.

On the fourth ring, she picked up with a wet and stuffy, "Hello?" She sounded close to falling apart.

"Hey, Rebecca, it's me, Jonathan. We haven't seen each other in a while, but I'm—"

"Tyson's friend," she interrupted, sounding a little happy to hear from me. "I remember you."

There were a few seconds of quiet, and I clenched and unclenched the fingers of my free hand, popping my knuckles with agitation, then asked, "How is he?"

Rebecca sniffled and struggled to give a coherent answer. "He's in the E.R. right now. The plane wasn't too high up before it crashed, and he was right in the middle of the plane, so he's not in the worst condition, but..." She blew her nose, excused herself, and continued. "His right lung collapsed, one leg is broken in three places, his spine is bruised, he's got a concussion, and he almost lost three of his fingers."

I gulped, growing closer and closer to tears with each listed injury, even as Rebecca's voice became nearly unintelligible.

"Mom and Dad are fine. Both of them just have a few sprains and fractures. Tyson's tough. He'll make it."

I nodded, then remembered I was on the phone and reassured her. "Yeah. He's a rebel. He'll come out of there with a smile on his face and a joke at the ready."

Rebecca laughed and agreed. We waited for each other to say something else, and when we didn't, we said goodbye. She promised to keep me posted, and I promised to spread the news to Nikki and the others. After that, I didn't feel like sticking around at school. I barely endured the rest of the English lesson, then skipped out early, walking home and texting my friends as I went to fill them in on Ty's condition.

When I got home, I tried to watch some TV, made myself a sandwich that I didn't have the appetite to eat, picked up the garbage and empty beer cans in the living room, and flipped through my new books a little more, but nothing helped to distract me from what had happened. Would Tyson be okay? Was my best friend dying at that very moment? I had just taken out the garbage and put the lid back on the garbage can when Dad came peeling in the driveway, his rusty pickup rattling.

A spike of alarm and fear pierced my chest and my hand shook a little as I replaced the garbage can lid. Usually I timed it to where I was out taking a walk through the woods behind my house when Dad came home. I'd been so wrapped up in my thoughts that I hadn't been paying attention to the time.

I watched Dad stumble out of his truck, cursing when he almost slipped on the gravel, holding as still as I could. If I left him alone and ignored him maybe he'd just go straight inside.

Dad looked up, belching, his face covered in rough stubble, his skin pale and sickly. "What the hell are you looking at?" he said in a slurred growl. "Your disgusting old man? Your...failure of a father? Come on, say it!"

Quickly, I looked away, my hands going clammy, hating myself for the weakness I felt. The fear. I started walking along the wall toward the back of the house but Dad beelined and met me at the corner, his steps uncoordinated and aggressive. He blocked me and the stench of alcohol came off of him in a cloud.

"You got a problem?" he hissed.

"No," I muttered.

"Lookit me when I'm talking to you!" Dad shoved me against the side of the house, hard enough to rattle the window beside my head. Pain rolled up my backbone where it had struck the siding hardest and all of the frustration, anger, anxiety, and grief that had been building up inside me for the past few days started boiling over. I looked up and met Dad's eyes and something in my face seemed to arrest him.

"Yeah, I've got a problem," I said, real low. He blinked at me stupidly. "You. You're my problem." I pushed him off of me and my voice was rising as I spoke. "Who do you think you are? What are you even doing here? This isn't your house. *I* pay the bills. *I* clean up after you and your shitty friends. You're just a rat crawling out of whatever tavern will still have you to grab some food and sleep before starting over again." Dad started backing away and I followed, outrage continuing to swell inside me. "And I'm glad Mom's not here to see what you've become because you know what you are? You're *worthless*."

Dad's face went slack as if I'd shot him and something dark and hot deep in my chest crowed with pride at the reaction I'd elicited. Then, so quickly that I didn't have time to register the danger I was in, Dad's expression went from wounded to a broken and agonized kind of fury. He hit me across the side of my face, and I went down to the gravel hard, skinning my cheek and the bridge of my nose. Instinctively, even though blotches of color marred my vision and my head swam, I curled up and scrambled as quickly as I could to my feet to avoid any further blows, one hand going up to my face.

Ice seemed to seize my guts in a sudden deep-freeze. Dad had given me some excessively disciplinarian slaps and beltings before; pushed me or thrown things at me, usually while shouting himself hoarse with despairing rants of self-loathing. But he had never hit me like that before, on purpose with a closed fist.

He trembled, but not with anger anymore–that had gone as quickly as it had come. His mouth was a mortified "O" and his eyes were just as round and filled with the same guilt I'd seen countless times before when his anger passed, after he realized what he'd done.

"Jonathan! Oh, I'm so sorry, I–"

I pushed past him. Tears of pain and a cocktail of other feelings had started to well up in my vision and I didn't want him to see them.

"I'm staying at a friend's for a few days," I said as I walked. "You can do whatever the hell you want."

Dad didn't come after me, didn't say anything, and I didn't look back once as I made it to the end of my driveway and started walking up the street.

Of all of my friends, Vince was the one who looked after the group's emotional wellbeing. He was a big guy from Mexico who couldn't claim a spare ounce of fat, and he was a beast on the football field, but his eyes were as gentle and warm as those of the horses he and his family raised. It was Vince who had been the one to drag me to football tryouts my freshman year, and in all honesty, it had probably saved my life.

Everyone needs an outlet, some way to vent, to get away from their stress. Between Garrett at school and Dad at home, I didn't have that. In middle school I had started getting edgier, shorter-tempered, picking fights with Garrett's stupid friends, blowing off homework. High school didn't look too bright for me. But after I'd made the team, a combination of Vince's encouragement, the coaches' strict rules about maintaining grades, and falling for Nikki a few months later, turned me around.

I owed my every smile to Vince, and whenever I tried to thank him for being so selfless, for having been so patient with the jackass I used to be, for showing me that I could make a different future for myself, he would just roll his shoulders bashfully and change the subject.

After the fight with Dad, I had considered going to Nikki's, but once I felt the bruise growing on my cheekbone, I decided on Vince instead. His parents wouldn't ask too many questions about what had happened and Vince, who would know what had happened, wouldn't ask the questions I didn't want to answer and wouldn't fret like Nikki's mother would. I didn't go to school the next day to give my face a bit of time to heal, and when Nikki called later to see what had happened, I explained the whole thing. She came over and she, Vince, and I took some of his horses on a trail ride along the edge of his property.

Rebecca texted me halfway through the day to say that Tyson was still groggy from his operations, but he would pull through. My spirits lifted considerably and climbed higher when I woke up on Vince's couch the next day.

It was Friday. Game day.

Everyone at school was pumped for the game. They were dressed in school colors; not an inch of clothing *wasn't* red, black, or yellow. Ben had coated himself in the hues and looked like a big multicolored mountain man in his layered garments. Terrified underclassmen, when they saw him trundling down the hall shouting the school's alma mater proudly, ducked behind teachers and snack machines. Most everyone had "Play for Ty" worked into their outfit in some way: with paint on their faces, bedazzled onto their shirts, or on homemade armbands.

Nikki had convinced some of her friends to join her in wearing little lion-like griffin tails and tiny feathered wings. When we passed in the hall, she winked and wrinkled her nose at me. I curled my hands into talons and tickled her, wrapping her up in a quick, tight squeeze.

Right after school, the team met in the locker rooms to change into our gear for practice. I slipped my breeches over the hip and leg padding and laced up my cleats. Tightening the bulky shoulder pads and tossing on my jersey, I faced Vince and asked, "How do I look?"

"Ready to slay some Minotaurs." He grinned. "How does your face feel?"

"It's sore," I said ruefully, gently sliding my helmet down over my face and grimacing as it dragged across my swollen cheek.

"Can you still fight?" Vince asked. I showed my teeth in a wolfish smile. He was reciting our team's mantra; our battle-chant.

"Hell yeah."

"Can we still win?"

"Oh, we're going to win."

He held his hand up and we clasped forearms. "Then let's go, Griffin," he said.

Already, the stadium was filling up. No one was sitting. No one probably would for the whole game. The Minotaurs' school rivalry with us was bloody and legendary.

The band was practicing on a platform beside the stadium. Vince was getting a little jiggy, and when the band struck a raw note and started a different song, he stopped and dejectedly hung his head.

"Poor Vincie!" I heard Coach bark. "Drop down and give me thirty!" He turned to me. "You too, Captain, for keeping us waiting." I obeyed and did as I was told, though I felt like I could've done a hundred more. Energy was coursing through me, my adrenaline building as if I was about to charge off into bloody combat.

I may not have had a place I could exactly call "home," but this was the closest thing to it. The Astroturf was where I belonged. This was my battlefield, where I could slay my dragons. No matter how out of control my life was, here, I was in control.

After I'd finished my pushups and jogged to the sidelines to get a drink of water, I noticed a figure standing conspicuously against the railing of the stadium, leaning over it with arms crossed staring at me, chewing some gum. It was Garrett.

I blinked at him, astonished that he'd suddenly made an appearance after his lengthy absence from school. And as far as I knew, Garrett never showed up to sporting events. A smile crawled up his face. It was a sinister and secretive kind of smile; something challenging and cold and snakelike. He winked and tapped his wrist as if to indicate a watch. I knew what he was saying, even if he hadn't used words: *After the game.*

A wicked kind of hunger filled me. After everything that had happened, Tyson getting hurt, fighting with my dad, my weird dreams, this would be good. I'd have to face Nikki's wrath once she found out about the fight, but Tyson had been right about this being a long time coming. Garrett had hit me where it hurt in the diner, mocking my family, gouging my self-esteem and he'd almost added manslaughter to his rap sheet, sending Carl up the mountain. Even worse, he hadn't cared. Well, I would make him care. I flashed him my own savage little smile and nodded.

Eventually, the other team showed up on a bus and came spilling out onto the field. The mascots looked ready to beat the costumes off each other. Our griffin mascot shook his fists at the rival, his wings flapping as he jumped up and down on the spot and imitated aiming punches like a prize-fighter prepping for a match. The rival Minotaur mascot pointed at the horns of her mask and then at the griffin, her posture tight and intense, locked like a bull bracing to charge. The griffin put his hands on his stomach and pantomimed guffawing.

By the time Coach pulled us in close for a huddle, I had worked myself up into a kind of bloodthirsty frenzy. I had taken all of my anxiety and anger and given it a physical form to be defeated: the Minotaurs. The stadium lights shone unflatteringly on the bald dome of Coach's head as he bent, looking heatedly at each of us.

"Okay, boys. You've made me proud so far this year. Don't let me down now. Remember, even if we lose, we want everyone to think back on this day and know that we didn't go down without a fight. Jon, Vince"–we looked at him–"you two sure you don't want to sit this 'un out? I understand if Tyson's accident is too fresh–"

"If anything, Coach, I want to do this *for* Tyson," I interrupted with the fierce bloodlust contact sports bring out in a man.

"What about you, Vince?"

Vince nodded solidly, lips pressed into a firm line. The coach looked proud enough to cry. I'm pretty sure his chin wobbled.

"Alright, then, Griffins. Vince, I want you and Manuel to keep an eye on Jonathan. Those linebackers of theirs look tough. Jonathan, run as fast as you can. Let's show those Minotaurs, okay?"

I stepped in with an extended fist and roared, *"Who's ready to fight and win?"*

The team piled their hands on mine and yelled, *"Gooooo, Griffins!"*

We broke apart, and I loped over to the opposing team's captain where he paced by the referee. Smiling through my mouth guard, my ears picked up the sound of the cheerleaders coaxing the audience into our school chants. I reached out to the opposing team's captain to shake his hand, as was customary. He briefly gripped mine while holding my gaze as if trying to get across the fact that he wanted to crush me into the grass and then step all over me.

"Heads or tails?" the ref asked, holding out a quarter.

"Heads," I said.

The quarter flipped in the air and thumped onto the ground. We all kneeled to see the upward side. Tails.

I grimaced and the Minotaur captain's mouth quirked into a small smile. "We'll kick off," he said.

I clenched my jaw. This gave the Minotaurs two advantages: they would get the kick off after half-time. And secondly, after having gotten the measure of my team and knowing how and where to hit us, they would get to choose which side of the field to play from. Our field, though looked after lovingly enough, was notorious for being windy at its western side where it faced the sloping, open fields. On rainy days it also tended to accumulate puddles, but we wouldn't have to worry about that until a few weeks more. Still, the Minotaurs were aware of, and would exploit, our weaknesses.

The Minotaurs jeered at me as their captain returned to them. *For Tyson,* I thought. *Keep it together for Tyson.* I turned away and, just for a moment, drank in the atmosphere, pulling in every sound, sight, smell, and sensation, and embracing it. A group of people in the front row of the bleachers started to rhythmically chant my jersey number, stomping their feet in time to the chant. I spread my arms at them and bowed as I stepped forward into motion again, earning a collective laugh of audience appreciation for my trademark playful arrogance.

But as I moved, as the chant melted into a toneless wave of breath and excited shouts of near-pandemonium, the most curious sense of deja-vu came over me and I remembered my strange dragon-slaying dream with alarming clarity.

For a long, disorienting moment, dream and reality meshed and I had the strange, disconnected feeling that I was in both, as if I'd just been baptized in my own imagination and was feeling it cloud over me. The brilliant colors of the waving banners and pom-poms became torn pennants snapping in a foul, smoky wind. The cheers became a solid, wavering note of misery and pain from a demolished village. The stomping feet became steadily approaching, flapping wings...

"He-klarr!" Vince shouted. I came to, shaking my head, and the deja-vu feeling dissipated slightly, though it wavered at the fringes of my mind. It was no wonder that I was mixing the game with the dream—sometimes the heat of the game was a lot like a battlefield.

The stadium was now full, and the air was beginning to freeze into nighttime. We got into position for the play. I crouched, fingertips snarled in the grass and leg muscles tight, still a tad dizzy from having my dream come flooding into my mind. The whistle was blown, and the game began.

I bounced off of a left fielder and scurried backward, heard the distant *pop* of a Minotaur kicking the football in our direction.

Merging into a clear space, I looked ahead to find Vince. The ball sailed through the air, canting oddly as the wind caught it. But Vince jumped like a cat, snaring it in his fingers. I burst into motion, close behind him. He turned and lobbed the ball laterally to me. I caught it and tucked it against my stomach just before Vince was crushed beneath twenty-five million Minotaurs. I poured on the speed, heading toward the endzone.

I almost thought I heard the clash of metal armor, the ringing of swords and shouting of fighting men. The lights of the stadium, flickering in my vision as I turned my head, put me in mind of dragon-fire. Rather than let myself become overwhelmed by the strangeness of the poignant daydream, I embraced it and channeled the euphoric battle-fury I had felt as a storybook knight about to face down a fire-breathing monster.

Keeping light on my toes, I extended a leg to sprint for a touchdown. But like a dragon's claws around an unlucky knight-errant, I felt thick arms clench tightly about my legs. A helmet dug behind my knees, and I collapsed and skidded a ways. I flopped over and came face-to-face with a Minotaur fielder.

He stuck his grill into mine, the plastic clicking together, and shouted, *"Waz up?"* Cheering, he ran to join his whooping teammates.

I struggled to my feet, furiously dusting myself off and rubbing in my grass stains. The stadium loomed in the corner of my eye, stringy verses of an encouraging chant drifted past my ears. Was Garrett up there in those bleachers? That'd be great; he showed up to his first football game ever in time to see me fail. After all, the vision swimming in my head was nothing more than the ghost of an epic dream. Reality was a much harsher, colder mistress—here, I was no chivalric knight. I was just...little old me.

We adjusted the line of scrimmage, and this time the Minotaurs intercepted the ball, running it back for a touchdown, and added the extra point on the kick. They were up 7-0.

I tried not to seem too discouraged. Coach slumped deflated on the sidelines. I stood tall, ready to run to him and receive a play but he noticed, shook his head, and gave a series of gestures. I hesitated but nodded and returned to my position. The Minotaurs were winded after their hard work. It would benefit us to avoid a huddle and defy them a chance to rest and catch their breath. I envisioned myself as the knight in my dream, side by side with comrades in arms, leading them into the charge. Maybe I wasn't really some armored hero, but Firestone needed this win after what had happened to Tyson. *I needed this.*

I returned to my position behind the center and squeezed the shoulders of the guys behind me as I went. One of them, Manuel, his chest heaving and breath leaving him in clouds, gasped, "Damn, they're quick!"

"Tomahawk Down Hot!" I shouted, my breath exploding from my helmet like dragon's breath. "Tomahawk Down Hot!"

Okay, Griffins, I thought, replacing my mouthguard, *we let them have that one.* The Minotaur defense was fast and tough. But with the right holes plugged and Alex and Drew flanking me I could do a pump fake, acting a pass, sprint through, and try to get us back on the road. Alex, one of the leanest guys on the team, was our speedster. I could see through his helmet that his bright, pointed face was alight with the thrill of the game. Drew, about a hundred pounds heavier, would be an unyielding wall of muscle defending us.

The whistle was blown, and after the snap the center thrust the ball back into my hands. I gripped it and joined Alex and Drew.

Faking as if I'd passed Alex the ball, I slowed down to a jog, and Alex sped up, beelining right. The Minotaurs' linemen veered to chase him, and Drew strayed away to tackle someone coming up on my tail. Now I picked up speed, twisted and turned, flying over the grass.

A great weight pulled on my leg, and I looked down to see the same Mr. Brawny who'd taken me down before. The dream-dragon in my mind roared its fury and snatched at me with its great talons. But I was so close, and I would not be defeated. I dragged us both forward and fell over the line. Touchdown.

The Griffins screamed in ecstasy, the school colors flashing in the stadium.

I looked the disgruntled Minotaur in the eye where he was still leeched to my leg and shot cuttingly, *"Waz up?"* He looked away and strode off stiffly, a dragon defeated.

After that, we fell into our usual rhythm and even the dream faded reluctantly in clutching tendrils. My worries about Tyson, fighting Garrett, and Dad all coalesced into an imaginary foe there on the field. If I could win the game, I could overcome my other troubles as well. Every time I ran the ball, my eyes zeroed in on the goalposts, urging me to move faster, dodge sharper, remain positive. When on defense, I prowled the sidelines like a general surveying his troops, scouring the Minotaurs for an advantage we could use.

The ref started to dole out penalties as the game progressed and became more violent. But despite the false starts, the players trying to discreetly stomp on one another's legs after a tackle, and the increasing attempts the Minotaurs made to hit me hard enough and bring me down violently enough to put me out for the rest of the game–despite all of that, the score ended up with us winning 48 to 26.

The Minotaurs wore stricken stares. The griffin mascot ran sideways before the stadium, pumping his fists. The cheers were rekindled, the band struck up. The football team hustled together, hopping up and down in a roaring mass, many shouting Tyson's name. Some of the school spilled onto the field.

This was what I had craved for years–to be the object of people's adulation, not their sympathy. The world at large may have been falling apart, Tyson may have been in the hospital, but now I felt brave, fierce–ready to challenge the next calamity that dared rear its head to confront me. And that calamity was Garrett.

I pulled away from a noogie from Vince and trotted over toward the locker room, spitting out my mouth guard and removing my helmet. The cold air felt good in my steaming hair.

Nikki came up from behind and hugged me, squealing, "We won, we won, we won! I'm so proud of you!" She swung around and gave me a kiss that I tried to return just as passionately, but I was still in battle-mode, riding the high of the game and ready to channel it into crushing Garrett, slaying my next dragon. I scoured the crowd and Nikki searched my face.

"What's wrong?"

I was torn. Should I stay and celebrate with Nikki and my teammates? Or go find Garrett? The desire to fight was so strong that my hands shook. It felt as if the hair on my neck was standing up like the hackles of some rabid animal.

"Babe, are you hurt?"

I looked down at Nikki, trying to cobble together a believable excuse for leaving her on the field and going to pulverize Garrett, but then I saw the worry in her face, drawing her eyebrows together. She was looking at the bruise on my face and she said gently, "We should get some ice on that."

The boiling bloodlust churning in my guts cooled to a simmer. I couldn't leave Nikki behind just to go and pick a fight with some bully. I didn't want to disappoint her and turn into someone who thought the epitome of greatness was whoever could throw the hardest punch. The vision in my head of myself as a knight in shining armor, a hero, drifted lazily across my mind's eye as if in gentle reprimand.

Garrett was no dragon stooped over the remains of a decimated village of innocent victims. He was a sadistic bully that wasn't worth the effort it would take to beat him up. I wasn't going to become my father, and I wouldn't stoop to Garrett's level.

"Ice sounds good," I said. Nikki smiled and we put our arms around each other, walking back toward the whooping and cheering throng to join in the celebration.

CHAPTER SIX:
RANKERS

After I'd washed up, and after we'd helped to scarf down a pizza with my team at the busy Firestone pizzeria, crowded with other postgame revelers, Nikki and I went for a walk through the park nearby.

I picked a hot-pink bee-balm flower and tucked it behind Nikki's ear.

She leaned on my shoulder and murmured sleepily, "Read any good books lately?" From the sly tone in her voice, I knew she was referring to the ones Josiah had given me.

I watched a bug drone by and replied offhandedly, "You could say that. For one thing, did you know that werewolves have fur the same color, length, and volume as their human hair? It's what helps people identify who's infected and who isn't."

Nikki was quiet, and then said, "No, I did not know that." She pulled away from my arm and looked sideways at me. "'Helps people'? Present tense?"

I cringed in the dark shadows of the trees beside us. "Well, I mean, helped. Or would help. That is, hypothetically."

"Getting a little too into our research project, Jonathan?" Nikki teased.

I struggled to change the subject. "Getting a little into you!"

Nikki pulled in close, her face inches from mine. "A little? Is that all?" she whispered.

I inhaled her scent and closed my eyes. I couldn't remember ever feeling this peaceful.

"Maybe a lot," I mumbled into her hair.

She kissed my bottom lip and whispered playfully, "Good game, quarterback."

I hugged her tight, our hearts bouncing dizzily off each other's. And what a magical moment it was...for about a second or two.

Cold hands wrapped around my shoulders, pulling me roughly away from Nikki. It was so dark! In a panic, I kicked out with my legs, tossed my head, bucked, and shoved at whoever was holding me. Nikki screamed. I saw silhouetted figures wrestling her still. With an animal snarl, I redoubled my efforts to get to her, towing my captors along a few feet, my muscles straining against their grip.

But they succeeded in shoving me to the ground, driving me down on my back into the frosty dirt, and when I fought to rise again, a muddy boot pinned my chest. I kicked my legs, then saw that the guy pressing me to the earth was holding something like a butcher's knife over my eye. *Oh.* I ceased wriggling and absorbed the details.

Two people held Nikki, who was whimpering in shock, and three stood around me, including the one with a boot on my chest. I also noticed with a sharp intake of breath that all five wore medieval-looking cloaks with hoods. I thought of the nightmarish creatures in my new bestiary book.

"Rankers?" I breathed to myself. The one resting half his body weight on my torso chuckled darkly and leaned over.

"Hello," he greeted in a voice that sounded vaguely familiar. "It's been a while, He'klarr."

"What? Who are you?" I tried to push the guy off of me but he wasn't budging.

"I'm not surprised that you don't remember. It's been a while," the man said. "You really hurt Garrett's feelings when you didn't keep your little playdate."

Nikki made an angry noise behind the hand of one of the guys holding her, and I asked falteringly, "Garrett? Did he put you up to this? Are you Rankers? Is he a Ranker too?"

The black-hooded head tilted to one side, as if intrigued.

"What's a Ranker?" he asked. His voice was playful, mocking. I was struck again by how strangely familiar it was. I searched my memory, trying to place it.

The man pressed harder on my chest and gazed hungrily down at me like a lizard with a tasty, bloody morsel beneath its claw. "If you're asking whether or not this is a nightmare, then I would have to say yes, I guess, figuratively, it is. But everyone knows that you can defeat a nightmare if you're brave enough. Are you brave enough, little griffin?" He removed his boot, and I gasped for air. His thugs yanked me to my knees, holding my arms, and I watched him stride coolly over to Nikki.

I felt like lightning had just zapped my skin. Now I remembered.

"I dreamed about you! I dreamed that you were the guy who killed my mother!" My legs were too weak with fear to support me. All I could do was cower there in the dirt, confusion and terror washing over me like peals of thunder.

"Now Jonathan, how could I kill your mother? That would mean I would have had to rise from the grave!" He snickered, and moved closer to Nikki, circling her slowly like a shark scenting blood.

"Then who are you? How do you know Garrett? Have I seen you before?"

"In a manner of speaking. Let's put it this way: you pissed Garrett off, so he sent me here to make you pay. You may be king of the school, Jonathan, MVP and beloved boyfriend," he paused to make a gagging sound and his companions chuckled darkly, "But not here. Here in the darkness, you're nothing. And that's what Garrett wants to make you...a nothing. A ghost. A memory. And he wants to do it nice...and slow...and painful..."

"B-but why? How?" I managed to ask. My voice sounded squeaky. "This has always been between Garrett and me, always! What is he doing bringing you guys into this? Bringing Nikki into it? What's changed?"

The man studied me, weaving around his companions like a snake through grass, the dark space beneath his hood fixated in my direction.

After a long moment, he said in an undertone, "You're a football player, so I'll say this in a way you can comprehend: In the first quarter, you test your opponent, try to gauge their strengths and weaknesses, see if they deviate from what you already know or have learned about them. You might let them win a few points just to lull them into a false sense of security. Goad them into hubris–into making mistakes."

He paced closer to me, his black cloak freckled silver in the moonlight through the sparse autumn leaves above us.

"The game only really starts in the second quarter, when you start to push back, when you rip that false sense of security out from under them and watch them tumble. And the big guns? You only pull those out at the very end, to pulverize whatever weak defense your opponent has managed to cobble together."

Now he stalked back over to Nikki, stroking her hair behind her shoulder tenderly. Nikki twisted her head away, her eyes narrowed. She kicked out but seemed to miss. The man laughed and pulled her face toward his, removing his friend's hand. "You and Garrett have similar tastes, Jonathan," he hissed. "He likes them feisty too…"

I clambered up to my feet and started jumping and twisting, renewing my efforts to help Nikki, and almost broke free, but one of the guys restraining me drove his fist into my kidney. I cried out, falling slightly before catching myself. My heart thudded so hard I felt it beating behind my eyeballs. Everything pulsated with a weird neon light. I felt detached from what was happening–drifting above everything and watching as if through someone else's eyes.

I couldn't let this happen. Not to Nikki.

When I looked up, the man was looking at me. "Some changes are going to come your way real soon, He'klarr, and we'll have the upper hand." His tone became casual. "Have you ever seen fresh blood? Bright from the arteries?"

I felt like if I opened my mouth to answer, I'd throw up. A squirmy tendril of premonition swam in my innards.

The stranger looked from Nikki to me and back again. "What would it take to break a prince's heart? What would it take to crush a hero?" he asked no one in particular. I felt the grips on my arms slacken as my captors became distracted by what would soon happen.

The man held the knife to Nikki's throat. "What does a hero become when he's lost everything?"

"*Jon!*" Nikki screamed.

I ripped away and jumped at the man, pounding his back and neck with my fists. He stumbled to the side, flinching. I scrambled back, warding off one of the thugs with a wild haymaker, and stood in front of Nikki protectively. The knife-wielding stranger wasn't even fazed.

"Lucky shot, Jonathan. But you won't be able to protect your little girlfriend forever—"

"Hey, what's going on?" I heard hurried footfalls coming along the path as a group of people, other kids from our school taking a walk after watching the game, approached.

The man from my nightmare gave a prim little sigh and said, "If you intend to become any kind of threat then you have a lot of work to do, Jonathan. I'll be seeing you again very soon."

They departed down a trail, and I collapsed onto my knees. After a few quiet seconds I felt Nikki's shivering hands helping me up, heard her sobs.

"C-come on. They—they left," she said.

"Sshh," I soothed, getting myself up. "It's alright, baby. We're safe, sweetheart."

Supporting each other, we waited for our inadvertent rescuers to come over and tried our best to make sense of all that had just happened.

By the time Nikki and I were done talking to the police, it was close to two in the morning. Everyone at Vince's house was already asleep, but even though I felt exhausted, stiff, and sore, sleep was the farthest thing from my mind. When I finally made it to Vince's house, I collapsed on his sofa and turned on the news, trying to calm down, trying to relax, pressing a bag of frozen corn against my swollen face. But if anything, I grew tenser with the incoming reports. There had been a slew of savage murders overnight by some unknown assailant in a small town in Oklahoma. Only a handful of residents out of a little more than a hundred remained alive.

On closer-to-home news, a girl about six years old had been kidnapped from a town not far from mine. She was presumed dead, and no suspects had been named. The tearful parents just said that during the night they'd heard their daughter crying out from her room. When they'd entered, she was gone. They were astounded as to how the intruder had been able to commit his crime. The girl's room was locked from the inside and seemed untouched when they had gone to investigate. The super-religious family ventured to say that they suspected evil entities to be involved in the incident.

Nothing ever happened in Firestone, and yet, tonight, Nikki and I had been jumped by people that looked a lot like the Rankers I'd read about in a make-believe book, and Nikki had almost died. Even more bizarre was the fact that the man with the knife had sounded exactly, impossibly, like the man in my nightmares. And now Garrett wasn't just interested in having your average school-yard brawl; he had recruited a gang of roughs to harm Nikki solely because that would hurt *me*. Now Garrett and his new cult, or whatever they were, seemed to have crawled right out of a book about monsters like a nightmare come to life.

I shut off the television and fell back, massaging my face and finding my eyes damp. I didn't know if it was because of the sad reports or the stress of the day. What had happened to turn the world inside out? And why did I have the feeling that it was about to get a whole lot worse?

CHAPTER SEVEN:
FIGHTING GARRETT

I couldn't avoid the inevitable any longer. Although they didn't complain, and I tried my best not to be a nuisance, Vince's family couldn't house me forever. I desperately needed a change of clothes, and there was a pile of homework biding its time in my backpack that I needed to complete before Monday. After what had happened in the park, I also wanted to get a hold of the three books Josiah had given me and see if they said anything more about Rankers, like whether or not they had attracted a cult of followers over the years. The man in the park the previous night hadn't admitted to being a Ranker, but he'd known what they were—had compared them to nightmares. Even if he wasn't one of the monsters from my books, that didn't mean he and Garrett weren't affiliated with them in some way.

The problem was, if I wanted my schoolwork, fresh clothes, and answers, I needed to go home to get them.

To my surprise, the lights were on in the house. Usually Dad spent his Saturdays either out visiting a barstool or hung-over inside in the dark. If the lights were on, someone cared enough to want to see and interact with the environment around them. Maybe it was a concerned neighbor. Unlikely, seeing as the closest neighbors were a mile away.

I quietly opened and closed the front door. Pop's graying stubble matched his bushy, unkempt hair, and his eyes were wild as he shot around the wall from the kitchen.

"Jonathan!" Relief suffused his weary, mysteriously sober features. He sagged against the kitchen entryway, closing his eyes and rubbing his face with his hands. "I was so worried. Where have you been?"

Intense dislike wriggled behind my ribs like a cornered, venomous creature. "You. Were. Worried." I said quietly, letting each word drop from my mouth like lead. I'd left the house for days at a time before, without letting Dad know where I'd gone or when I'd be back. This was the first time it had ever concerned him.

Dad stepped toward me, and I took a few paces back. When he spoke, his voice was uncomfortable. "I had no idea where you were, or if you were coming back or not, and...I wanted to know if you were okay."

"I'm just dandy," I said.

Dad sighed at the ice in my voice and rubbed the back of his neck. "Son, I didn't mean to hurt you. You know that I'm trying to get better–"

I was already short-tempered and irritable because of the previous night's trauma, so I blew up at his excuse, the words he always said but never meant. "Yeah? Try harder! Drinking a case of beer every day is not going to bring Mom back and if you think that kicking me around the house will change anything, then you're living in a fantasy."

Dad stared at me, aghast, and I noticed that his eyes were watering. If anything, it made me angrier.

"But here," I said coldly, "let me give you a dose of reality. Did you know that we almost lost this house, *Mom's* house, twice? I had to work overtime for a month at the lumber mill to make payments and I almost failed my junior year because of it. Yeah, that's another thing—I'm graduating next year, maybe with a football scholarship. I'm in love with a girl that I want to marry someday, and you?" I sneered disdainfully. "You've missed all of it." I stopped, red in the face.

For a second, I thought Dad was going to hit me again, and I got ready to take it, but then he took another deep breath, and his voice shook when he murmured, "I'm going for a walk."

I blinked and shuffled around him, moving for the stairs. At the last moment I looked at him over my shoulder in time to see the front door snick closed behind him. Dad's attitude perplexed me. He must've been really sober. Of course, it wouldn't last, but it was nice once in a while to complain and yell at him without him hitting back.

As I'd suspected there was nothing helpful in Josiah's books. Even though I'd already finished reading them all, I scoured them again, cover to cover, skimming passages about fearsome gargoyles and places like Fairies Waterfall, a lush haven of pure water and bizarre plants. But I found nothing new to add to the cryptic page on Rankers in the bestiary. I couldn't even find anything online about them, no matter how deeply I scoured the internet. Maybe I was wrong. Maybe the Rankers had nothing to do with anything. But I wanted to talk about it with Nikki anyway.

At the beginning of September, the school had planned a senior trip that would count toward the volunteer hours necessary for graduation. The next day, Sunday, a bus took Ben, Kitty, Nikki and I, along with a group of other upperclassmen to the Arrow Creek homeless shelter where we were to help out all day cleaning up and preparing food. It would be an excellent opportunity to talk with Nikki about everything that was happening away from the insanity that Firestone was becoming. My spirits were relatively high, considering the circumstances; we'd gotten a call from Tyson's sister saying he was already improving–breathing on his own and talking in short spans. He had asked for me, and I'd spent most of the bus ride to Arrow Creek discussing the game and how school compared to hospital life before he went to sleep. I hadn't mentioned the happenings in the park the previous night.

It was a wonderful, sunny day, and I could almost convince myself that I'd imagined the horror of the previous night and that the weird dreams I'd been having were nothing more than the result of stressing about Friday's football game. Almost.

Ben and Kitty were taking their lunch break at a table nearby, but they were busy talking, so Nikki and I were able to discuss things in private.

"Alright," I said, "Let's sum up what we know: someone Garrett knows attacks us in the park dressed like a Renaissance fair headsman. His voice is the same voice as the guy's in my nightmare who kills my mom. I dream of a guy who has the same name as the man who wrote the books Josiah gave me and he warns me that weird things are going to happen. Then lo and behold, they do! Am I missing anything?"

Nikki nodded, tapping her fingers against her mug of chai tea. "I was thinking about it last night...all the weird crimes suddenly happening all over the world...only really started around the time we saw Garrett on the mountain." My eyes went round. I hadn't considered that. "Tyson said that the other survivors of the plane crash are all reporting that they didn't see anyone go up the aisle to the cockpit to hijack the plane. There were no sounds of violence, no warning from the pilots. No proof of mechanical failure. The thing just nose-dived from a half-mile up."

"You really think it's all connected?" I asked, leaning forward over my coffee.

Nikki looked grim. "I don't think we should rule out the possibility."

"But *Garrett?*" I asked with disbelief. *"Garrett* having people attack us in the park with a knife? Garrett almost killing a kid on the mountain? Garrett somehow affiliated with the terrorists committing these mass attacks and bizarre disasters?" I asked. Up until Friday night, he would have been last on my who's-who list of criminal masterminds.

"He could be just a part of the bigger picture. Maybe he knows people; maybe he's a member of a terrorist group or a cult–"

"Maybe he's a Ranker," I interrupted impulsively. I hadn't meant to really say it out loud.

Nikki gave me a skeptical look. "Hold on, Jon, what would that even mean? You read about Rankers in a book about myths and legends. So he knows people that have dark robes and he wants to hurt us. That doesn't make him mythological evil incarnate."

"He almost killed Carl on the mountain and he *laughed* about it. He didn't just have a pair of his friends TP my house or key your car, they had *knives*. And the guy in charge...I knew his voice. It was the same voice as the guy who killed my mom. That isn't possible."

"The same voice as the man who murdered your mother in your *dream*, Jonathan," Nikki said. She spoke delicately, as if afraid that I'd break like glass.

I frowned at her. "Nikki, you're the one who mentioned the weird timing of all the world-catastrophes. Are you really willing to rule out a supernatural explanation here?"

She swept a hand through her hair and said, "Okay. You're right. All of this is too weird for there not to be...*something* extra going on. For the sake of this discussion, let's say this isn't just ultra-organized crime or a weird cult. Let's say that Rankers *are* after you. Why? What do they want? And why are these things happening to you? What did you do? Do you know something you shouldn't?"

"Mmmmmm...no, not anything criminals would want to hide. I know a load about the mythological, but...nothing to really astonish anyone. Probably enough to have me locked in a padded cell but not enough to have me killed."

Nikki wouldn't meet my gaze. She carefully chose her words. "Why did he call you a prince?"

I thought back to the park and the weird things Garrett's friend had said: *What would it take to break a prince's heart? What would it take to crush a hero?* And Peter, in my dream before that, had said something about me being chosen to sit on a throne.

I scratched my chin. "Oh, that's right, he did call me that."

Nikki smiled sympathetically. "You're a good guy, Jonathan. There are a lot of people that don't like good guys. Maybe he was being facetious. Mocking you."

I squeezed her hand. "I don't know. I'm going crazy trying to understand all of this. I would never have imagined that Garrett had this kind of influence. But back in the diner, his eyes..." I remembered the scarlet glow that I'd glimpsed in his pupils and sank lower in my chair as if to hide, shaking my head. "There's something wrong with him. I always thought he was just some sociopath but then I learned about Rankers and...I can't explain it but it fits."

Nikki tilted her head at me, supportive despite her own doubts, encouraging me to continue with a dip of her head, her eyes attentive.

I kissed her fingers gratefully and said, "Imagine that you'd never seen a tiger before, but you'd read about them in books. How they look, how they act. If you saw one in the wild after that, it might not fit the picture you had in your imagination, but you could recognize it by the information you had, right?"

Nikki appeared thoughtful.

I added, "With Garrett and the Rankers, it's like that. But even if Garrett isn't in charge, even if he is just a cog in a bigger machine, why is the bigger machine acting out now? We need to figure this out before things get even worse. Maybe we can piece together enough of the puzzle to help the police put it all to an end."

I took another sip of coffee and saw that Ben was gazing at the town annex across the street with his mouth open, bobbing his head every now and then to keep it in his sights as vehicles scooted by. I made a face at Kitty, who smirked back and shrugged, as oblivious as I was as to what could be so fascinating about some old building full of papers. Then Ben frowned, shut his mouth, and his focus suddenly became extremely intense.

"What's up?" I asked, trying to spot what was distracting him.

Nikki followed Ben's line of sight and pointed up at a small civilian helicopter droning in the sky, just visible above the roofline of the annex. "How low would you say that's flying?" she whispered.

"Too low," Ben said.

The whopping sound of the helicopter's rotors drummed out over the sound of traffic, loud enough to begin drawing the eye of others around us. To my sight, it seemed to be tilting erratically, swinging side to side. Was the pilot having fun or having a heart attack? Or was it even more sinister? I thought of the conversation Nikki and I had just had and felt chills.

Every conversation had dwindled to a halt. People were leaving their tables to squint up at the helicopter, shading their eyes, murmuring cluelessly. The little chopper dropped lower, so sharply that we all flinched. I thought I saw something like a small black cloud funnel out away from where the cockpit was, like a tiny tornado of smoke. But it wasn't smoke. Nikki's sharp glance at me confirmed it. She had seen it too. There was nothing normal about that darkness.

"Rankers," I whispered.

At first, I thought the chopper was going to crash into the plains behind the annex. It was close enough now that its rotors were deafening. Some vehicles were stopping, their drivers pressing against the windows to stare. I heard a couple of cars collide but didn't look away from the helicopter. No, it was going to crash into the trees not forty feet behind us.

"Shit," I muttered.

The helicopter glided over us; the air vibrating loudly, rattling the windows. We covered our ears. As it swept overhead, I forced my eyes open, tracking the glass bubble of the cockpit. I couldn't see anything within–the inside of the glass was blackish red and glistening, as if a giant paint bomb had gone off inside.

"*Get down!*" I bellowed, shoving the table over and yanking Nikki beneath me behind it. I peered over the top to see that my order had been followed–Ben and Kitty had ducked behind their own table and those who weren't running for their lives were doing likewise.

I felt myself begin to tremble with adrenaline and glanced at the chopper once more, just in time to see it smash into the trees. Its engine whined, and then with a horrible, protesting shriek, it was torn to pieces in the branches and trunks. I heard a small explosion, but it was mostly confined in the trees. The worst part, the part I had expected, was the rotors. Bits of them flew like shrapnel around us, razor blades of metal that struck our table with sounds like nails being launched from a high-powered nail gun.

Someone running past me went down with a strangled cry. Spots of blood swelled into puddles through the dark shirt over his back, and he screamed again.

Ben appeared beside us with Kitty, both of whom looked whole and uninjured. He began to examine the wounded guy, using his pocketknife to cut the tattered shirt away. "You and Nikki should go check for others who may be wounded," he said, his dark eyes glancing our way. "Kitty, call the police."

Ben could take care of the situation here. Kitty fished her cell phone out of her pocket, her hands trembling as badly as if she'd just pulled them out of ice water. While she watched her boyfriend work, she edged nearer to him as if to receive protection, finding solace in his confidence and detached, clinical manner.

I took Nikki's hand, and we went to check out the damage. The fireball spread, swelling as it ate the dry autumn foliage. It didn't look like any buildings were in immediate danger, but they would be if firefighters didn't get here fast enough. All that remained of the helicopter itself, and its poor pilot, was charred, blackened metal and foul-smelling smoke.

Most everyone had been able to escape the brunt of the explosion and the deadly barrage of shattered metal. Some people still sprinted past me, eyes wild with animal panic, a few with hands pressed over bloody wounds that hadn't penetrated through the shock to their awareness yet. Many began to wander back, drawn like moths to flame, hands over their mouths and cell phones pressed to their ears or held in shaking hands, recording the chaos.

Not everyone had made it, though. A handful of people lay around us, also stuck with shrapnel. Moans and anguished weeping began rising to a crescendo. One man nearby rolled a woman's body over, shaking her, calling her name hysterically when she didn't respond. The smoke was now too thick to make things out clearly, but there also seemed to be a few unlucky pedestrians who had been walking along the street beyond the cafe and got caught in the worst of the damage. I surveyed the carnage, put my hands on my head, and tangled my fingers in my hair. My breath started hitching, and I didn't know whether to weep or scream my frustration at my own helplessness. Something in my expression made Nikki reach over, take one of my hands, and give it a shaky squeeze.

"Come on," she said to me. "I've had first-aid training. Not as much as Ben, but I know how to treat some wounds." She spoke soothingly, as if I were one of the traumatized victims, calm and collected–or at least doing a decent job of pretending to be. She took the hair tie from around her wrist and began pulling her hair back into a ponytail. I followed her toward the bodies spread across the pavement beyond the cafe, watching her evaluate the injured at a glance, deciding who needed immediate aid the most. I hovered uselessly at her shoulder until she had me press a pad of someone's wadded-up jacket to the gash in their side. Nikki told me I was doing a good job the same way a doctor might coddle a child who had just been given an injection without screaming, and then she started speaking conversationally with her "patient," despite them being obviously out of it and incapable of responding. After a time, Nikki just started humming a slow, pretty, lullaby-like tune.

I watched her and Ben work, mute, watched them rush from person to person, mindless of gaping wounds, blood, and screams, watched Nikki tear strips from her skirt to make tourniquets or staunch bleeding, staining her fingers red, talking to those in shock, and generally healing.

That black smoke streaming from the gore-spattered cockpit kept popping into my mind like a jump scare. The crash wasn't an accident. Somehow, the Rankers were involved, and if that was the case, then how many other terrible things happening in the world were their fault? And if Rankers were real, then were the other things in the books Josiah had given me also real? Did unicorns and mermaids and griffins exist too?

Nikki backtracked to check on one of her "patients" and I trailed after her, gazing forlornly around us at the carnage and hating my helplessness.

There was someone leaning against the trunk of a tree across the street in the front yard of a large model home and for a horrible moment I thought that maybe they'd been pinned there by a stray piece of wreckage. But when I did a double-take, straining to see if the person was wounded or not, I recognized him.

Garrett.

He stood there under the fiery-colored maple leaves, the picture of unconcern, grinning in my direction. As I stared, astounded that Garrett had shown up here, of all places, he spread his arms as if inviting me to take in and enjoy the tableau of carnage around us, then kissed his fingers and spread them in the air like he found it all delicious.

Pressure built in my head and eyes as a fury more intense than anything I'd ever felt before consumed me. My ears rang with it, my heart pounded, and energy sang through my body. Without a backwards glance or a word to Nikki, I sprang forward, sprinting toward Garrett with one thought in my mind: I was going to take him apart.

With a gleeful skip in his step, Garrett spun around and ran into the model home. I burst in a few steps behind him, head low and fists up, but he was gone.

"*Garrett!*" I roared, only half aware of what I was saying. "*Garrett, get out here! Did you do this? Did you cause the crash?*"

There was no response. I started prowling through the rooms, listening for a breath or a footstep, and stalked upstairs, trailing my hand on the railing.

"Come on, Garrett," I growled, pausing at the top of the stairs, "I know you've wanted this as much as I have. You almost killed Carl, you had your friend in the park pull a knife on Nikki. But you think that makes me afraid of you?" I laughed, a loud, harsh, and mocking sound, moving down a long hallway. "You've pissed me off, Garrett. *You* should be afraid of *me.*"

"Hey, Jonathan"–Garrett grabbed the back of my shirt and threw me against the wall, holding me there with his elbow–"you should watch where you're going."

Before I could do or say anything, he tossed me to the ground, sending me skidding along the wood floor. I scrambled to my hands and knees and tried to get to my feet, but Garrett planted his shoe against my back and pushed me down again.

"'My friend in the park,'" he snorted. "Yeah, he's good at what he does. He takes people who consider themselves brave, and he breaks them. You think you know what's going on?" He ground the heel of his shoe into my backbone. "So arrogant. So damned *heroic.* I'm sick of coming to school and seein' you there, surrounded by your admirers. Prince Jonathan, the popular one."

Listening to his snide voice, I could barely breathe. It hit me how earnest it sounded, how it was full of loathing. And I knew that this wasn't going to just be a cathartic little fistfight. Everyone was occupied with the emergency outside—no one was going to enter this house for weeks until the destruction had been taken care of. Garrett had lured me in here because he was going to try and kill me. That realization sent an icy shiver down my spine and an electric tingle up my limbs. Nausea made my skin go clammy. I dug my fingers into the floor and strained to pull away, like a mouse tearing itself out from under the claws of a cat. His fingers curled themselves into my hair and gave a vicious yank. My roots screamed in protest. I was pulled up to my knees and twisted to face Garrett's eyes. He was enjoying this.

Garrett stared into my face for a while, searching for something. "Nah," he said, as if disappointed. "You aren't *ready*, yet! Get angrier, Jonathan!" Then he laughed and hit me hard in the jaw.

I was surprised it didn't snap; my lower face went numb, and fuzzy dots danced tauntingly in my eyes. The force of his strike flung me backward and my back hit the railing leading downstairs. I put my hand on it, trying to concoct a plan of defense. All that came to mind were images of Garrett in the diner, the men in the park threatening Nikki in Garrett's name...

That got my blood pumping again, and I felt a pinprick of anger. I grasped it and let it blossom, filling up my body with a warm and excited buzz. I looked over to see Garrett stalking closer, his hands flexing.

I lunged down the stairs and ducked behind the wall, at the base of them, tense. Garrett's loud, confident footsteps came closer and closer. Suddenly, his fist smashed around the corner and right where my face had been seconds before. I'd been expecting his move and ducked, shouldering into his chest so that he collapsed with a loud grunt. I tugged him back up, punching him onto his butt at the bottom of the stairs. He leaped to his feet and football tackled me around the waist.

We plunged into the neatly arranged sitting room, hitting the coffee table, rolling off it, and taking out a lamp. We writhed and snarled on the carpet like two feral dogs finding each other on the same territory.

Strategy. I need to think strategy, I thought. What were my strengths?

Garrett had me by the shirt front and, as we grappled, seemed to be trying to steer me away from the front of the house and toward the door leading down to the basement. *Is he moving us somewhere that no one will hear us?* I wondered. That sent a strange chill down my spine. How could he actually be capable of that kind of rationality at this moment?

When I felt my back touch the door to the basement, I desperately channeled my football energy and bent low, hefting Garrett up and throwing him down like a sack of potatoes. As he still had hold of my shirt, I went with him, yelping in alarm and frustration. I tried to pin him, maybe give myself time to turn my impotent panic and anger into the rage I'd felt in the diner after saving Carl on the mountain, but all I saw was the green flash of Garrett's eyes as he rocked his head forward to butt it against mine.

Red splotches blossomed behind my eyes as I clutched my face. I rolled off of him, and Garrett, completely unfazed by anything like what should've been a killer headache, dragged me up onto my feet by the back of my shirt, pinned me against the refrigerator, and drove his fist into my gut. I doubled over. He chuckled wheezily and straightened me back up.

"Your friends aren't here now, are they, Jon?" Garrett hissed, his eyes alight with savage joy. "It's just you and me." He leaned in closer to whisper, "And this is only the beginning." His face seemed to glow red, but then I saw something like a red light reflected in his eyes. Was the light coming from *me*?

Garrett gave a joyous laugh. "Yes, Jonathan, there you go! I knew you could do it!"

"What are you talking about?" I gasped, still trying to get adequate air into my lungs.

"Your eyes are red. And glowing like the steel in a forge's fire. You know what that means, right?" He hit me in the stomach again, shoving me into the fridge and making it rattle. "It means that you're ready to play the game."

I held my hands protectively around my body and kept my head lowered, spitting up syrupy blood and watching it fall to the linoleum: a small red puddle on the off-white tiles. That blood, my fear... it made me think about the people outside...the victims of Garrett's sadism...Carl and Nikki...people in pain, people who suffered while

Garrett just stood there like a king surveying the ruin of his enemy's kingdom and laughed.

A roar built up in my throat, and my hands clenched at my sides. I ripped away from Garrett, batted aside his fist that was coming at my throat, swung back my arm, and shot it at his face, letting loose with another animal roar just as I felt his nose shift under my knuckles. I heard a popping sound and saw Garrett's eyes go big, his nose slightly off-center and pouring blood.

He fell to his knees, touching a hand carefully to his nose and staring at the scarlet fluid it came away with. I was too insanely exhilarated to see at the time how he was more surprised than in pain. He should have been crying in agony or passed out, but instead he just pinched the bridge of his nose, inclined his head, and looked curiously up at me.

My voice was shaky. I swallowed hard, pointed a trembling finger at him, and said, "I don't want to hear from you ever again. It's over, Garrett. I'm calling the cops and your ass can rot in jail where it belongs." I shuffled my sore weight, trying to see if I had more to say, but instead spun around and headed back toward the living room where my phone had fallen out of my pocket.

I'd done it. I had finally stood up to the guy who had mocked my grief after my mother had died, taunted me when I came to school tender and depressed after a beating from Dad, insulted Nikki for caring about someone he called pathetic, a wimp, a loser...

My cheeks felt warm and wet, and I pulled my shirt sleeve up to siphon away the blood, but there was none. I wiped at my tears with the heel of my palm and blinked furiously.

It was over. That was what mattered.

A splintering throb of pain burst in my lower back, below the rib cage and to the left. It stung like a hornet's tail, all sorts of agony.

I fell to my knees and reached back to feel the handle of a steak knife half-buried in my flesh. My shirt was soon soaked with red. *There's a knife in my back,* I thought, but that truth felt detached and distant from me like I was dreaming about something that had happened to someone else.

Toppling to my side, I watched Garrett limp around to glare down at me. "Next time I'll make a frontal approach, Jonathan," he said with a giddy smile and a red glint in his pupils that this time seemed to come from inside his eyeballs somehow, "None of this cloak and dagger-in-the-back stuff. I want to stare into your eyes as you die."

Everything seemed to pulsate once like a heartbeat. A red haze descended from the sky like mist or the light from a lunar eclipse. I heard his steps dwindling, heard the front door open and shut, and I lay there bleeding out on the carpet. I tried to move, but the pain was intense; it tore through me and I gnashed my teeth and screamed, collapsing back down again.

Something clattered loudly upstairs. Was there someone else here?

"Help!" I cried. My voice was weakening. But whoever had made the sound must have heard because they came bounding down the stairs. I waited for a pair of shoes to round the corner into the living room. Instead, a brown, speckled creature the size of a weasel with large, round eyes and long, mule-like ears came hopping in and perched on the coffee-table above me, gazing down at me with concern.

I knew right away what it was, but I couldn't understand it: a charlatan, a clever critter known for its cunning, speed, and clownish tendencies. I'd read about it in Peter Malone's book on mythological beasts. What was one doing here in reality? Was it a weird hallucination? Maybe I'd finally snapped after everything that had happened, and I was really still in bed, catatonic, having some vivid dream.

It sounded real enough, making a comforting cooing sound. It reached down and ran its paw down my face in a soothing gesture. It *felt* real enough.

"Help, please," I murmured. "Get help." The charlatan chattered like a squirrel and leaped away toward the kitchen. I heard it rummaging around, heard the clank and clatter of dishware and pots being shifted.

"I must be crazy," I muttered to myself. "This is crazy. Everything is crazy. What am I doing?" I tried to get up again but couldn't manage the strength. The blood from my back had soaked, warm and sticky through my shirt and was crawling up the carpet to about my elbows, saturating everything crimson.

I heard the charlatan return dragging something behind it. Hell, maybe it was a first aid kit. But when it came around within my field of vision, I saw that it was lugging along a giant frying pan. Aiming carefully with its tongue sticking between its teeth, it hefted the frying pan up into the air by its handle, balancing on its two back legs.

"Wait, no!" I yelped.

"We'll take care of you, my prince," the creature said solemnly in a high, squeaky voice, and the frying pan came rocketing down at my skull. I heard a loud clang and experienced a feeling of wonderful, pain-free weightlessness before I left *this* world completely.

CHAPTER EIGHT:
I Meet A Gaggle of Griffins

Warm water seeped over my tongue. I was thirsty, so I took a few weak gulps. The water was salty, but it cleared up my achy head. My first thought was that maybe my blood had pooled up toward my face and gotten in my mouth and I tried to push myself off the ground, but there *was* no ground. Water continued to pour into my mouth and nose, and I spat it out, trying to keep my head aloft.

I opened my eyes and saw that I was floating in an ocean, the sky was brilliant blue and cloudless, and a bright, hot yellow sun beat down on me...which led me to my second thought: the little charlatan rat had knocked my brain loose. I would plot some appropriate revenge when I was out of my current predicament. Calming down as best I could, I paddled in a circle, looking for shore. Behind me a short distance was a beach of golden sand. It was already getting closer as the tide pushed me in.

Up the beach a ways was a line of tropical trees and jewel-green foliage. To the right of the beach was a behemoth cliffside covered in small trees and shrubbery. An archway of stone populated by droves of shrieking seagulls protruded from halfway up the cliff and arced down into the water. I couldn't see anything beyond the edges of the beach; it curved around beyond my field of vision.

Though I had never been here before physically, I recognized the location from Peter Malone's book. It was called Pebble Embark, and it was where, supposedly, many heroes of legend had made their beginnings. That book had obviously been a work of fiction. So was this another vision? Another dream?

I swam hard for shore, surprised at how ungainly I was. Normally, I was a pretty good swimmer. I didn't feel any pain in my back from the fresh knife wound—more proof that I was tripping. When I felt mushy sand under my feet, I tried to stand, but my legs felt stiff and a great weight pulled at my back. I fell forward, reaching out to catch myself, and got the shock of my life.

Instead of my hands digging into the sand in front of my face, I saw monstrous bird talons.

"What the heck?" I blubbered, sitting back on my heels to examine my appendages. My skin was rough, scaly, and yellow-brown. My "fingers" were sensitive and nimble and guarded by long, curved, ebony-black claws. A fringe of fine coppery-colored feathers started at my wrists and thickened farther up my arms. I wriggled the talons. They moved like human digits, and I dug the wicked claws into the sand, then watched the salty seawater fill up the holes.

Flopping around, I found my reflection in the water. A long, curved beak, half open to allow my frantic breaths, was set into a fierce raptor's face with pure-white eyes and small ear tufts. My eyebrows had lengthened and turned bright yellow, fanning above my head. I cried out, my heart starting to race and my stomach to churn, and scrambled away, twisting my head to see huge, tentlike wings folded out above me. Then there was the tail, which ended in a bushel of long feathers. I moved them up close to my face, fanning them out like a peacock's tail.

"No, no, no, no!" I whimpered, spinning in circles, trembling with fear, muttering my denial, clenching angrily at the sand with my claws, and then cycling back to fear again. Finally, utterly worn out, I sat back like I'd seen Nikki's cat do and wrapped my tail around me.

I had to do something. Maybe there was someone around who could help me. I hoped I was capable of human speech and that I hadn't just chanted desperate repetitions of the word "no" and a few swear words in some monster-bird language only I understood. I doubted any poor person I came upon would patiently wait while I spelled everything out for them in the sand.

With that plan in mind, I made to venture into the trees, but something moved atop a steep, grassy hill to the left of the beach choked with stones and tree roots, and I looked up in the hopes that maybe someone had come to *me*. Instead, I saw a large beast that looked exactly like me but bigger and easily more majestic. I brought myself to think the word: "griffin." We were both griffins.

The jungle climbed up to fringe the base of the high, rocky hill, trees standing precariously on the edges of the drop-off, and the griffin was almost invisible in their shade. He had rich, dark, chocolate-colored feathers. His ear tufts were larger than mine and more pointed, and thin, whiskery hairs wisped back from his eyes and beak. One white streak ringed each eye, making the gray irises stand out.

He seemed to be amused, watching my antics with his beak quirked up at the corners just under his eyes where they were fleshy and mobile. Rearing back, he flared open his wings to reveal cream-colored undersides striped raggedly with bars of chestnut brown.

I wasn't sure what to do. I balanced on the tips of my feet, paws, or whatever they were now, and got ready to bolt should the need arise.

The griffin dropped forward gracefully off the hill and soared over the sand to me. At the last moment, he pulled back, flapping his wings hard and buffeting me with their gusts, and touched down on his hind lion paws. When he had come down on all fours, folding his wings after preening a few choice feathers with his beak, the griffin turned his silver eyes on me. I felt like I was being inspected by a UFC heavyweight—someone who could take me down in a second and slurp what was left up a straw.

The griffin opened his beak and spoke in a deep, bass voice. "Calm down, Jonathan. I am sorry to be blunt, but the Rankers have gained the upper hand and plan to use it. I assure you that you will eventually master the ability to shift into your human form, but you must adjust to these changes that have come over you first."

I watched his beak blankly as he talked. It took me a few extra seconds for his words to sink in. When he had finished, I said, "I understand you," feeling unbalanced—like I was standing on a very thin, wobbly wire, about to topple off of it into a chasm of insanity.

"Well, that makes things a whole lot easier, doesn't it?" the griffin remarked with mirth.

"You can talk," I stated again. My words dropped from my mouth—beak, now, I guess—in a dull monotone.

"Keen observation," the griffin teased again.

I registered what he had said and narrowed my eyes suspiciously. "How do you know me?"

The other blinked. "I know a lot about you. I've been watching you. My name is Peter." He dipped his head in greeting.

I tried to move back but did it too fast and fell over, crushing one of my wings. When I boosted myself back up and shook myself to clear away the sand lodged in my fur and feathers, I asked, "Not the same Peter who wrote those books Josiah gave me?"

Peter rocked back on his haunches and spread his wings, holding his talons out to the sides as if to present himself. "The very same," he said, falling back onto all fours. "I had Josiah give those books to you, to help prepare you."

"You know my school counselor?" My voice dripped with dubiousness and I started looking around as if for a portal or doorway that I could take back to the real world. I was bleeding out on the floor somewhere with a knife in my back and Garrett on the loose. I had to wake up and get help–and give that charlatan a good kick if it was still there.

"Josiah frequents these parts," Peter chortled, as if at some inside joke. "He's one of the few people out there with the ability to dream lucidly."

"Sure he can," I grumbled. "So a giant griffin who just so happens to know my guidance counselor wrote a couple of books for me. Because that makes all kinds of sense." I gazed down at my talons, still tensed to run if Peter tried anything funny while my gaze was averted and imagined Peter scribbling with a pencil the size of a yardstick clutched in his lethal talon.

Peter chuckled and said, "We are actually excellent scholars, but haven't you been listening? I am human."

With that, his shape shifted and blurred, becoming a cacophony of colors. Next thing I knew, he stood tall, a bald, dark-skinned man of African descent with a snowy-white beard and mustache and big calloused hands resting around his suspender straps. He studied me with a very kind and gentle warmth in his eyes, like a proud grandpa. When I had gotten an eyeful he blurred and blended back into the big grizzly griffin.

"I've seen you before!" I cried, pointing at him with one talon and this time maintaining my balance. "In my dream at Nikki's! You gave me that focus-mint and told me to get ready for change when my..." I stopped.

"When your eyes reflect your heart," Peter said. "And, unless I'm mistaken, they have. You've demonstrated the righteous fury of one chosen to rule as griffin-prince; an anger born from witnessing injustice and yearning to punish it."

I thought of what Garrett had said about my eyes changing color–remembered seeing his skin bathed in a red glow that had seemed to emanate from my own face.

"Mmmm, no," I whimpered. "This can't be real. *You* can't be real." I lifted one of my hand-like talons and shook the claws at him. "*I* can't be real!"

"Why not?" Peter asked. "What's real? Is it something that you see? Something you feel?" He slapped my shoulder with the fan of feathers at the end of his tail.

"Something that makes sense!" I cried hysterically.

"Not everything that's real makes sense," Peter argued.

"Listen, Socrates," I snapped, "I would love to have some long, philosophical discussion with you about life and death and humanity and crap, but I'm kind of losing my mind right now, so if you'll excuse me, I'm going to try and find a phone."

I stood up, looking from the ocean on one side to the jungle on my other, wondering helplessly where the nearest town would be. I took a wobbly step toward the trees.

"You want answers," Peter said mildly.

I stopped and looked at him. "That would be nice, yes."

The corners of Peter's beak twitched like he wanted to smile. "Very well. Let's start with your arrival here. Once the Rankers discovered that you are next in line to rule, they started watching you, biding their time, waiting for the opportune moment to send you here, waiting until you were ready to become a griffin."

I raised one of the frilly tendrils that served as my eyebrow. "They *wanted* me to turn into...this? Why?" I asked curiously. Why would the bad guys want me to become a beast that was five times more powerful than a human being?

"You're the only one who can stop them. Here, you're out of the way of their machinations in reality. Being a griffin is...like wearing your finest suit to a party. Folks show you deference because they can see the suit's fine make and that as its owner you must either be well-to-do or you worked long and hard saving up enough money to afford it. During the party you would be careful not to stain the suit or tear it. You would move with dignity and grace.

"But the griffin in you is balanced with your humanity. Your human-ness is what makes you special; unpredictable. But it also makes you weak. Griffins are incapable of being *sinful*, of acting on feelings of lust, pettiness, greed. To do so would break the transformation and turn you back into a human. Here, your human-ness can be manipulated and you can fall prey to all manner of corruption. Here, you can be crafted into a "Dark Griffin," a creature of evil and brimstone, a foul creation that would bring the minds of Men into ruin and insanity. You could become the most powerful weapon in the Rankers' arsenal. After all, that's what they wanted to do to your predecessor. But Rankers greatly underestimate the hearts of griffins." He sounded a little sad, as if remembering a tragic memory, but my new ear tufts twitched at the word "predecessor" and I remembered all of the mumbo-jumbo in my old dream about sitting on a throne.

"What are you saying?" I asked. "What do you mean only I can stop them?"

"You are the prince and protector of this land," Peter smiled, "Until we can get you to the capital city and Michael can perform the ceremony that will make you king."

I didn't know what he expected me to do—dance around for joy? Not happening. But we had finally made it around to the crucial question that I'd been avoiding.

"Uh...huh. And where exactly is 'this land?'"

Peter's gaze turned thoughtful. He looked around and replied in a voice dreamy with some emotion I wasn't quite familiar with (maybe a sort of adoration?): "This is the Land of Dreams. All dreams past, present, and future are here in this place. Though there are some good dreams, there are bad ones as well. Those with dreams of bravery and heroism appear here as superheroes, or knights"– he gave me a sly side-look through his intimidating silver eyes–"or griffins."

"So, I'm dreaming?" I asked, "Everyone here is dreaming?"

Peter turned to glance into the trees, then said, "Well, sort of. Without intense training and practice, you can't utilize the unlimited power of the dreamworld while asleep. We don't have that kind of time, and neither do the Rankers. No, right now you're in a heightened form of dream–like a coma. You have been called into the minds of others to vanquish a spreading evil. Some others that you will see in this world are also from reality, like you and I, but only a select few are actually aware of the ongoing Ranker war. Most think they're just having dreams or nightmares. But nightmares are fast becoming a reality for all. You have noticed how terrible things have been in the world lately, correct? How terrible some people have become?"

I nodded.

"The Rankers have been encouraging evil for a long time," Peter explained. "Our world is becoming more and more corrupt and dark, and they have chosen this time to finally end it all."

That made me gulp. "End?"

He gave me a serious stare. "In blood and fire." My eyes grew big, and from the pressure building behind them and the white glow shining off of Peter's dark chest feathers, I didn't doubt that they had changed color in response to my emotions again. "From the ashes of our lives, the Rankers will rebuild an empire of shadows. Rankers are born of evil minds or thoughts. Pure evil."

Something in my chest burned hot, and even though his name left a nasty taste in my mouth, I choked out, "Garrett?"

"He was sent to spy on you all these years."

"Is he a leader of the Rankers?"

"The best, and the most evil."

Of course, I thought. It was hard to imagine that the guy everyone had hated since primary school, the bully who terrified other bullies, had enough brain cells to *lead* anything. Then again, it was hard to imagine me turning into a big fat Macedonian myth too. I guess I had to work on my imagination a bit.

"Well, who made him? Can't we just go and...fix that guy?"

Peter gave me a fond smile. "It isn't that easy, unfortunately. Anyone could have made Garrett, and if he's strong enough, has collected power enough to be acting independently from his creator, then that creator could have died centuries ago and we're stuck dealing with the manifestation of his wicked heart."

My heart was sinking lower and lower in my chest. "My friends and family..."

"You'll see them again. And your body will be taken care of too. You have a job to do first," Peter said reassuringly.

I cocked my head. "Job?"

The dark griffin nodded. "You must go to the capital to be crowned and meet the White Griffin. He is very wise, and he's advised many griffin rulers before you. Along the way, we shall gather more troops and, hopefully, discover the Rankers' whereabouts and plans.

They've been leaving clues—and thanks to the efforts of your predecessor, we know where to look. And now you're here to lead us."

I looked behind me, wondering who he was talking to, because it was just too bizarre for me to even test the idea that he meant me. It clicked an instant later, however, that he did mean me, and I felt as if I'd just swallowed a golf ball.

"Yeah," I laughed. "Too bad I *can't*! I can't lead a battle. I'm no prince!"

Peter disagreed. "You can't fight who you really are."

That was finally too much. "Bullshit!" I cried. Peter recoiled a bit as if taken aback, but it was hard to read emotions on a griffin. "For all I know, this is a fever dream brought on by an infection from Garrett's knife. I mean, me turning into a monster?"

"Griffins aren't monsters," Peter interrupted, sounding defensive.

"And the world is falling apart because of Rankers? Which I read about in a book right next to the fairy and unicorn entries?"

"They exist too," Peter said mildly.

"And the idiot who's been making my life a living hell at school just so happens to be the mastermind behind some evil plot to take over the world?" My voice broke a little with borderline hysteria.

"Essentially, yes," Peter confirmed.

I took a bracing breath, closed my eyes for a beat to listen to the whispering of the waves, then said with forced calm, "Who I am...is Jonathan He'klarr, football player at Firestone High, regular Colorado teen, and I don't want any of this."

Peter's low bird-of-prey brows dipped even lower, as if he were disappointed, and I don't know why that bothered me a little. "If you're wanting proof, all you have to do is stick around. Truly, that's all you can do. There's no going back the way you came. And whatever your personal feelings about this situation, Garrett and his troops must be stopped or they will break the hearts of humanity by consuming our dreams, conquering our hopes, crushing our minds—feeding even further off of our worst nightmares—until they have the strength to move on the waking world en masse, and it will collapse under their power."

"I–I don't want to do this," I said, as firmly as if my words were a brick wall. "You can't *make* me fight for you, or be a prince, or whatever."

Peter inclined his noble head, looking irritated, and I forced myself to remain still and not appear intimidated. "No, you're right. I can't force you to do anything. But I can't force you to wake up either. You're in a coma. I'm afraid you're stuck with us until you... wake up. And no one knows when that will be."

I stared open-beaked at him, feeling black-mailed. I didn't know what to believe. Everything *felt* real enough. Option A: I was dreaming a very strange dream. Or option B: I was indeed in a frying-pan-induced coma, because I sure as heck couldn't seem to wake up no matter how hard I tried. Either way, I couldn't do anything about my situation at the moment. I was stuck.

Peter looked back into the trees, and suddenly I was suspicious.

"Is it a coincidence that you just happened to be here when I arrived?" I asked, standing up and inching away.

Peter shrugged. "I don't know. I was originally here to wait for a squadron of soldiers and two other griffins to catch up with me. It was an added bonus when you popped up."

Good for you. I grumped.

"The Rankers were here earlier to leave a message for their allies, but I saw them leave it. The soldiers and griffins are going to assist me in intercepting it." He looked back into the trees with ear tufts perked forward and added, "Ah, here they are."

I peered over at the tree line with anticipation. I was curious to see what sort of military this place had. My raptor-eyes picked up shadows slowly separating from the dark interior of the jungle.

Around twenty or twenty-five armed men and women emerged into the bright sunlight a few at a time, marching toward us and blinking rapidly in the change of light. I was surprised to see such a variety, but then, people don't all dream about one single type of warrior. There were sailors that could have come straight out of the navy, looking relieved to see the ocean. Stocky marines in camouflage, eyes wary, scanned their new surroundings. Army men hefted their rifles and stared down at the sand. There were armor-clad knights and gladiators, a couple of Amazonian-women-warrior types in tunics and what resembled reptile leather from a lizard that had to be the size of an elephant. I even spotted a few serene-looking samurai in colorful padding.

When they saw me, the warriors all bowed as one and shouted, "My prince!" They stood straight and stiff at attention.

"Yo," I said, astonished, flicking my head in greeting. Some of them exchanged looks, but they remained standing rigidly.

Peter nudged me, and I added, "Oh, at...ease?" It worked, and they all relaxed, still with looks on their faces like, *Why doesn't our prince sound like he knows what he's doing?*

Two griffins came out from behind the squadron. One was female; her form was dainty and slim, and her coloring was a soft pink. She had large eyes, and a jeweled, golden collar glowed from around her neck.

The other griffin was a male about my size but stockier. He was jet black with purplish spots on the insides of his wings. He wore a defiant look and held his thick, ruffed neck stiff. When he saw me, he immediately sized me up, and his large, tufted ears perked toward me. The female's face lit up, and she bounded in my direction with enthusiasm, skidding to a stop when she reached my side. The other followed her in a lazy lope.

"Hello!" the female greeted me boisterously in a thick French accent, and graciously lowered her head, curling a talon beneath her. I nodded uncomfortably back. "I am Mariah. Very pleased to meet you, Prince."

I winced. "Please, just call me Jonathan."

Mariah beamed and looked up at Peter. "The charlatan did his job well."

Peter smiled, and once more, I felt a sudden urge to break something.

"He's working for *you* guys?" I asked, incredulous. I'd been laboring under the delusion that the little rodent had been working for the Rankers...

Peter nodded. "Charlatans are magnificent messengers. The one who brought you here was the same one who brought Josiah my books. It took Michael a while to muster the power to send him into reality. It's a lot easier for nightmares to cross over and become reality than it is for good dreams because evil is simpler to harness, to summon. But ever since he was a young kit, that charlatan claimed to have dreamed and desired to help fight for the cleansing of his land from the Ranker filth. And so he has—he's sent you safely here to us before the Rankers could send you here and claim you. We'll have to thank him when we see him again."

A strange feeling of guilt coursed through me. The inhabitants of this place had apparently been through terror and tyranny. They were ready to put a stop to the madness. This was a lot to ask of me. I knew next to nothing about where I was, why I'd been chosen to be a prince, and—most concerning of all—the enemy. But were ignorance and naïveté ever an excuse to not do the right thing? Despite Peter's opinion, I was no prince...but couldn't I at least stick around and see if there was something I could do to help? If only because the trouble affected my own world? I remembered back to the moment in the park—the stranger slinking around Nikki with the knife clenched tightly in one hand. I shuddered, imagining that event on a larger scale, the Rankers ruling over the earth. My hackles spiked up. Mariah gave me a sympathetic look.

I waited expectantly for the black griffin to introduce himself, but he turned to Peter instead and asked, "So, we finally get to see some action?"

I was surprised to hear that he, like Mariah, had an accent. It was lilting, soft, and melodious. Maybe Irish or Scottish.

Peter frowned sternly. "Let's hope not, Kayle. This isn't a game."

Kayle grinned impishly, his tail swinging side to side like a lioness's when she's ready to pounce. "Life's a game."

Peter transformed into his big, thickset human form and patiently waited for Kayle and Mariah to join him.

Mariah became a girl about a year or so younger than me with long and silky dirty-blonde hair. Her collar had turned into a necklace, and her feathers and fur had been replaced with blue jeans and a shirt with billowing lace at the sleeves. Clasping her hands behind her back, she smiled at me and blushed, rocking back and forth.

Kayle's appearance wasn't bizarrely unexpected. He wore baggy jeans and a thick black sweatshirt. A black beanie was pulled down over his gingery-brown hair. His eyes were an intense, penetrating brown, almost maroon. As soon as his talons had shortened and thinned to human fingers, he reached into the back pocket of his pants and pulled out what seemed to be a sort of wide silver Zippo lighter with what resembled a bird engraved into it. I waited for him to pull a cigarette out of somewhere and slide it between his teeth, but he just opened and closed the lighter over and over again, delicately moving his fingers around it, always just avoiding the wisp of flame that came to life with each igniting *click*.

His eyes met mine, and he flicked his eyebrows as if to show off how much tougher and more badass he was than me–the guy who was supposed to be the grand, imperial leader of the Land of Dreams.

I ground my beak and glared, hoping my eyes were scarlet red and freezing his cold blood.

Kayle didn't seem at all perturbed. He turned behind him to the squadron and shouted, "Gather 'round!"

The men briskly trotted closer to Peter. Mariah was sitting on the sand with her legs stretched out. Kayle folded his legs beneath him, vivid eyes watching Peter's face as the man waited for everyone's full attention. My head was up to about everyone's chests when I was on all fours. I sat moodily on my haunches.

Stroking his beard, Peter gave us his report. "Just days ago, at oh ten hundred, a trio of Rankers gathered on this beach. They were water types. Water-proof cloaks, lithe bodies, and they spoke by means of dolphin-like clicks and whistles."

"But what were they doing?" Kayle asked, looking between the soldiers' legs at the ocean.

"I'm getting to that. Two of the trio went over to those trees and shaved off the bark until they had created two smooth planks of wood. Using these boards, the pair of Rankers floated out onto the water and dropped an object I couldn't make out into the depths. The last Ranker was sitting on the sands of the shore, facing his companions. He was playing a complicated tune on some panpipes. I believe he was summoning something to guard the item. When the song was finished, those on the water rushed back to the beach and burned their boards, disposing of the ashes."

"What do you think the object was, sir?" a marine asked.

Peter turned to gaze thoughtfully at the sparkling sea and replied, "A clue. The Rankers' reinforcements don't know the location of the Ranker base, and the Rankers have no clear means that we know of to reach or even locate all of their potential allies individually. They're trying to take advantage of King Brody's death to gather in secret and swell their numbers. Like Michael told us, these clues have a dark spell cast over them, meant to call to their allies, to draw them in. I think that, within a month, the Ranker reinforcements were going to retrieve it, and it would lead them to the next clue, and so on, through places of dark power, in a chain that would eventually end with the revelation of their master plans and the location of their base. Then whatever monsters have chosen to ally with the Rankers would know where to go, and the Rankers would have their army." He added more quietly, "Just as King Brody had said they would."

Mariah sat up. "So if we were to get it first…"

Kayle flicked his lighter harder than was needed, and the flame burst into fruitful life, making me jump. He seemed to get some enjoyment out of that and clapped the lighter closed. "We would scare them sh—"

"Kayle?" Peter's brows popped up patronizingly, and Kayle tightened his lips. My mouth—er, beak, as I guess was the case—twitched. You had to admire the fellow's spirit.

"Have you ever surfed before, Jonathan?" Peter asked.

"Yeah," I replied a little proudly, glad I could contribute. "Yeah, I'm pretty good at it." I'd had the privilege once of going to California with Tyson and his family and getting a crash-course in surfing. After a fair few times of getting a lungful of sand and scampering out of the water like a pansy–Tyson constantly teased that there were sharks–I'd gotten the hang of it.

"Well, let's hop to it! We don't know when the Ranker reinforcements could come!" Peter clapped his huge hands together. He looked down at me and the other two kids. "Mariah, Kayle, Jonathan, come with me."

The warriors parted to let us through. Peter led us toward the jungle. He and the other two transformed into griffins and studied some trees, at a loss as to where to begin. Using his shoulder, Peter leaned against a tall, thick tree and pushed into it, feet braced and wings tightly tucked in. With a few great creaks, the tree toppled with a thud into the sand, quaking the ground. Without saying a word, he paced speculatively around the trunk. When he had found a good spot, he carved an oval into the bark and set to work.

CHAPTER NINE:
I Make Out with a Monster

What would normally have taken several hours to create by hand, Peter finished in one and produced a semi-long, crude surfboard. Within forty-five more minutes, using the same pattern as the first, Peter had made another. By now, almost the entire tree was used up. In close to another hour, while Kayle and Mariah dozed and I fought to empty my mind of the questions and concerns parading through my mind like a circus, Peter had scraped out a board longer than the other two and handed it to me.

"Wait, what?" I asked. I'd assumed they wanted me to give them a few pointers, maybe some coaching on how to get started–not to get out there with them!

"We'll need you out there with us, just in case, so we're close enough to protect you. Just until you can take care of yourself," Peter explained, and I once more found myself watching his beak move. It was so weird–almost like talking to a freaky pet-store parrot with a large vocabulary.

I dragged my eyes up to his piercing silver ones and suggested frantically, "Uh, wouldn't it be safer on *land*?" I didn't know what the hell kind of monsters the Rankers might have summoned to protect their "clue," and it wasn't like I knew how to fly or fight. I may have looked like a griffin, but at the moment, I felt like an overgrown dodo bird.

Peter's eyes flicked to where the squadron stood looking back at us. One of the men waved.

We all turned away again, and Mariah said in a hushed voice, "We can't trust them all yet. Not everyone has really had a chance to prove their worth. If we had time to interrogate them and do cross-references, we would, but, of course, we don't, so you'll have to have faith in us instead."

"There is a griffin code of honor," Peter said proudly. "The three of us pledged to protect you."

I glanced at Kayle in disbelief. He was pointedly preening his ebony feathers. I didn't want to look like a coward, so I relented.

Peter put his talon on the last board and said to Kayle, "Stay on the beach and watch the squadron. If any enemies come, you know what to do." Kayle's beak almost moved into a smile. His ear tufts swept back, the tips slightly curled like devil horns.

Tapping the decimated log that had once been a tree, Peter said, "Burn the remains, and this time control it!"

Kayle broke into a sheepish grin. *Hmm...inside joke?* I wondered. I didn't know if I wanted to hear the story behind that or not. Kayle galloped over to the soldiers, and the rest of us pushed our boards along in the sand until we were knee deep in water.

Mariah and Peter changed into humans and sat on their boards, their feet dangling in the water. I struggled onto my own, inhaling some salt water and gagging, my soaking pelt clinging to me. My legs dangled over the sides, and I rested my beak on the wood, waiting placidly for what came next.

Mariah looked amused, tracing the grains in her board, and said, "I thought you said you were good at this."

I defended my dignity. "This is a lot harder when you have four legs, muscle mass equal to a grown bull's, and wings the size of Dumbo's ears." I teetered dangerously far to the left, and my right wing automatically extended to balance me. It worked, and I was able to lay flat again.

"Who's Dumbo?" Mariah queried, loftily splashing her fingertips in the ocean. I shot her a surprised look.

"The baby elephant...you know...from the Disney movie? Do you not own a TV?"

For some reason, Mariah looked offended at this and turned her gaze away, features crestfallen.

Peter braced himself. "Here comes a wave."

We all hunched forward shakily, and the others pushed through it while I positioned myself to ride over it. Having my wings open seemed to help, so I spread them a bit, the long pinions touching the water. Having wings felt awkward. They were built like an extra pair of arms that came out behind my shoulders.

The wave carried us over and through, and we were able to relax before the next set. Peter and Mariah were already soaked, but at least they looked confident. I always got a little nervous when I couldn't feel the sand beneath my feet, hovering over the crushing watery pit that was the ocean. I was glad humans were created with the ability to swim.

"Some friends of Garrett's jumped me in the park the other day," I said tentatively. "They almost hurt Nikki, my girlfriend, and they kept talking about breaking me. Were they Rankers too?"

Mariah and Peter exchanged grim looks.

"Sounds like something a Ranker would do," Peter admitted. "They'd want to break your spirit, turn you into that Dark Griffin I mentioned earlier. And what better way to do that than hurt those closest to you?"

"Can you describe the people who attacked you?" Mariah asked.

"Only the guy in charge. He had the same voice as a guy I've had nightmares about. But that's not possible. The guy in my nightmares is dead in real life."

"Certain Rankers possess different powers," Peter explained. "Some can mimic your worst fears, some can craft particularly powerful nightmares, some can work subtle manipulations on weakhearted folks and convince them to perform dark acts or speak cruel words."

"Have you seen his true form?" Mariah pressed. A fish the size of a football with trailing sapphire-blue fins and what looked like tiny trees growing on its back flitted through the shade under her surfboard and vanished into the turquoise depths.

"No, I don't think so. But in my dream he has these shark-like teeth and black eyes."

I shivered, feeling the feathers on my neck and shoulders lift up like hackles.

"Hmm, maybe a gargoyle Ranker," Peter speculated. "One of the more powerful types. Let me know if you have any nightmares about him while you're here, Jonathan. Now that you're in the dreamworld they can do a lot of damage if they get to rootin' around in your mind."

I nodded, but I wasn't too pumped about sharing nightmares about my mom getting murdered with total strangers.

"This is about where the object was dropped," Peter said, after we drifted a little further. He pointed straight down next to him. "We need to be careful. The enchantment that was cast with the song from the panpipes can be either offensive or defensive Dark Magick. We'll need to be able to improvise on the fly as we figure it out."

"How do we get the clue, then?" Mariah asked.

Peter shrugged. "Jump in."

Ironically, just as he said that I slipped and one of my talons plunged into the water. I lashed my tail and leaned to the other side, flapping my wings, tugging myself back onto the board. I almost fell off the other side and squashed my front half tight against the board, my rump in the air, using my hind legs to brace myself. I took a few deep breaths, then felt shivers steal over me as the water soaked beneath my feathers in tickling streams. An instant later, something stirred the water's surface about three leaps away.

The three of us grew rigid, watching the horizon, scanning the spot where we'd seen the water disturbed, waiting for some great calamity to strike. I expected a kraken's tentacles to sprout from the depths, or maybe the saurian head of the Loch Ness. (I remembered from Peter's book that neither creature was very nice.)

Instead, I saw rapid flashes of color just beneath the water's surface.

"Whoa," Mariah murmured, eyes big.

The colors were getting brighter as whatever they belonged to came closer to the surface. They were moving so fast, I could only make out random features: a long arm, tendrils of silky black and blonde and red and brown hair, lithe bodies.

Then came the music.

It didn't really have a tune, but it was melodious all the same: a soothing croon, an inviting pitch, a lullaby-like song with indiscernible words. My eyes blinked slowly. I felt so comfortable...like I could totally sleep right there on the ocean and everything would be just fine...

I heard Peter shout, "Sirens!"

Hmm... Sirens were bad, right? But why? If only my head wasn't so foggy. Would the others mind if I just let them take care of the situation? I was content to lie there and let the music lull me to sleep. I sighed contentedly, tilting my head and tail side to side in time to the music. I couldn't remember ever being this completely relaxed.

I looked behind me at the beach. Everyone in the squadron except for the Amazonian women was swaying in time to the music. One man took a few steps forward with his arms longingly stretched toward the water. Kayle frantically ran over and herded him back among his fellows, proceeding to pace in front of them like a Rottweiler. Why? The man could do as he wanted, right?

I had started to sway as well.

"What are you doing?" Mariah asked me. *Ew.* Her voice was totally different from the beauteous, angelic ones below me. I shook my head, frowning.

"I feel weird," I was able to say drunkenly.

She turned to Peter and shouted, "Those filthy temptresses have him under!"

So what if they did? Of all the people on the beach and in the water, she was one of the only ones not at all affected by the music. Even Kayle and Peter were ignoring things pretty well, despite shaking their heads every now and then as if to dislodge a bug.

I yawned and watched one siren swim beneath me, studying me with her gem-blue eyes. We exchanged smiles and she playfully brushed my hind paw with her hand. The contact sent a thrill through me, like someone had zapped me with a cattle prod. But in a good way.

Mariah leaned over and pulled painfully on the short feathers on my side. "Snap out of it!" she cried.

I growled at her, and my eyes flashed red. Mariah leaned away from me. "This is not the time, Jonathan!"

"He is still more boy than griffin!" Peter said, and he actually sounded worried. "Fight it, Prince!"

For some reason, the word "prince" swept away some of the fog in my brain. I blinked hard and felt something vibrate in my chest. Was it a growl? A purr? Could I do that now? I giggled at the thought, still feeling a bit loopy and detached from what was happening. But I tried to ignore the music and stood up again.

"Does anyone know what to do?" Mariah shouted.

"They can only be defeated if you run them through with a water-based tool," Peter said. "We need a trident or a harpoon…"

"A surfboard is a watery tool…" I slurred. My tongue seemed too big for my mouth.

Peter guffawed and slapped his thigh. "Great thinking!" He swung his arm in a beckoning arc and said, "Let's get to work!" in a fierce, predatory way.

We split apart and swooped over the next wave. The sirens' song intensified, and I found myself struggling to ignore it. Angling my board, I aimed for a siren. She was sticking out of the water, watching me with her thickly lashed eyes–which were an almost fluorescent green color.

Closing my own eyes, I plunged forward, felt a dull thud, wetness splatter on my talons, and nothing more. Looking down, I saw that the siren, when hit, had collapsed into a spray of water. It had slicked my board. I slipped and felt myself falling. I caught my reflection in the water and saw that I had tousled hair and skin. I was a human again. Though I was insanely shocked to discover this, I realized that it also meant whatever griffin strength or willpower I'd been using had broken. I had given in to the siren's call.

The salt water rushed up to meet me. Someone called my name–Mariah? And then I was choking on salty ocean water and trying to get used to my normal body again enough to swim up for air.

My clothes were pulling me down; the water was getting colder the deeper I went. I caught a glimpse of sand far to my right dotted with coral and an object I couldn't make out. My surfboard was floating above, too far away to reach. I stretched up my hand and tried to grasp at it, but to no avail. *Okay, now what?*

I kicked my legs and moved up. *Oh yeah!* Now I remembered. Slowly recalling how to swim, I paddled upward, toward the sun, the sky, the friendlier waters. Maybe a little too friendly.

A young woman blocked the sunlight. Her hair was the color of chestnuts and long enough to obscure most of her body except for a few tantalizing peeks as it drifted like lace in the current. Where had she come from? Where was I?

She swam—seeming rather to fly—down to me so we were at an eye level. I felt my expression go completely blank. I didn't understand what I was feeling. I reached out for her, and suddenly she put her hands on my cheeks and mashed her face to mine. A thrill coursed through me. I was hypnotized by her embrace and utterly triumphant that I had pleased her enough to make her want to kiss me at all.

We went on and on like that for what seemed like forever. Little by little, I became aware of an aching burn in my lungs and a stinging pain in my mouth. I tried to break away from this wonderful female, but she held me tighter. I gave in and went on kissing her, ignoring the pain.

For some reason, I was once more getting sleepy. My eyes were swimming with a black mist, and images were popping up in an irritating slide-show fashion in my mind.

I saw my mother holding a Christmas ornament up to my face. I was about two, and I was giggling and reaching up to touch it. Time passed, and I saw my pop coming home soaked in rain with blood on his hands and shirt. My babysitter rushed up to meet him, and as if I sensed their sadness from where I played with my toy trucks on the floor, I burst into tears. I saw me, Tyson, Vince, and Ben racing each other on the playground. I was shrugging off questions about my black eye and challenging the others to a football game. I saw myself running upstairs to my bedroom to collapse on my bed and beg fiercely of a God I hardly knew to take me away and end my misery. I saw myself going to high school, a freshman. Saw Garrett mocking me for my upbringing and watched as I stood up for myself for the first time. I saw Nikki, her face pure and loving.

Nikki!

With a great effort, I ripped away from the siren. Her eyes furrowed in anger, and she bared her teeth. Her beauty seemed to melt away to reveal fleshless bones and a grinning skull with sharp fangs. Her teeth came at my throat, and I threw up my hands to defend myself, closing my eyes tight. Nothing happened. When I opened my eyes, there was a cloud of funneling bubbles in front of my face, and I saw a glint of silvery scales as some fish or other flitted into the darker depths, but the siren was gone.

I swam for the surface, and this time, I was able to break through and fill my lungs with air. My mouth was bleeding, but not badly, and I came to the disgusting conclusion that the siren had been trying to devour me while I'd been under the impression that we were making out. My tongue was cut, and a bit of my chin and bottom lip as well.

On the beach, Kayle was shoving men into the sand to keep them out of the water. The Amazonian women were trying to help him, barricading the men with their weapons, shouting at them to stand down. Kayle spread his wings and gave an eagle scream. From this distance, he seemed to be letting off smoke for some reason. I shook my head hard to clear it, feeling terrible: dizzy, sick, and just plain dirty. I had cheated on my Nikki! It's not like I could ever expect her to believe my excuse.

At a snail's pace, I started swimming for the beach, wallowing in guilt and self-pity, until a hand grabbed the hood of my sweatshirt. Frenzied, I started slapping at whatever was holding on to me until I saw that it was Peter.

"Calm yourself," he scolded, seeming amused. "You're alright now." With one great heft, he had me slung across his board.

As I left the water's crushing weight, I was finally able to take great, fresh breaths and gargle some water to clear away the blood. The salt stung my wounds.

"Got bit," Peter observed. He had a small smile.

"Enjoying this?" I asked sourly.

Peter raised one eyebrow and said more seriously, "It's shown me that we have a lot of work to do."

I wasn't too sure how to take that, so I rested my chin on the board and forced myself to stare only at my reflection. I didn't want to look up and see a condescending sneer turning up Kayle's beak, making his maroon-brown eyes gleam. And I didn't want to see the dazed and longing faces of the once powerful squadron brought to foolish boyishness at the sirens' song.

Feeling a tad silly being slung over Peter's board like a hunted deer, I played with the idea of swimming the rest of the way, but my feet suddenly dug into sand. Clambering off, I waded to shore and fell onto my back, staring at the sky. Kayle and the squadron gathered silently around me, conversing with Peter.

Mariah had dived for the object I had seen in the coral when I was under. She reappeared, swimming gracefully to the sand as a griffin, using her legs and wings to paddle with. She held something gray in her beak. I sat up, and we all watched her approach in apprehensive silence. Shaking her pale feathers and fur, Mariah dropped what she was holding and set about the task of preening. Kayle picked the Ranker clue up in his talons and carefully measured its weight, prodding it and rolling it around. It was a square package wrapped in thick, oily gray paper and bound with a thin cord of seaweed.

"Seems safe to open," Kayle finally said. "No enchantments, nothing moving inside, no odd smells or sounds." He tossed it over to Peter with a flick of his talon. I was sort of glad to find that I could still understand him, not being in griffin form myself. So we weren't speaking bird, after all.

Peter caught the package in his huge hands and was about to tug on the knot holding the seaweed together when Mariah interrupted, "Hey, let's first give thanks to those who saved our prince's life!"

As one, we all whipped around to face the ocean. Weird-looking things with long tails were just chasing off the rest of the sirens, brandishing tridents and using them on the ones that were too slow. I heard one sailor sigh to his buddy, "The angel of the sea. I've never seen one. This *must* bode well for us."

Peter swiftly changed into a griffin and beckoned for me to follow him down to the shore to meet the heroes. Kayle and Mariah flanked us. Mariah was still wet; her fur clung to her, making her look almost bony. Her feathers were quicker in drying, but they were fluffed out to do so and gave her a darker-orange-tinted look.

Kayle had his head low, his neck straight out into a continuation of the ram-rod spine. His tail was slung into a J shape, and his face was empty of emotion. I was beginning to really wonder what his deal was. Peter was so much bigger than all of us. His head was high and arched like an Arabian stallion's, and his gait was leisurely. I wondered about him as well. Why was he so cool with everything? Didn't he want to go home too?

The squadron hung back, unsure of what to do. As our rescuers slowly came into view, the knights peeled up their metal visors to see better. Four heads came up out of the water, giggling at the befuddled soldiers. They belonged to mermaids. So it hadn't been a fish I'd seen earlier, swimming away. Now I felt self-conscious about being the tallest in the near vicinity (my neck was up to Peter's head) and the only human. I felt naked, like my feelings were scrolling across my forehead in neon letters.

The mermaids had long curly hair in vivid coral shades: bright pink, blue, green, and yellow. One had a starfish holding her hair away from her face. Their eyes were large and expressive, the pupils almost fully shrunk, making them seem nonexistent. Their lips were full and pulled back over their large canines. Their webbed hands were wrapped tightly around the poles of three-pronged tridents made from some weird kind of mineral. One mermaid had her tail lazily sticking out of the water and curved over her back.

Peter, Kayle, and Mariah bowed, leaving me to be the confused fool standing with his head in the clouds. When they stood straight again, Peter jerked his tail at me and said, "Forgive him. He's still getting used to transforming."

The mermaids nodded understandingly. I leaned over to Kayle and whispered, "Is that bad? That I can't transform at will?"

Out of the corner of his beak, Kayle answered, "As a human, you can't fully understand the magic of your surroundings. If you're a griffin or other type of mythical, imaginative being, you can sense the magic around you and understand different tongues and cultures better. Plus, it's respectful. Mermaids enjoy seeing such powerful creatures, like griffins, bowing to them."

"Oooooh," I drawled and stepped forward to bow, one hand across my torso, the other behind my back. The mermaids burst into another bout of laughter. I frowned, insulted. Was my fly open or something? Sheesh, it couldn't be that hilarious to be a human.

The mermaid with the starfish silenced her companions with a raised hand. Her face was serious. Sticking the butt of her trident deep into the sand beside her, she crawled closer to us. Her voice hit my ears in strange tones. One second, it was pure and clear and very feminine, the next harsh and quiet and croaky. I think me being only part griffin had something to do with it. I noticed that they all kept at least halfway in the water. I had a feeling that their tails had to constantly be wet, like a fish had to continue circulating water through its gills.

The serious mermaid rasped, "Those foul creatures will not return. That package you found is evil. We could smell it from afar. It called us to you." She looked up at me and said, "Come."

I was frozen in place. Kayle head-butted me hard behind the knees, and I stumbled forward and fell, nearly face-to-face with the mermaid. Her skin was olive green and moist, and I couldn't tear my eyes from hers. She reached behind her and pulled forward my surfboard. My eyes flicked quickly to it, then back to her. What was she going to do?

The mermaid extended her long arms and placed a cold, webbed hand on either side of my face. Looking deep into my eyes, she said, "Jonathan. You will do great things... Many will stand in your way, but only you have the power to move them. The legacy you leave behind shall be everlasting, and shall reach back to the very foundations of the Land of Dreams and the throne of griffins... You are the herald of our most terrible and most beautiful age: the Age of Miracles." She let go of me and bowed deeply.

Looking surprised, her friends followed her example. Then she pulled my surfboard in front of her, closed her eyes, and rested the head of her trident on top of it. Suddenly, the board grew smaller and smaller, its sides coming out and a ring opening in the center. The color turned white and mottled yellow, and the texture became smooth and pliable.

Leaning forward, the mermaid looped the surfboard-turned-necklace around my neck, her face so close that I could smell her salty breath, and explained, "This is sun coral. It grants upon you a special power. A griffin's power will awaken on its own after a time, or it may be presented to them by a mystic being."

I touched the necklace and whispered, "What is *my* power?"

The mermaid shrugged. "It is for you to discover. Good luck, Prince." With that, she slid backward into the water, and she and her fellow mermaids vanished.

Kayle scoffed snidely. "He doesn't deserve a gift." My stomach sank. He was right. I hadn't done anything helpful. But to protect my dignity, I got to my feet, dusted the sand off my jeans (since my clothes were still wet, I ended up rubbing in the wet muck and salt from the ocean instead), and looked down at him.

"Apparently the mermaids thought so. Whatever problems you have with me, whether it's because I'm a prince, or an American"–his eyes narrowed–"shove 'em."

Kayle's collar of thick feathers bristled. "Maybe you should try not talking to me."

"Maybe you should try uppers," I shot back. One of the soldiers up the beach busted up laughing and then tried to cover it up by coughing.

Kayle looked ready to carve my heart out of my chest, but before he could, Peter stopped him.

"Fighting isn't going to help anything. Let's see what's in this package."

I led the way back toward the squadron with my hands shoved into my pockets in fists. I wanted to teach that goon a lesson, but it would be weird beating up a griffin. Plus, I needed a nap first. Like, really bad.

The soldiers had formed a circle around the clue, their weapons nonchalantly pointed at it. They cleared a path for us, most staring at me and taking in my human appearance with something close to cynicism.

Peter, of course, was the one we assumed should open the package. He once more picked it up in his talons and readied to untie the knot. Everyone took a casual step back. Peter unpeeled the wrapping and turned it upside down.

What fluttered to the ground surprised us all: a slip of paper followed by a small key. Peter stabbed the paper onto one talon and squinted, holding it up to his eyes. He read, "Ingredients for the Bowl of Bemusement: Four chopped up shiitake mushrooms, handful of leeks, extract of swamp-rat, clump of moss, pinch of mold, scoop of mulch, a quart of boiled mud water."

"Eeeewww!" Mariah grimaced squeamishly, her crown feathers popping up like a cockatiel's.

"How is a recipe a clue?" I asked. I'd expected something more along the lines of a map: "turn left at the talking tree," or, "go twenty steps past the dragon and then go right."

"The Rankers' clues appear to intentionally lead their allies through places where they can gather power. Who's to say what this recipe does, or whether it's a code of some kind that only the Ranker's could decipher. But we're going to find out."

Peter passed the key around, and when it got to me, warm from being in so many hands, I was surprised to find how heavy it was, like it was lead-infused iron or something. It looked old-fashioned, and the base was stained with rust and moss.

"Pocket it," Peter said. "It'll be safest in your possession."

"How so?" I asked, still a bit thrown by everything the mermaid had said, making out with a siren, finding a new frenemy in Kayle, and everything else, so I had a hard time keeping my tone civil.

"Like we said, we took an oath of honor to protect you," Peter said. "Every one of us here would die before we'd let anything happen to you." One of the women in the squadron was gravely nodding her head, and I felt strange all of a sudden—like I wanted to cry. I wanted to say something, but I didn't know how. So I just obediently shoved the key deep into my jeans pocket and pulled my sweatshirt down over it.

Peter spoke up for all of us to hear. "Those ingredients, I'm afraid"—*uh-oh, that was never a good way to start*—"can only be found in the Melancholy Bog of the Reekwood Swamp."

Yikes. I remembered reading about the bog in Peter's *Locations* book. It was a mysterious place—people sometimes vanished out of thin air there. A haunting myth clung around the swamp, but none of the natives liked to speak of it. The people and beasts who lived there weren't hospitable, and the area was permeated by noxious green mists, muddy wallows, and rotted trees.

Peter was saying, "We must be careful, the bog is one of the sheltering zones for nightmares. Even if we don't meet any Rankers we're very likely to see minor creatures of darkness."

One soldier swallowed hard, his Adam's apple jumping. "What... sort of nightmares, sir?"

Peter looked at him out of one eye. "The kind where you're running and running and you just can't seem to get away. The kind where a snorting beast waits for your back to be turned. The kind where you feel yourself changing into something hideous and broken, something that reflects your every perceived internal flaw, and against your will you become a tortured monster—you become the very thing in the world that you most hate and fear." His casual tones did not keep a sense of ominousness from leaking into the air.

"We'll camp up in the trees for the night and then set off at dawn," Peter said.

I looked out behind me at the water, wondering about my father and Nikki. Was anyone looking for me yet? Suddenly, I fell forward and felt familiar weights tugging at my back. I was a griffin once more.

"Get used to it," Peter said in response to my plaintive expression. "The more you shift, the more you'll be able to do so at will."

I moaned. Things were not turning out the way I'd wanted them to. The next time I saw that charlatan...

CHAPTER TEN:

MEANWHILE, BACK IN REALITY

Ethan He'klarr's eyes popped open. He jolted up onto his feet from where he was lying on the couch in the living room, massaging a crick in his neck, and rushed throughout the house calling his son's name. Then, clinging to a frayed thread of hope, he went to the front door, threw it wide, and ignoring the evening's chill, he called out, "Jonathan!" But he was only answered by the distant baying of a loose dog.

Ethan walked out onto the porch and looked all around his yard, which was bathed in the blue-gray light of a full moon. It was no use wishing. His son had not returned. He must have been dreaming.

The police had arrived at Ethan's house that morning to question him, just as he was getting ready for work. One of the officers had scowled at the stench of alcohol on his breath but the other had maintained her composure enough to professionally inform him that Jonathan had been reported missing the previous day.

"Do you know anything about that?" the first officer had asked, still with a look of disdain on his face.

"No, I...I thought he was at a friend's!" Ethan replied. An old fear had seeped through him like cold sludge. Memories of the night he had lost Esther had flickered through his mind. After the policemen had informed him that Jonathan had apparently vanished after a helicopter crash, that they had found his phone and his blood on the floor of a nearby model home, Ethan fell onto the sofa, his head thundering with terror for his son, and with pain from the previous night's binge. Once the officers had finished questioning him and left, Ethan had rolled onto his side on the couch, shaking with the same, visceral despair that he had felt only once before, and eventually drifted into a light sleep disturbed with nightmares of strange sounds and fleeting glimpses of Jonathan.

Now, making some coffee, Ethan trundled upstairs to his son's empty room for the first time in years, clutching the hot mug tightly in his cold hands.

The bed-sheets were mussed and the window open. Setting the coffee on Jon's bedside table, Ethan stared at the mural of the football player on the ceiling above, tears forming in the corners of his eyes. He had known so little about Jonathan—been so absent from his own son's life.

After endless minutes of morosely admiring the brushstrokes forming the work of art on Jonathan's ceiling, Ethan forced himself to confront the one question hovering at the forefront of his mind: *Did this happen because of me?*

Ethan took up his cooling coffee and went on to search his son's room, looking for clues as to his disappearance and little trinkets with which to soothe his sorrow.

In a corner of one of Jonathan's wardrobe shelves was a crumpled-up ball of paper with Nikki's phone number on it. His girlfriend. Ethan guessed that maybe his son had memorized the number and no longer had any need for the paper.

But if anyone could tell him more about what had happened, Nikki could.

Rushing out into the hall so fast that he practically dislodged the rug from where it had molded to the floorboards, Ethan jumped downstairs and ran to the phone. He dialed Nikki's number and waited impatiently during the dial tones. After two rings, someone picked up and Ethan heard a young, feminine voice, sounding miserable, ask hopefully, "Hello?"

"Miss Nikki?" Ethan asked.

There was no answer, then, "Yes."

Ethan knew that she wished to say more and waited.

"This is...his number. I thought..."

Ethan took a deep breath and said, "I'm his dad. I was wondering if you could tell me...what happened? The police came by today and they didn't say much."

"His dad?" An uncertain silence.

"Please?" Ethan added.

He listened as Nikki described the charity work they had been doing in Arrow Creek, the crash, and Nikki looking over her shoulder to check on him while she made a tourniquet for someone who'd been injured and finding him gone.

"Did you know that they found his cellphone?" Ethan asked.

"No, they did?" Nikki's voice brightened even as Ethan's spirits plummeted. She wouldn't know, then, about the blood. And he didn't want to be the one to tell her. They spoke a little longer, but quickly ran out of things to say. After a particularly long pause, Ethan waited until he thought he was in danger of being hung up on and said as consolingly as he could, "It'll be okay. The police are still looking."

Nikki gave a tremendous sniffle and said, "Yeah."

"I'll keep you posted."

"Me too."

With that, they disconnected.

Ethan picked up his cold coffee, setting the phone back in its cradle with a dejected slowness. He stared out the window, poured his mug out into the sink, and retrieved his truck keys from the floor by his armchair. The police had no doubt already combed Arrow Creek for any clues as to where his son might be, but it wouldn't hurt to give the town a drive-through himself.

CHAPTER ELEVEN:
TREE SPIRITS

What would it take to break a prince's heart? My sleeping mind was assailed by feverish visions of the helicopter crash, Nikki with a knife to her throat, Garrett's eyes glowing red like lasers. Everything was disconnected and nothing made sense. First I was squatting in an icy cavern of wet rock, and thunder was roaring loud enough to rattle my skull. Then I was running toward the man who had killed my mom. Then I was in pitch-darkness and things were howling eerily somewhere nearby.

"Do you feel brave, little griffin?" The mocking voice of the man from my nightmare, the man from the park, chased me through the winding chaos of my dreams. *"You finally made it to the dreamworld, I see. Are you prepared to protect your kingdom? Against the mighty evils of forsaken Man?"*

At times I caught a glimpse of shark-like teeth, eyes like obsidian, gray, stony flesh. The Ranker's laughter pursued me.

"What do you want with me?" I shouted, my voice shrill.

"Don't you know, yet?"

A horrible feeling encompassed me, like claws were wrapping around my ribs and crushing the breath from my lungs, and I opened my eyes to the cold night. I could see as well as if it were dusk. The countless stars formed an array of constellations, some known to me and some not, across the heavens and a moon as round and full as could be was reflected in the sea below it.

I watched the water lap at the shore and fought the urge to let it lull me back to slumber and nightmares. I wanted to go somewhere. I wanted to move. The quicker we got to the White Griffin, the quicker I could go home.

I stuck my rump in the air and stretched like a cat, yawning. Shaking myself, I turned to see what the others were doing. My coat of feathers and fur was keeping me comfortably toasty; I felt bad for a group of knights and gladiators shivering in some ferns nearby.

Something moved, and I jolted, my talons digging into the ground. But it was only Mariah. She stopped and looked at me, eyes glowing green like a cat's in the moonlight, then smiled and continued on toward the cold men on the ground.

I tried to remove my talons from the dirt with dignity, wondering what she was doing.

Mariah circled the men a few times, stepped so carefully in among them that they didn't awaken, and lay down. She spread her wings out on top of them like a blanket, and almost immediately, they stopped shivering.

I joined her and opened my own wings; one lay atop her left one, and the other covered a few huddled marines. They were dressed warmer, so I didn't know how much help I was, but it was an ice-breaker, and it didn't hurt to help just in case.

"How is it that I can still have dreams in the Land of Dreams?" I asked in a hushed whisper.

Mariah giggled, a pretty trilling sound from her beak.

"You ask all of the right questions," she said. "Your brain still needs to process all of the stress and sensory input from the day somehow. Sometimes that manifests as what appears to be a dream, but while you're here, it's really just memories or a string of tangible thoughts. Other times you have dreams-within-dreams, where you confront the deepest parts of yourself."

"And nightmares?" I asked. Mariah looked at me sharply.

"Did you have a nightmare?"

"Maybe."

"That's not good. The Rankers know you're here and they will try to twist your mind and break your spirit. You need to be careful not to let them find out where you are and what we're doing."

"How?"

"The longer you're here, the more you discover what it means to be a griffin, the stronger you will become. After you discover your power, that should help greatly. Until then, I'll pray over you before you go to sleep each night. Rankers detest prayers."

I thought of my friend Kitty with a pang. She had prayed for my friends and I on multiple occasions, usually when we were about to do something stupid like jumping from Tyson's roof and onto his trampoline. There was something pure and bright in the casual way she, and Mariah, vowed to do something so personal and compassionate.

"Thank you," I said.

Mariah bobbed her head.

"So," I began in a hushed whisper. "How long have you been in this place?"

She answered casually, "A while."

I couldn't keep from asking her a flood of questions. "What's it like? Have you been all over? Who've you met? What happens if you get hurt–"

Mariah cuffed me gently over the head with the "wrist" joint of her wing and messed up my crown feathers. While I smoothed them back out, she laughed. "It has been an awesome experience. At first, I had difficulty adjusting, just like you, but I'm a fast learner, and Kayle helped a bunch."

"Yeah, what's his problem?" I asked.

She sighed. "He doesn't like change. He knew your predecessor well. We all miss him. Kayle's frustrated that you would rather go home than embrace your destiny."

A bunch of new questions came to mind about my predecessor, but Mariah changed the subject.

"The creatures and places and events people dream up are amazing and terrifying. Sometimes it feels like we're intruding on their minds, but Peter said they aren't bothered. To them, we are just another part of their dream. If they only knew..." She took a breath as if to say more, then held it, looking at her jeweled collar.

When she went on, she was hesitant, and her words were slowly chosen as if she were uncomfortable. I watched her intently, but not enough to make her nervous.

"I saw my mom," she began, "but she ignored me when I called her name. She didn't recognize me." She gave a dark laugh. "I've been gone from the real world for two years."

"*Two years?*" I croaked in a strained whisper.

She smiled wryly again. "Yes. Sometimes I wonder if I'll ever wake up again... But I like to help protect people. Rankers try to gain numbers by influencing the darkness in our hearts through dreams... giving humans nightmares so horrible that they are driven to wickedness, even madness. When a person loses his or her mind, their destroyed consciousness can create multiple Rankers. There are hundreds–thousands–maybe millions of them out there."

I remembered watching the helicopter crash when I had been trying to puzzle everything out with Nikki, then thought of that terrible event multiplied by ten. Monsters tearing cities apart, demolishing buildings with whatever horrific powers they possessed, massacring with abandon.

Watching me try and process, Mariah said, "Rankers want to strike from the inside out–they'll start here, in our minds, in our hearts, but they're gaining power and slipping free into the real world. But some people have willpower so strong that they can fight the Rankers here in the Land of Dreams and wake up perfectly normal if not a bit startled. The dreams you have when you jump start and are jolted roughly awake? Those are caused when a Ranker tries to attack you but your mind fights it off. The brain is a powerful thing–a miracle. It understands that something is wrong and so shuts it away from you."

"So, humanity has a hope?" I asked, my voice meek.

"*We* are humanity's last hope. Not everyone is equipped to fend off a Ranker, let alone an army of them. The griffin-hearted dreamers have managed to keep the beasts at bay so far, but as the darkness in humanity increases, so the Rankers' power builds. And those who have stood against the demons in their dreams will be made slaves when the Rankers are strong enough to enter the real world together as one physical army. I pity them then. The Rankers will show them no mercy."

It was a lot to take in. I felt overwhelmed. "I'm not sure I understand." *I'm not sure I want to.*

Mariah crossed her talons daintily and said, "You will. In time."

When I took a breath to question her further, she shushed me and began purring. Apparently, griffins *can* do that. My anxiety threatened to escalate to full-out explosion mode, but her purring was as soothing as a lullaby. I took a long, deep breath, letting it hiss out through the nostrils of my beak. What I needed was a plan—and not whatever plan Peter and the others had all cooked up together to vanquish the Rankers. I needed something smaller...something to hold on to so I could keep sane until I figured out how to get back home, or at least find whoever the hell I needed to talk to to get answers.

Answers, I thought, *That's what I need. Something tangible I can bring back with me to my friends—a way to keep them all safe.* I felt a bit better with that tiny goal in mind, letting Mariah's kitten-esque purrs flutter against my ears like butterfly wings. Despite all of my concerns, we trailed off into a comfortable silence for a few peaceful minutes, listening to the crickets and the distant waves stroking the shore. There was also quite a backdrop of raucous snoring (marines have the lung capacity of a bull elephant), but even that seemed peaceful in a way. It was the sound of calm.

"So, you saw your mother?" I asked.

Mariah said, "She was dreaming about flowers. We were traveling through a meadow of them, and there were multitudes of people meandering around with dazed smiles on their faces. One was my mom. She was picking petals off a daisy and...humming to herself a lullaby she always sang to me. I wouldn't doubt it if you see some people you know here, especially since you're going to be on a lot of people's minds. But you may not recognize them. Sometimes people have dreams where they appear as something else. I had a dream once that I was a puppy..."

I sighed slowly. "This is my first time as a griffin."

Mariah peered sternly through her brow at me. "*This* isn't a dream. This is a world that mankind has collectively created where dreams are *born*."

I turned the corners of my beak down and messed with my new coral necklace, straightening it against my downy white chest.

I brushed my longest right pinion against Mariah's collar. "Were you presented with that? Have you found out your gift?"

Mariah nodded proudly. "Yes, the dwarves gave it to me. When we passed their volcano, Peter asked for directions to Pebble Embark, and one pointed at me and said that he had long ago made this for someone, but only then knew it had been me."

"Dwarves?" I bit back a laugh, imagining tiny, chubby old men with beards and spectacles.

Mariah gave a disgruntled sniff and said defensively, "They are the most skilled of craftsmen. Many gorgeous gemstones are discovered in their mountains. I am honored to have this trinket."

I gulped back another laugh guiltily. Now that I remembered from Peter's book of mythical creatures, I knew she was right. Comparing them to the seven Disney dwarves was like comparing a pit bull to a poodle.

Mariah added, "I can grow things," with an edge of finality—like she wanted me to quit talking about it, so I changed the subject slightly.

"And what of tall, dark, and gloomy?"

Mariah understood that I meant Kayle and said, "He found out his power on his own just like Peter. Peter can blend in to his surroundings. He and Kayle were ambushed in human form by a batch of Rankers on a scouting trip, and suddenly Kayle was pinned down by one. He pulled out his lighter to burn the Ranker away, and discovered he could manipulate the fire. When he's a griffin, he can become fully combusted, like a phoenix. It's a spectacular gift. He destroyed that whole group of Rankers. Peter owes him his life."

That explained why he had seemed to be setting off smoke on the beach. I made a mental note not to anger him any more than was deemed necessary unless I wanted to be cooked medium, rare, or well done.

"And what about your human life? How did you get here in the first place?" I asked.

A dark cloud fell across Mariah's face. Her eyes narrowed. She clicked her beak, shifted almost imperceptibly a few inches away, and muttered, "That's private."

Almost right after that, Peter climbed out of a patch of berry bushes and shook himself like a great, shaggy dog. Flapping his wings a bit to stretch out the kinks, he shouted, "It's time to move out! Open your eyes and stand ready, men, we have before us a long day."

Faster than I thought possible, everyone was up and awake.

The warriors placed their armor and smoothed the creases from their uniforms. Kayle slunk out of the trees, looking wide awake. Maybe he hadn't even slept at all.

Within minutes, we were all packed up and moving on down an overgrown trail. The sun was abnormally large, but just as bright and warm as the sun in reality. It turned the sky (seen only barely through the canopy) a pale blue and pink. We kept on maneuvering around thick and mossy trees and stumbling over knobby roots–feeling like the jungle was trying to stop us, preventing us from traveling into its dark heart.

The day wore on slowly. We took random breaks to eat some fruits and vegetables that Mariah grew straight from the ground. (I couldn't stop staring at her for a while afterward until she gave me a really venomous stink eye.) And soon after, we moved on.

My feet were sore. I longed to change back into a human, but no matter how hard I tried, my feathers and fur remained. I had pestered Peter about it earlier on, and he had shrugged and told me that I had to learn how to do it on my own–there were no instructions, no trick to get it to happen. My mind needed to "adjust to the new way things were" first.

The lush leaves above us kept us shaded, but because of how closed the jungle was, humidity seeped from every clump of moss and flora like steam in a hot shower.

On one of our breaks sometime around noon, I was starting to feel a little weird. My heart was beating faster, and I was filled with an eager sense of anticipation. I was avoiding Peter, Kayle, and Mariah for various reasons, so I only had the gladiator sitting beside me and whittling what suspiciously resembled a siren to ask, "Do you feel that?"

In a thick accent of some sort, Greek or Roman maybe, he queried, "Feel what, my prince?"

I was too distracted to tell him not to call me that and stared into the jungle, replying vaguely, "Like you're being watched, but by someone that you know...?"

The gladiator set aside his sculpture and clenched his knife tighter in his hand. He saw Peter watching from across the glade and gestured for him to join us, his strong-featured face a mask of concern. Peter appeared at my side, his talons and paws making no noise on the earthy jungle floor. We both gazed into the gloom of the shrubbery, ears cocked forward.

The squadron quieted their conversations and warily took up their weapons. Kayle's eyes glowed a dull red; rivulets of smoke coiled from his nostrils like gray snakes. Mariah's face was blank. Slowly, she placed a talon over her heart and closed her eyes.

I was tilting my head every which way, striving to pinpoint a sound or sight–anything to explain the emotions I was feeling.

Peter's rigid form relaxed, and he breathed, "Tree spirits."

At his declaration, an invisible wind shook the branches, and a few leaves fluttered meekly to the dirt. The trunks swayed side to side, creaking so loudly that I was afraid they might snap and fall over on us. But just when I was about to retreat into the open somewhere out of the way, the creaking stopped and shimmering, ghost-like people stepped out of the trunks of five trees nearby.

Two were female. They wore silver dresses, and crowns of brambles, leaves, and berries graced their locks. One had ringlets, and the second, long and thin tresses.

The other three were men. Two were younger, about the women's ages, wore gold-tinted pants and tunics, and had shoulder-length hair. One had his hair pulled back and tied with a band of pine needles and sap.

The third man was so old that it looked like another gust of wind would send him flying. His skin was very wrinkled, and I observed his thin shoulders beneath the white robe he was draped in. He leaned on a knobbly staff, and his wispy hair hung down to his waist. From the way the other four shot him occasional reverent looks, I could tell he was the leader.

While we stood there staring at each other, I fought to remember what I had read about tree spirits. Their human appearances resembled the tree they resided in. As a human, they couldn't be hurt. They could only be destroyed if the tree they were connected to was somehow killed. Peaceful and wise, they assisted the lost and weary traveler, provided the most delicious and replenishing fruit, and had super-thick bark. The only time they were known to be dangerous was when their tree was being threatened: then, they used their arsenal of fingery knife-sharp branches as defense.

"Oakpaen," Peter said warmly, arcing his tail into a sinuous S shape, and the five tree spirits broke into small smiles. "I was hoping to find you."

Oakpaen's voice was breezy, and I had to strain to actually hear the syllables he was forming when he chuckled and said, "You did not. *I* found *you*. But what is your business here, Peter Griffin-Scribe?"

Peter replied airily, "To get directions."

One of the women asked in a voice like fresh autumn air, "Where to?"

Peter stepped back and extended his wing to brush my side, saying, "The prince has arrived, and our quest begins in the Melancholy Bog."

All five tree spirits bowed and curtsied at me. The little old man shakily bent forward with support from his staff.

"Then may you go without hindrance, and the Golden Griffin with you," he said. "Journey northeast and follow the path. You should reach the bog by tomorrow evening."

Peter thanked him and ordered the squadron to make ready. One of the younger male tree spirits took a hasty step forward and outstretched a halting hand.

"Forgive me, Prince, but I must ask, if only to settle my foolish curiosity, how go things in your reality?"

My face fell, and I tried to find something to say that wouldn't seem too morose or depressing.

"Well," I began lamely, "things are…changing. That's for sure."

"Ah, yes," broke in Oakpaen, "things are forever changing; I can feel it in the wind. But 'tis true, the change you mention, sire, is a cold and foul breeze indeed."

"We're ready to leave, Peter!" Kayle called over. He shook his black feathers, eager to move on.

Oakpaen noticed the crestfallen look on my face, and the way my tail drooped, the tuft of feathers at the end slapping dismally against the ground. A warm breeze stirred up, nudging me beneath the chin like a grandfather chuffing his favorite grandson, and I looked up at him again.

"Do not abandon hope, young prince," the elderly man murmured, "for through the thorns of sorrow and strife emerge the most beautiful blossoms." I caught a whiff of spring in that breeze, not the kind of spring a jungle might have but the smells of spring that I remembered from my childhood back home: roses, lavender, barbecues, and the fresh, clean rain misting down from the mountains. My heart swelled in my chest, and a powerful swing of homesickness almost knocked me over. But I felt bolstered too, comforted.

"Good luck. We of the jungles and forests wish your journey to be a success," Oakpaen said.

I was sincerely thankful to him. What he had said had been wise, kind, and encouraging. I don't know even now where the words came from, but I found myself saying, "And may your life branch long and full of splendor, King of Trees."

Peter gave me a mildly surprised look out of the corner of his eye. The tree spirits' faces lit up with pleasure.

As one, they bowed their heads, and Oakpaen cried out in a voice stronger than what he had used before, "Come, my sons and daughters; the tree folk must meet and discuss these new events." And with another invisible breeze, the spirits dissolved into clusters of flowers and vanished among the trees.

Peter and I stood there together and let ourselves be filled with that weird emotion the tree spirits had given us. Finally, Peter turned around and strode to the head of the patiently waiting squadron. I followed but stopped.

Kayle and Mariah shot me cold looks, and the soldiers were all talking among themselves. I didn't want to be a third wheel, but I didn't want to walk by myself and pout either.

So, as our sore feet returned to the endless pattern of marching, I trotted past everyone to the fore of the column and tentatively joined Peter's side. He didn't acknowledge me except for lazily arching his tail and turning one ear toward me.

"Is–" My voice came out sickeningly high-pitched, so I tried again. "Ahem–is this spot taken?"

"No one's name is on it," Peter said with the hint of a smile.

I matched his stride, and for a while we listened quietly to a pair of samurai arguing behind us about whose sword was sharper.

Then Peter asked, "Any idea where that came from back there?" In response to my confused look, he explained, "That poetry that you impressed our friendly tree spirits with?"

"Oh," I mumbled. "That. Yeah, I don't know..."

Peter's smile stayed frozen on his beak, his silver eyes twinkling, but he didn't say anything more. I followed his lead and fastened my eyes on the trail ahead with a firm determination.

We made camp that night off the trail in a lush nest of vegetation. I felt miserable as I nibbled at my watermelon, rubbing my scaly talons together, trying to relax my sore and cramped muscles. Wincing when I accidentally jabbed a claw into my palm, I stretched out and fought long and hard to fall asleep.

CHAPTER TWELVE:
I Find Out My Wings Work

The next morning I was still very achy, but loathe to admit it. I had to remind myself that I was doing this for my friends. For Nikki. *Answers,* I thought, *I need answers.* I once more joined Peter's side, and, in silence, we resumed marching after a quick breakfast of dried meat strips and nuts one of the warriors was packing.

After traversing nearly two miles in mutual silence, eavesdropping on a pair of Amazons chatting behind us about what the Rankers' key might open, Peter casually asked me a question.

"How much of my books did you read, Jonathan?"

I was a tad taken aback and struggled to force my face into a serious expression before answering, "Everything."

"How much have you taken to heart?"

"Everything."

Peter made a contemplative noise in the back of his throat and shouted behind him, "Sergeant Flaherty!"

A stocky marine appeared beside us. He removed his hat to reveal a neat crew cut and waited politely to find out why he had been summoned.

"Keep the men in this direction. Make sure Kayle has everyone covered in back. Jonathan and I will return by evening." Peter veered off the overgrown trail. The marine gave a snappy salute and took his place.

I ran to join Peter, grimacing every time my sore feet pounded the ground. "What's going on?"

Peter was smiling at me. "We need to practice, son, for what lies ahead." He started to lead me deeper into the jungle.

I followed reluctantly, stubbing my talons and paws on stumps hidden beneath a carpet of ivy and moss. "Yeah, but *where* are we going?" Was he taking me away somewhere to kill me? My steps faltered at the thought.

"Guess you'll have to wait and see," Peter called back. From his tone of voice, I could tell he was grinning.

Getting my dander up, I shouted back, "But why all the secrecy? Don't you think I *deserve* some clarity?" I hurried to get closer to his side in case he wasn't catching my drift. "I mean, any more being kept in the dark, and I'll have an aneurism."

Peter said, "I sure hope not. That would be terrible. Besides, you know what they say, actions speak louder than–"

"Than words, yeah, yeah..." I groused angrily, my low eagle brow furrowing over my flickering red eyes. Peter just threw back his head and laughed heartily.

In about ten minutes, I was able to see clear blue sky through the tree trunks ahead. Five minutes more, and we were out of the claustrophobic jungle and perched on a rocky cliffside.

I inhaled deeply of the fresh, salty air, eyes closed to the sun. An immeasurable drop below us, ocean waves slapped the sandy base of the cliff. I felt free and strong, high above the world.

Presumably, this cliff was an extension of the hill we had climbed back at the beach. Far to my left, it continued as far as my eagle eyes could see. It was an ominous marker to the long distance we had traveled. But to my right, the cliff gradually sloped down and broadened into a vast forest punctuated and ringed by snowcapped mountains.

"Is this an island?" I asked, my words almost tossed away by the fierce wind.

"In the same way that Australia is an island," Peter said in a distracted way. "I've traveled far and still haven't seen all of it." He was studying the insides of his cream-colored wings, neatly straightening crooked feathers and flexing the powerful muscles. When he was done, he locked eyes with me and asked fiendishly, "Are you ready?"

I looked at him uncomprehendingly, a stupid smile still plastered on my beak. "What?"

Peter flapped his wings feebly. "Are you ready?"

"For..." I trailed off as my eyes wandered suspiciously to the edge of the cliff.

I started to back off, my heart doing flips and my breath coming in short bursts. "Awwwwww–no!"

Peter gave me an *oh come on* look. "Jonathan, you'll have to do it sometime, and this is the easiest way to teach you."

"*Fly?*" I squeaked.

"Well, you're a griffin, aren't you? Ya got wings!"

I frowned at him, something that was becoming a habit, and fumed, "Alright, first of all, I am not a *griffin*, I am a *kid*, a hu-man *kid*! Second of all, I cannot fly. Just because these huge, feathery things pop out of my back, it doesn't make me Orville!"

Peter grew more serious as I became closer and closer to losing it. He said gently, "There will be times when you will have to fly. It's easy, it's fun... You aren't scared, are you?"

To be honest, it had been a dream of mine to fly someday. I squirmed and inched closer to the drop-off, completely terrified of it now that I was supposed to jump off it.

"Let me show you," Peter said quietly.

I swallowed and looked over at him, sitting back on my haunches.

Peter backed about twenty feet away from the edge of the cliff. Then he pushed off his hind legs, the muscles tensing. He ran swiftly toward the edge, as graceful and powerful as a cheetah on the savannah. His wings opened at a measured pace as he calculated his distance from the jump. At the last minute, he placed his hind paws right on the edge of the cliff, stood up so that his upper body was suspended above empty space...and fell, just like that, with his wings clamped close to his sides.

"*Peter?*" I rushed over to where he'd dropped just in time to see him snap open his wings from where he had plummeted fifty feet down. Wind cushioned up beneath him, and he teetered a bit, but steadied and quickly rose up past me.

I gasped. It was an amazing sight to see: Peter's immense wingspan, the sun dashing white zags on his dark feathers. On land, Peter had seemed aged, if not ancient, but in the air, he was transformed. A mythical beast of legend reborn.

Peter had said in one of his books that the griffin was king of the land (being part lion) and king of the skies (being part eagle).

Watching him carve intricate arcs and pirouettes in the air, I began to believe it.

He spun to face me and dove down to land next to me, a look of peace etched deeply into his features. "Do you see?" he murmured.

I opened my beak to say something, closed it again, and twitched my head by way of an understanding nod.

He instructed, "Open your wings."

I worked the muscles in my chest and back, and with a soft rustle, they spread wide. It felt like I had an extra set of arms, but they were heavier and fingerless and huge. For the first time, I examined the insides closely. They were a warm honey color with rich brown spots and pinions.

"Wow," I breathed.

"Indeed," Peter chuckled amiably. "Now let's see you flap 'em."

I began to swipe my wings up and down, a cloud of dust billowing up around my face. Over the loud whooshing sound, I heard Peter coughing and shouting, "Stop! Stop it!"

I slowed my flapping to a stop, hacking on the dirt and blinking it out of my third transparent eyelids.

"Only in cartoons do birds flap up and down," Peter said, shaking his whole body free of grit. "In reality, you must paddle, pushing the air beneath and behind you like so..." He demonstrated by raising his wings and performing the motion slowly. I followed his example, and he complimented my success. The motions repeated themselves in my head: *forward, down, and back, forward, down, and back.*

Peter added, "If a thermal, that is, a cushion of air, suspends you so that you don't have to flap at all, that is when you glide—stilling your wings and moving effortlessly."

"Okay." I had seen some of the birds of prey around my house glide before.

"When diving, as I was doing, fold your wings close to you. You have deflectors in your beak that will keep too much air from being pumped into your lungs at once, but it'll still be a bit jarring the first few times. And always clean your feathers. I cannot stress that enough! *Always.* Or else one of these days you'll try flying and your dirty wing feathers will be too messy and heavy to support you."

I gulped and pinned that little note front and center on my mental bulletin board of things to remember.

"Now, let's try it," Peter encouraged softly.

I sighed and stared up into the sky as if for support. Peter's voice came again; he had moved closer to one of my ear tufts.

"Jonathan, things like this take more than willpower. They take faith..."

I backed away from the ledge until my tail brushed against a tree trunk, then gathered myself together and lunged forward, running toward the drop-off. My heart was racing like it was trying to run away from the cliff; a numbing, surreal sense stole over my brain; my body was in a state of shock, fighting mind over matter in disbelief that I was actually going to hurl myself into the abyss.

This was it! I reached out my claws, digging them around the rocky ledge. Like a rabbit, I hunched my back legs forward on either side of my talons, bracing against the ledge while I pushed forward with my upper body. My talons were curled under my chest now, my haunches slowly extending, my body parallel to the sea so many leagues below. It was too late to pull back now.

My wings were half open, but now I reeled 'em back in close to my ribs. Without their levitating stability, I suddenly nose-dived, my lion paws dragged off of the nice, safe ground.

The sudden force of falling made me dizzy and weak. The wind ripped viciously at my face and talons. The water didn't seem to be getting any closer, but I could tell by the rocky wall flashing past me how fast I was falling. My organs felt all bunched in my stomach, my mouth was dry, and my transparent eyelids were automatically working overtime, flashing over my rapidly drying eyes, which were being pressed back into their sockets.

I had a fleeting thought about how bad it would be for me to suddenly transform into a human right then.

Wow. This is not at all fun.

Someone shouted. I wrenched my head to the side and saw that Peter was free-falling right next to me.

"*Open your wings!*" he bellowed, the wind almost completely obliterating his voice.

Oh, yeah. Wings.

I struggled to stick them out but found that I couldn't. Were they stuck? Did I still have them at all? I assumed I did and cried back, "*I can't!*"

"*You must, Jon! Fight your velocity! Spread them wide!*"

I was feeling nauseous and developing a tiny headache, but I would take that over being crushed wafer thin by the water any time.

So I forced my wing muscles around. It felt like fighting against ropes that bound my arms against me.

Finally, I had opened up my wings enough so that the air flew differently over them, and was able to gain full control again. Invigorated, I burst out my wings with a soft *snap* and my body was yanked roughly downward by my change in direction. It was painful, the wind sharply filling up my wings and straining at the muscles. I grunted and watched the rock wall begin moving down past me.

Warm air floated me up. I didn't even have to move my wings. I stared down at my paws and drooping tail, then past them at the shrinking sea. The adrenaline kicked in, and energy raced through my blood and nerves. But now, something was happening: My wings shook—I wobbled side to side, losing support. The air pressed into uneven pockets under random areas of my wings, threatening to collapse them.

Once more, Peter floated beside me. "Flap now," he said, looking relieved and surprised at how well I was doing so far.

I pushed down and successfully shot up. I could look over the jungle now, hovering around fifteen feet above the ledge from where I'd jumped. Wobbling again, I flapped and rose even higher, so that the treetops seemed to blend into a large green quilt punctured by mountains and surrounded by water.

Curious, I moved up to where I could get an eagle-eye view of the land. I saw mostly forests and mountains, but through the tops of trees, I could glimpse lakes sparkling in the sun, dry and yellow-grassed meadows, and even what I thought were modern buildings. Smaller islands were speckled behind the mainland in the north, but they were either old volcanoes coated with black rock, or sloping, barren sand dunes.

I flapped higher, wondering if I was just imagining the air thinning. Where was that Peter when I–

"Straighten out your body, Jonathan! Start flapping down and back to right yourself."

I did as suggested, having to dive down a few paces from the stratosphere, and was soon gliding and flapping in wide circles at a more comfortable altitude parallel to the ledge.

"Wow," I gasped, a wide smile stretching the flexible corners of my beak. I felt more blissful than I ever had in my whole life. I could sail like this forever.

"That's the only word I can think of to explain it too." Peter laughed. He was loftily surfing a wave of air beneath me, first rising, then dipping in a U pattern.

Within the hour, I had shaped up to be a pretty decent flier. It helped that aviation was so addicting. Peter was tracking the warriors' progress from the air, catching them through gaps in the tree branches. My wings were beginning to get tired, and I wanted to land, but I had a feeling that Peter had me up here for another reason. Plus, this was the perfect time to ask some questions that needed immediate answers.

A crushing blow suddenly barreled into my chest, sending a sharp ache bruising through my rib cage. The breath was squashed out of me, and my wings collapsed. I started to spiral crazily downward, black splotches melding in and out of my eyes. Wind whistled through my beak, wreathed through my feathers like grabbing fingers as I tumbled and twisted. It took a lot of effort, but I sucked in a deep breath, and the dots started to fade, replaced with a nauseating sight similar to what the world looked like from a high-speed carousel: a spinning blur of color and shapes. With a determined growl, I spread my wings and flapped up, regaining my balance.

"Peter!" I coughed. "We're being attacked!" I looked around for him and saw the great griffin watching me from up and to my right with an apologetic, sheepish smile. I came to the instant conclusion that it had been he who'd hit me.

"*What was that for?*" I scowled indignantly. Maybe he really did want to kill me...

"I wanted to see how you would react to an air attack."

"Oh, really?" I groused, but my interest was piqued. "Well, how did I do?"

Peter squinted, unsure of how to answer. "Announcing that we were being attacked was sort of stating the obvious, don't you think?"

I mumbled irritably under my breath.

"What was that?" Peter asked, gliding closer.

"I said, 'How was I supposed to act?'"

Peter soared over and hovered in front of me. "You should have fought back. Attack me."

I almost forgot to flap. "Attack you?"

He nodded, eyes keen. Shrugging, I flew at him, vowing to go easy, but he somehow avoided me and kicked down into my back. I fought for composure, resuming my position in the air, and protested loudly, "Ow, man, c'mon!"

Peter circled around with a warning gleam in his eyes. "Now I'll try!" he called. Swooping over, he struck out with his fishhook talons. I made a split-second decision and pushed to one side with one wing, flipping into a roll–like I was in the heat of a game, dodging a tackle. Even then, one of Peter's talons clipped my wing, leaving raw scratches and pulling some feathers loose. I yelped, and he pulled into a sharp about-face to pursue. With football tactics fresh in my mind, I snatched desperately at which of my skills I could apply in this instance. Peter was powerful, but I was smaller. Faster.

The dark-brown griffin stretched out his talons to grab at my wing again, and I instantly closed them–maneuvers coming only half-baked into my mind. I dropped backward, for a moment suspended upside down in the sky, but before I could rocket into another vomit-inducing nose-dive, I opened my wings again and performed a midair backflip. Peter sailed over where my wing had been an instant before, and I came up right behind him in time to swat at the feathers spread at the end of his tail.

He fumbled a bit, wobbling, but I may as well have been a kitten playing with its mother's twitching tail for all the damage I did. Still, he tossed me a small, proud look that gleamed in his silver eyes before spinning and nipping me in the shoulder with his long orange beak.

"Yowch! Enough!" I exclaimed, examining the tiny bald spot that had been inflicted.

Peter seemed a bit troubled and mused, "Perhaps that was too tough. You did just learn how to fly."

"Yeah," I agreed heartily.

"All things considered, that wasn't too bad. I think you learned a lesson, though."

"Not to take my eyes off you," I shot.

"Or any enemy," Peter added sternly, then: "It's a good start."

Although it may not have seemed like it, I had taken Peter's lesson to heart and also learned to dodge in the air. I knew that would come in handy. So I added it to my rapidly filling mental bulletin board.

"What are these dinky little tail feathers for?" I asked Peter, swooping low to skim some tree branches with my claws.

"They perfect maneuvers to the letter. If you go into a roll, as you did when I feigned an attack on you, the movement is slow, clumsy. By spreading those feathers and positioning your tail, the roll is sharper and faster. It's very handy in battle." He demonstrated for me, and I tried myself, dizzily discerning which way was upward and vowing never to try it again.

I found out the names of some of the other creatures native to this strange place as I flew. When I asked what the little flying lizards jumping from holes in the cliffside below were, Peter answered, "Wyvern hatchlings. Looks like they're out for their first hunt. Not the friendliest creatures...we must be getting close."

"So," I said, wishing to get answers to some questions before we landed or my aching wings fell off. "If you're dreaming–having a nightmare–and the Ranker causing it dies, what happens to the person dreaming?"

Peter answered cheerfully, "Their minds are freed and they wake up and start over."

"Who kills them?" I asked, though I suspected I already knew the answer.

"We do," Peter said. "The good guys who dream about defeating the 'bad guys,' and, of course, 'bad guys' being Rankers in disguise."

I pondered that. It all sounded so...gosh darn heroic. Fighting bad, good always wins, and that sort of stuff.

"That collage of faces in one of those books you sent me? The griffin one. Were they...like us? Who were they exactly?" I asked.

Peter's expression turned sad. After taking a moment to coast on a warm late-afternoon breeze, he said, "Brave young people who died before their time. They all had great hearts. They would have done the world plenty of good if the Rankers hadn't killed them."

I felt myself grow chilly, and a sour taste filled my mouth. How sad. And *I* was expected to do something about these monsters?

As if reading my mind, Peter said, "Jonathan, everyone has a darker side to them. But some choose to ignore it for the most part and act on the other side. They have an obligation to those who might be caught somewhere in between–to protect the innocent and defeat the wicked."

I was reminded of the little girl who had vanished under mysterious circumstances near where I lived. Anger filled me–no, not anger, *hatred*. I needed to understand this enemy. Peter's book had told me some of the how (–the dark powers the Rankers used)–and the why (–the wickedness that drove them),–but I needed to understand more about the *who* if I was ever to confront the monsters again.

"So, they have allies," I said. "They have an army, or they're trying to amass one, which implies a martial chain of command. What weapons do they use? What are their battlefield tactics?"

"No," Peter interrupted. "Those are good questions, but you're trying to put them in a box. Rankers don't fit in a box—they aren't constrained by the rules men at war must follow in reality. Rankers are a dark force, and until now, they have never struck out in such numbers, with such cohesion. Yes, they have allies—evil always will—and, yes, they seem to have fashioned for themselves a semblance of military ranks, but most of the information we are now acting upon was brand-new intel as of only a few years ago. I'm not exaggerating when I say that you know as much about them as we do."

Alarm raced up my spine and made my wings shake a bit. I pinned my ears back and forced my voice to remain steady.

"And yet you seem confident that we have some sort of edge or advantage."

"We do—we've intercepted their clues. If we can find out their plans, and the location of their base"—he shook his head—"that'll be a gold mine."

"Sounds like quite a gamble." My voice dripped with doubt.

"Maybe it is. But we also have an ace in the deck—"

"If you say me, I swear to—"

"You."

"Oh, for shit's sake..."

"Jonathan." Peter angled his wings so that he dropped back level with me, our wingtips almost touching. His silver eyes pierced me beneath his low eagle brow. "You heard what those mermaids said. You are the herald of a new age. Now you got a lot of folks that believe in you, including me. How long before you start believing in yourself?"

I felt my face grow hot under my feathers, and didn't answer, wrestling with my own discomfort. *I'm a football player whose mom died and whose dad knocks him around. How can I be anything more than that?*

Something caught my eye below.

The tree line dipped down and stopped with a few clustered rows of sickly and twisted bare trees. Here, earthy ground was replaced with pools of burbling greenish-gray soup pockmarked with islands of muddy, weed-choked slush. The small valley dipped back up a hill seemingly in danger of crumbling in on itself, then grew dark and misted into the foggy depths of more unhealthy trees.

"What *is* that place?" I coughed out disgustedly. The noxious fumes hit me even up here. It smelled like decay.

"Our destination," Peter said gravely. "The Melancholy Bog."

CHAPTER THIRTEEN:
MEANWHILE, BACK IN REALITY

AT ST. PAUL'S HOSPITAL

Nikki sat at the windowsill, looking at the busy traffic crowding the road eight stories below her, studying the colorful life.

Life. What a word. The hospital seemed so devoid of it.

The room she was in had reddish-brown walls and warm lights that couldn't be turned on too bright. A small TV was tucked behind a panel on a shelf. Chairs, a table, and a couch covered with a rumpled bed-sheet were squeezed by the walls.

The adults were out getting dinner. They took turns spending the night there and only rarely remembered to feed themselves.

Lights were just beginning to wink on in the street lamps outside. Restaurants turned on their neon signs. People bundled up cozily for the cold stayed close together on the sidewalk to avoid the water from puddles thrown up by the racing cars.

Nikki swallowed, blinked, and raked a hand through her bangs, trying to stop thinking about the homework load that waited for her at home. It was as if teachers didn't care that the whole world was collapsing on its knees. Maybe they thought homework would keep everyone from going insane.

"Have you found anything out yet?" a small voice asked from the center of the room.

Nikki jumped and turned around. "Tyson! I didn't think you were awake!"

Tyson twitched the hand with the IV in it. "Am I?" he teased.

Nikki shook her head in mock exasperation and took the chair by his bedside. Tyson's girlfriend Lia was in a chair keeled over across the edge of his bed asleep with her arms folded under her head. Lia was usually the most well-kempt of their group. Her bright blonde hair was usually silky, her makeup spot-on, her clothes trendy and flattering. But not today. Today, her hair was thrown into a messy bun and she wore one of Tyson's grubby old sweatshirts.

"How do you feel?" Nikki asked softly, trying not to wake Lia up.

Tyson had recovered extraordinarily fast from his list of wounds. His mother and father had been released long before and now hardly ever left his side except to eat and give him and his visitors privacy. His eyes had deep shadows, and cuts were scattered on his face like red pen marks. Both arms were heavily bandaged, and his leg was suspended in a sling from the ceiling. Gauze encased his head, torso, and the hand with the reattached fingers. Now it was all painful therapy.

"I–am–fi-nuh," he enunciated, with the air of having answered this question many times.

Nikki carefully patted the back of the hand nearest her. "I just worry about you. You've been through so much. That plane...you were right in the middle of it. The doctors said it was a miracle, and I know those happen, but still–"

While she talked, Tyson slowly slid his head sideways against the pillow. He stared blankly ahead as if dead and parted his lips to emit a long steady, "Beeeeeeeeeeeeeep," as if his heart rate monitor was reading zero.

"Oh, stop it!" Nikki laughed, leaning back.

Tyson chuckled weakly and said, "Then stop avoiding the question! I guess the police couldn't find any sign of Jonathan?"

"No. The news crew put out a story today."

Tyson's eyes roved to where the television set was shut behind its doors, as if thinking about whether to turn it on, but instead he returned his focus to his friend.

"I wonder... Have you seen any sign of Garrett?"

Nikki had to dig her nails into her arms to keep from visibly shuddering. She would never forget that day in the park when those... whatever they were...had jumped her and Jon. She hadn't mentioned Rankers to any of the others yet. Too much had happened since that conversation with Jon. "No."

Tyson growled menacingly. "I wouldn't put it past him to have done anything."

Nikki shook her head. "No, me neither. But the police couldn't find any sign of him or his family when I told them he was a suspect. It's like he moved away or something. They're looking for him too. And you know what?" Her voice dropped lower, and she leaned forward. "One police officer who was searching in the woods outside Jon's house yesterday looked up and came face-to-face with a pure-white horse."

"A horse?" Tyson raised a brow.

"Uh-huh, and he told Mr. He'klarr that, after he saw it, he got a weird feeling that...everything was going to be okay."

A wry smile twisted Tyson's mouth. "How did Mr. He'klarr take that?"

Nikki widened her eyes. "He yelled at him to get back out and look for his son, not imaginary animals. But when he went out to look for himself, the same thing happened. He looked at the horse and felt almost hypnotized. He just turned around and headed back. *Everyone* who comes close to it turns right around. The whole thing was on the news today." She became quiet and twiddled her thumbs uncomfortably.

A nurse came in with some Jell-O and set it in Tyson's lap. She checked him over, gave him a fond smile, and left.

Ty exchanged an exaggerated, worried look with Nikki when he spooned up some of the bright-red gelatin. Experimentally, he stuck out his tongue and poked the food with its tip. Satisfied, he wolfed the spoonful down.

When he could speak again, he said, "Weird. Have they called animal control?"

Nikki replied, "Yeah, but when they got out there, it was gone. No one's seen it since. Mr. He'klarr thinks it found its way back home."

Tyson sank back into his pillow a bit. "Ever since he left, everything's been more messed up, huh?"

"Yes, it has," agreed Nikki. She thought again of that night in the park with Garret's friend. "Actually...ever since we saw Garrett on the mountain..."

"You think so?" Tyson asked, surprised. Then he blinked. Frowned. "You know, I guess you're right." He sat up straighter with a grimace of discomfort. "You don't think *he* has anything to do with everything else going on, do you?"

Fear made Nikki feel hollow—insignificant and weak. There had been something about the way those strangers had talked to them that night. And Jonathan had spoken about Rankers the following Sunday. He'd challenged her skepticism. *Are you really willing to rule out a supernatural explanation?*

"I think that there is more going on here than we're aware of," she said, choosing her words carefully. "I think that everything that's been happening...the violence, the disappearances...it's all connected somehow."

Tyson nodded slowly. Thoughtfully.

"There was a kid in the room next to mine," he said. "Perfectly healthy except that he was recovering from a minor concussion from a fall. He was always visiting me. We became good friends. Then one day he was gone. No one knew where to or how. One of the docs would've seen someone come or go, and nobody had checked the kid out of the hospital. It was like that story in the news about that kidnapped girl. Real spooky. I felt awful for his family. They cried like they were dying slow deaths." He sighed through his nose and added, "I don't think people are just disappearing. The news is making it sound like they're just getting up and walking away, because that's the only thing that makes sense. But...I think they're being taken."

Nikki looked up sharply. "Why do you say that?"

Tyson shrugged one shoulder, confusion puzzling his face as if he couldn't completely understand his hunch himself. "Just a feeling. What would kidnappers want with a bunch of random people? What's the MO? It's more like people are being selectively removed. Taken out of the way of something."

"Jonathan too? You think he stood in the way of some nefarious plan?" Her tone may have been sarcastic, but Nikki's eyes were wide and honest, thirsty for truths that no one had, desperate for clarity. However far-fetched some might have found Tyson's suspicions, she felt that they made more sense than what the tabloids were saying. And she realized that she, too, could not explain why. It was as if she and Tyson stood on the brink of a discovery, but it was too slippery for them to grab hold of properly.

"I don't know," Ty said. A dark spark kindled in his brown eyes. He fiddled with his hospital bracelet, spinning it around and around his wrist, and murmured, "But as soon as I get out of here, I'm going to try to find out."

Nikki wished she had Tyson's bravado. What could they do that the authorities couldn't? She shook her head helplessly and leaned against the wall, reading the various get-well cards on Tyson's bedside table. She stopped on one with a neat sketch of an ambulance on the front. She could almost hear its flashing sirens, it was so realistic.

"We've got another one," Tyson murmured.

Nikki looked quizzically at him. His head was tilted to one side, his eyes directed out the window. "Oh," she said. She went to look outside again. She *had* heard sirens. Two ambulances raced by, getting curious stares from the worried people on the sidewalks.

Nikki had heard more and more sirens lately. Sighing, she rejoined her friend's side, sick with worry for Jonathan.

She really missed him.

CHAPTER FOURTEEN:
The Worst Vacation Destination Ever

I sort of crash-landed in the mud. Peter was too busy to assist me; he had to meet up with the squadron. He led them over to me, we bunched warily together, and we moved on.

The bubbly bog water was hot, almost unbearably so. I hated to think about the bacteria swimming around in it. The soldiers were steel-faced, but their feet had to be getting soaked through their shoes, and the gladiators had only thin sandals on their otherwise bare feet. I swallowed my own discomfort and muscled my way up the rise.

The trees swallowed us up with bony branches, their white-washed bark dyeing the surrounding atmosphere greenish-blue. No animal made any sound from the shadows. No wind brushed away the clogging humidity.

In time, a tall fence came into view. When we were closer, I was able to see that it was made of a row of logs stuck close together with no gaps and the tops sharpened into points. The wall was too high for someone to climb over, not that they could get a hold in the damp, moldy wood anyway.

"There." Peter pointed at a thin break in the fence some distance to our right. We made for it slowly, looking around us at the too-quiet landscape. Peter looked back and transformed into a man.

Kayle nodded and followed suit, looking made for the environment in his dark clothes, and then Mariah, after shaking the mud from each foot like a cat. I tried hard to transform but couldn't quite get it. One samurai gave me a sympathetic shrug, a hand ready at the hilt of his katana.

"Just follow along," Peter ordered.

We slunk to the tall break in the fence. Through it, we saw a moss-covered gravel road. On either side of it were buildings shrouded in mist, and shadows that were people shuffling dismally through the fog. Peter took a confident step forward.

From around one side of the fence strolled a tall man clad in black armor with a billowing violet cape. His helmet had a pointed chin and three horns. One spike-knuckled gauntlet rested on the ruby-encrusted pommel of a long sword.

My first thought was that this was a Dark Knight, one of the first creatures posted in Peter's book, loyal to the highest bidder and willing to sell their own grandmas up the river if there was a profit in it, so my second thought was:

This guy's going to ask for money.

Everyone gasped at the same time, and hands flew to weapons. The only thing holding them back was a look from Peter.

The knight looked every one of us up and down, like a farmer studying a choice stallion. Turning his head, he asked Peter in a gravelly voice muffled by his helmet, "Where do you and your patchwork collection of comrades think *you're* going?"

The warriors of the squadron were so stone-faced a poker player would've been green with envy, but Mariah was fretfully fingering her necklace, and Kayle had an incredulous sneer. His knuckles were white as if he were fighting the urge to pull out his lighter.

Peter kept his tone steady as he explained, "We seek lodging and food for a brief reprieve. We are on our way to sell this beast. We found him in the valley."

What? I glared at the hand Peter was pointing at me.

The knight's helmet tilted down at me. "That's not a beast," he said, in a guarded voice, "That's a griffin."

"Well, then he must be a dream-created one, because he hasn't transformed or spoken in the days he's been with us."

The knight made a sudden move forward; there was the scraping sound of metal being unsheathed. Before I understood what had happened, the knight's sword point was at my throat, holding up my new coral necklace so he could see it better.

As one, the militia reached for their own weapons, but once more, Peter stilled them.

The knight pretended not to notice the threat and asked shrewdly, "And where might this 'beast' have found such a fine accessory?"

Peter had an answer. "Maybe it's a collar. We suspect he is tamed. He doesn't seem to understand the situation."

The knight and I both noticed that as Peter implied my stupidity, my eyes flashed red. He was staring into my face when I saw a dull crimson glow form two rings on the sleek blade of the sword at my neck.

"Well, he understands *us*," the knight mused. He pressed the blade harder into my jugular and leaned forward to add, just for me to hear, "Don't you?"

Panic for my life made my heart beat faster, the blood raced through my veins. Some feral instinct to defend myself took over, and I opened my beak to shout at the guy to back off, but my mind blanked. What came out was a vicious hawk shriek. My head flicked bird-like to the side, and I snapped at his hand. He stepped back, almost fell, and leaned against the fence for support. The squadron laughed.

The Dark Knight composed himself and jabbed out an open hand, palm up. "Currency," he demanded shortly.

Peter extracted some gold coins from a pocket, still flaunting a small smirk. The knight grabbed them, and stomped inside the fence, vanishing around the corner. After a few moments of preparing ourselves for entering the bog, we fixed our eyes straight ahead and moved one muddy foot in front of the other.

The entrance was so narrow that we had to file in, in pairs. It was a clever setup. If we were an enemy, we could have been cut down easily from inside. The gravel, packed into the muddy soil beneath us, crunched loudly. It was an almost homey sound–like walking up my driveway. The soupy fog wrapped itself around us, patching up denser in some places more than others, so that, at times, we had glimpses of something in perfect clarity: a pile of rocks, puddles of water, or little street urchins pausing briefly to stare at us.

We eventually came upon buildings lined up one after the other on either side of us. Dull yellow, grimy lights were suspended from above doorways, shedding minor radiuses of brightness upon us as we passed and throwing shadows into the already dark alleys.

I tried to play the part of the stupid animal while at the same time inquisitively taking in my new surroundings. There were shops: a blacksmith's forge, its entryway lit with a red heathen glow. I saw an apothecary, its walls covered in some thick sort of ivy, and a butcher's displaying hunks of bloody meat in its windows.

The few people wandering the street were cowed and draped in ragged cloth. Old women hobbled witchlike on knobby canes. Bearded men stared fiercely, their stiff demeanors cold and unfriendly. Some people looked innocent enough, fearfully meeting our eyes only to totter off with lost and terrified expressions. I wondered if these were the people in the world having nightmares, and the other grumpier, mean-ish looking citizens were the results of the darkness in peoples' minds. Like Rankers, but not as bad.

We were halted by Peter. His thumbs were hooked in his suspender straps, and he was looking at a large building on our left with something close to satisfaction. "Here seems decent enough," he said.

I wondered who he was kidding, as this place appeared to be just as ramshackle as everything else. It was around three stories tall and just as wide and deep. A sign hanging from a post suspended out next to the doorway displayed a chipped painting of a thick worm twining itself in the words: "The Grub's Haven."

Promising, I thought sarcastically.

We entered cautiously into fuzzy yellow light. Two thin wrought-iron stands were positioned on either side of the door. Candles were set in branches at the top. The floor was coated in grime and cluttered with toppled chairs and rickety tables that gave the appearance of a recent bar fight. The stained-glass windows randomly interspersed in the walls would have been pretty if: they were actually clean, there was any *light* outside to shine through them, and if they didn't depict dark, haunted forests and creepy little demons and ghosts. Candles, wax clotting the wicks and dimming their feeble flames, were stuck in brackets in the walls, leaving the corners in shadow.

A trio of Dark Knights leaned casually in their chairs off to one side, hands curled around tankards of foaming beer. I *think* it was beer. I actually hoped it was, for their sake. I didn't want to know what the soda tasted like in this filthy, slimy, swampy place. Probably flatter than a sheet of paper. The knights stared at us coldly, their conversation cut off. A black cat sitting at their boots arched its back and hissed at me.

We approached the bar at the back of the room next to a flight of stairs leading up into the ceiling. The marines and sailors had removed their hats upon entering out of habit, eyeing the ceiling as if expecting hungry spiders to plop down into their crew cuts.

A man covered in coarse hair stood behind the bar, drinking deeply from a mug and watching us come closer with eyes curtained behind knotty brown-black bangs. He finally pulled his mouth away from his drink, set it down with a large hand, and smiled greedily.

I quickly looked down at my talons so no one would see my eyes flash white with fear. His teeth were sharply pointed, like fangs. He tossed his hair out of his stubbled face to clear his eyes. The irises were a deep green ringed with black and let off what seemed to be a faint glow.

In a feral, growling voice, he asked, "Can I help ye gentlemen?" Catching sight of Mariah, he added, "And lady?" His grin spread.

Mariah scowled. Kayle and some of the other more chivalrous soldiers glanced at Mariah and then glared at the bartender with barely concealed revulsion.

"We're just passing through here, sir. Do you have adequate rooms for all of us?" Peter asked courteously, though his eyes were stormy.

The bartender nodded slowly, taking all of us in with his tongue poking from a corner of his mouth. "Sure. Upstairs to the highest level, the four rooms across from each other." He rummaged under the bar for a roll of keys and handed them to Peter. The jingling of the metal reminded me of the key I held from the package. I wondered, not for the first time, what *it* opened.

"The beast can stay in the stables," the bartender added when we all began to inch toward the stairs.

Peter came to my rescue by warning, "I think you'd rather have him stay up with us. Griffins tend to get lonely and nasty in dark places."

The bartender sneered maliciously. "I'll send out one of my men to...keep him company. He touches so much as a keg of my ale, I'll have him whipped into submission."

"I don't think your 'man' would appreciate assisting you in the keeping of this inn with one arm," Peter replied.

"Fine!" the shaggy man snapped. "But if I find even one feather, you're out."

"Fair enough," Peter said with a slight bow.

We trundled up the stairs, then down a hall lined with thick doors, behind which we heard no signs of life. At the end of the hall, we turned right, up some more stairs, and faced down another hall. Mariah whimpered. Compared to this level of the inn, the second story was as homey as the Four Seasons.

Up here, the long red carpet extending from beneath our feet to the far wall was tattered and filthy. A fat, mangy rat chewed on an edge of it, but skittered off noisily when it saw us. Dark, creaky rafters dripping with moisture showed through a hole in the ceiling. We avoided the doors closest to us and made our way to the last four, careful not to fall through the floor in any places we suspected might collapse right beneath our feet.

Peter whispered to the marine who had led the squadron in his place when we'd been flying earlier, "Me and the kids will stay in one room. Divide the men into the other three. Be careful tonight, son; eat that bread we packed. Be ready to wake up early."

The marine nodded, saluted, and turned around to face the rest of the militia. Mariah, Kayle, and I joined Peter before the door to our room. Peter took out our key, inserted it in the lock, and turned it. With a heavy *clunk* the lock slid aside, and Peter pushed the door open.

It was almost pitch-black inside. The only light came from the lit candles out in the hall and Kayle's lighter.

"If you would, Kayle," Peter invited jovially.

Kayle shouldered his way through, the tiny flame he held in his hand dyeing his face orange, giving his eyes an inhuman glow, spreading shadows on his cheeks and hat. Cupping one hand around his lighter, he closed his eyes tightly in concentration. He parted his lips and blew out softly, caressingly. The flame flickered madly.

What happened next took place so fast I almost didn't see it. Kayle extended his cupped hand; I saw a ball of fire writhing in his palm. Then he closed it and clicked shut his lighter, at the same time curving his hand in an arc from his chest straight out, as if throwing a Frisbee. The fireball flew into the room and soundlessly exploded into tinier sparks, each zipping to a candle and curtaining the room in new light.

I found myself smiling. That had been the coolest thing I'd ever seen.

"That never fails to amaze me," Mariah said as Peter shut the door. Kayle shrugged but looked pleased and sort of out of breath, like he'd just parachuted out of an airplane.

I grimaced at our new, measly surroundings. At the left wall stood two beds covered in patched and wrinkled quilts. The colors had bled out of them, leaving them bleached white. The pillows were stained in places a dull brown color and ripped through. The faces of snarling beasts, writhing serpents, and other such cuddly things were carved intricately into the headboards. Three cockroaches clung to the bedposts, just sitting there...waiting...

One stained-glass window was set in the wall in front of us. The multi-colored panes glowed eerily in the new candlelight, showing the form of a beautiful girl on her knees, her head in her hands and her gown's sleeves and hem torn. Towering behind her, black wings outstretched, stood the Angel of Death, his hood covering his face, one skeletal hand reaching down to touch the crying woman.

The only decorations in the whole room were a vase of dead flowers on a simple table and a cracked mirror beside the door. I jumped when I saw myself in it; I still wasn't used to seeing that I had a beak and feathers. I hugged my wings snug to my sides for warmth and tucked my tail closer to my legs, the feathery tuft at the end brushing the floor and the inch-thick coat of dust layering it.

"What do you think?" Peter asked at length.

I sat down where I stood. "I don't think 'one feather' would make much of a difference," I replied.

Peter tentatively sat down on a mattress and said apologetically, "Sorry I treated you like a dumb beast."

I was about to accept his apology, but Kayle ruffled my crown feathers on his way past and remarked, "He's okay, aren't you, birdy?" He threw himself with vigor upon the other bed, folding his arms behind his head and pushing his beanie down over his eyes with a wily smirk.

"You ever wondered if your ego would get you a black eye someday, Kayle?" I asked, peeved.

Kayle ballooned his cheeks and breathed out, "Bollocks."

"Yeah, me too," I muttered. I had absolutely no idea what the heck that meant. I doubt it was anything nice.

My vision blurred, and I blinked furiously, assuming my eyes were dry. Everything whipped back to clarity, but things farther away were less detailed. I looked down and saw hands instead of talons pressed onto the cold floor. I jumped to my feet happily. "Yes!"

Mariah gave Peter a worried look, and Kayle straightened his hat, biting his lower lip. "I know that at this point the shifting comes automatically, but try not to let it happen too much in public, Jon," Peter said. "Now we have another body, and a missing griffin, to explain for."

"We could say he was one of the soldiers?" Mariah offered.

Peter blinked sleepily and began tugging off his boots. "That'll work for a while. Hopefully until we find what that key of ours unlocks. Still have everything, Jonathan?"

I reached into my pocket and extracted the folded recipe and mossy key. "Sure thing," I said. *Gosh, I love fingers and lips.* "Do you think this opens a door somewhere?" I held out the key.

Peter took it and held it close to his eyes, running his big, calloused fingers over the teeth. "No." He sighed, handing it back to me. "It's too small and brittle for these heavy locks. No, this key was custom-made for someone."

"Maybe we need to give it back to them," I mused, looking at my familiar face in the mirror. The crack warped it in half, but I was just glad to see it again.

"Maybe..." Kayle said thoughtfully.

"The main thing to remember," Peter said, raising his eyebrows seriously so that the firelight shone eerily off of his pale eyes, "is that as we try and figure out these clues, we have to also keep an eye out for any Rankers waiting to meet potential recruits here in the bog. Right now we have the advantage of anonymity, but if a Ranker catches wind of a griffin being sighted in the area, things can go south fast."

"And if they find out that that griffin is the prince of dreams..." Mariah trailed off grimly.

After that, we all dressed down to sleep (putting on clothes that Peter had packed) and let Mariah change in the bathroom. I accepted a white T-shirt and black sweatpants and headed into the bathroom after Mariah to take a bath. We'd all agreed that she and Peter would get the beds... And the cockroaches. Of course, I didn't care to think about what sort of creepy-crawlers made their homes in the floor.

Our small bathroom contained a hole in the floor for...you know what. A faucet suspended over a drain in the floor was the sink, and the bath was another crooked faucet over a basin with porcelain feet in the shape of animal paws. The water was cold but clean, and I stepped out feeling refreshed. Kayle and Mariah were sitting on the second bed facing Peter. I heard them pleading with him to tell them about something or other as I dried off and got dressed.

When I opened the bathroom door and reentered the main room, Peter was saying, "...can't think of any story I've not told you already!" He was lying on the other bed, smiling up at the ceiling while Kayle's and Mariah's voices overlapped.

"Tell us of the one about the fire-bird!"

"Or when you met the dryads in the spirit pond!"

"Or how 'bout the secrets rumored to roam the capital's sewers?"

Peter noticed me and asked, "What do you think, Jonathan? Any suggestions?"

I started packing my clothes from the day into one of the bags and offered, "How about...what it was like when you first got here?" Slowly, Kayle and Mariah looked at Peter with half smiles. Peter met my gaze uncertainly, his eyes switching from one detail of my face to the next, my eyebrows, my mouth, my eyes, trying to perceive my expression. I, however, was purposefully keeping my face stoic, blank of anything to give away my intentions.

The truth was, I wanted more answers. I hadn't even been told yet exactly *why* I was considered a prince, despite all of the times I'd asked on the way here. I got knocked out by a frying pan, and the next thing I knew, I'd washed up on the shores of a place fraught with danger. Then Peter appeared, took me in, taught me how to fly, and I was expected to obliterate the massing Rankers? That was like giving a three-year-old kid a calculator and telling them to sit down and do trigonometry. Peter had asked for a story suggestion, and I gave him one. It was *his* turn to give back.

CHAPTER FIFTEEN:
PETER'S SECRETS

I blinked at Peter expectantly, pasting a polite smile on my face to hide my desperation for answers, my thirst for the truth. Mariah and Kayle continued to stare at us uncertainly but I managed to ignore them. Peter gave me a sad sort of smile in return, then fixed his stare back on the ceiling and began to speak. I sat in the space between both beds, made myself comfortable, and listened.

"It was one day, some time ago, maybe about four or five months...a year and a half...three years...that I arrived here in the Land of Dreams. I had been sleeping one night, and I had a vision–I thought then that it had been a dream–of what looked like a grand pure-white eagle but with the hind body of a lion, watching me from atop a rock sticking out of the ground. His eyes were a penetrating shade of yellow, and when he spread his wings, I saw all my hopes and longings flash in them like they were television screens or something. But when I blinked, they were feathered and white. The next time I blinked, it was all gone. Everything was black, and just as had happened during recent nights, I was tormented with nightmares of men shrouded in black cloaks and hoods."

"Rankers," I said.

Peter nodded. "More and more, I had the vision about the lion-bird until it even pushed away my nightmares. One day, I had a dream that I was in a thick forest full of pines and firs, and this time I couldn't wake up. I discovered the hard way that I had changed into the same creature as the white lion-bird, and it confused and startled me. I wandered in the shadows and silence for what felt like an eternity, lost and scared."

Just like me, I thought.

"And just when I had given up hope of returning home, something bright caught the sun streaming through the trees. I spun around real quick and was shocked to find myself no longer alone.

"It was another creature just like me. He was thin—wiry, you could say—and built like a cheetah. He had a tuft of feathers that swept back on his head and sharp, falcon-like wings. He was the color of flame, a bright scarlet, and had a relieved look on his face. Sitting all calm-like on his back was a little weasel-type fellow." Peter glanced my way, and I saw his cheek twitch as if to smirk. "A charlatan."

"Did he beat you with a frying pan?" I had to ask.

"No."

"Coffee mug?"

"Uh, no. He seemed pleased to meet me."

"Hmmm." I settled down again as Peter resumed his tale.

"These new arrivals took me in and explained everything they could: who they were, how I had gotten there, where I was, and why I was there. The charlatan, whose name was too complicated to remember except for the first five letters, R-E-X-U-S, Rexus, told me that I was expected by Michael, the 'White Griffin,' a sort of guardian of the land. I was to be briefed on my mission to find someone: a young man who would save our lives, though at the time, we didn't know that that meant finding the new king."

I looked down at my legs uncomfortably.

"At first, I didn't want to go. I wanted to return to my own world, but there was no way I could until my job was done."

Again, I felt a strange and unexpected stirring of empathy for Peter. I couldn't imagine what it had been like for him to appear in the dreamworld all alone, just wandering around until someone found him. The stench of the bog leaking through the window, the unsettling sound of the floorboards—or something *beneath* the floorboards—clicking and creaking, faded away as I became more immersed in the story.

"The scarlet griffin worked closely with the White Griffin. Josiah was his name—your school counselor, Jon."

I shook my head with a small smile, mystified that my counselor, who played games on his phone during our meetings, could've kept such a secret from me. How many other people had I met in my life that were cognizant of the power of the dreamworld?

"He explained that, soon, I would be able to transform into my human form as well as the one I was already in, and showed me himself how easy the transition would become. I asked why the charlatan could not shift, and Josiah said it was because he was not of our world. He had been created from the mind of some sleeping dreamer and was a native of the land.

"So we traveled, through thick and thin, danger and calm. And as we went, Rexus and Josiah filled me in on the war with the Rankers, who and what they were, and the effect they were having on our world. Josiah told me to write three books as we journeyed. He told me that the books would help the mysterious hero be prepared for what lay ahead." Peter looked significantly at me, and I thought of the thick books that had appeared mysteriously in my room. Peter had made those just for me? I felt a gentle stirring of gratitude and offered him a wan smile that he readily returned as he continued speaking.

"For a time, our job was to constantly check on allied towns, supplying them with what provisions they needed to support themselves and rebuild after Ranker skirmishes, evaluating what fortresses we had across the land. It was at one of these fortresses that I met King Brody for the first time..." Peter's mouth stretched into a solemn line. His face betrayed such anguish that I found myself mimicking the expression in sympathy.

"He was older than you, Jonathan, by about five years. Strapping kid, healthy, real quiet. But, boy howdy, he had a way with words! Josiah and I joined his company for a few months while he went about inspiring loyalists with speeches both grand and honest. He was easy to talk to. We got along really well.

"One day during a routine patrol flight, Josiah and I were joined by two others. Kayle and Mariah, back from reconnaissance, who said they had arrived in the land shortly after me. We got to talkin', them and I, and Kayle told me more about Brody.

"Brody had been a brave, hard-working youth that was a few weeks into college in our world. He was hit by a speeding truck when he was on his way home from work. Nearly half the bones in his body were broken on impact, and he had to be life-flighted out of there to the nearest hospital. For days, he was in a deep, impenetrable slumber, hooked up to machines that were basically living for him. Then, he dreamed, and the White Griffin found him.

"Just as Josiah helped me, the White Griffin helped him get used to his new gifts and told him that he was to be the next king. For years, Brody led battles against the Rankers, concocted plans of defense, and, despite the fact that his physical body was comatose, he even stopped attacks in reality by warning important world leaders of Ranker-caused potential disasters through dreams."

"We can do that?" I interrupted, absently shooing a mouse-sized beetle away from my knee with a few lazy sweeps of one hand.

"*He* could," Peter replied gravely, and I settled in to listen further, in awe of my predecessor.

"Everyone thought that he was the one who would fulfill an ancient prophecy carved thousands of years ago into the foundation stones of the capital itself—we all thought he was the fabled Destroyer of Shadows, destined to cleanse the dreamworld of mounting evil. But one day, when I was out writing in my journals, I received word that the king was dying. I went to him as fast as I could, and got to his side just in time to exchange a few words and say goodbye. His ravaged body lost its fight with death." Peter bowed his head, his eyes anguished and tired. "And our hopes, our *desperation* that the prophecy was anything more than just ancient, silly scribblings, died with him."

What a loss. The king had lost his life; Peter, Kayle, and Mariah had lost a friend; and the kingdom had lost what sounded like a great guy and a much more capable ruler than the one they were about to be punked with.

"How did he die in reality?" I asked.

"It's a difficult concept to explain, but I will try to tell you as I told Peter," Kayle said, leaning forward to see me better. "If someone on earth is deathly injured, as the king was, as they lay unconscious, recovering, they dream and, of course, arrive here while their bodies try to heal. But sometimes the wounds are too extensive to heal and take a bad toll on the body, sapping its strength. So while his brain began shutting down, the Rankers closed in, killing his imagination, breaking into his dreams. In a last valiant fight, the Rankers slaughtered the king and his guards at the same time that his mortal body died. What affects you in reality affects you here. Does that make sense?"

My mouth was hanging open. I shut it abruptly and then said falteringly, "I think so..."

"Think of it this way," offered Mariah, gesturing as she spoke. "If you were having a nightmare in reality and, as you tossed and turned in your sleep, you bonked your head against the wall, then your brain would have kick-started, thinking it was being physically attacked, and in your dream the Ranker tormenting you would have struck out at you–possibly at your head–at the same time you bumped it in reality."

I jumped to my feet. "Well, *my* body is currently lying abandoned in a house! How do I know that wild animals aren't eating me *as we speak?*"

Peter brushed one of the huge, creepy cockroaches onto the floor where it scuttled into the shadows beneath his bed and said slyly, "You're being guarded, don't worry."

I settled down a margin, secretly hoping that my guardian wasn't that pan-handling charlatan. If it came down to wild animals catching a whiff of me lying unconscious like a free buffet all for them, I wouldn't trust him not to take the first bite.

"After many days and nights," Peter continued, "we all arrived in the capital city with Brody's body, and I beheld wondrous sights that no human has ever seen before. There is beauty everywhere there; trees and all other manner of flora cover the buildings. A magnificent palace, your palace, rises up into the sky, almost past the mountains surrounding it. When we arrived, all the people and animals crowding the streets and steps, enjoying the warm sun and fresh air of the day, stopped to stare as we passed. They saw the king's body and started weeping and howling with grief. I didn't know what to do.

"I had discovered by now how to transform at will and was in my human form as you see it now. I was trying not to weep, myself, scouring the faces and bodies for the White Griffin I was supposed to meet here.

"We came to the palace and passed under an archway into a courtyard. People in black clothes of mourning stood in the shadows there, their faces sticking out from between the columns, silent and sad. We followed the path that leads up to the castle doors. Two rows of men in blue suits stood by the steps, facing each other at attention across the path, waiting. The king's body was taken inside.

"Sitting above everything on top of the corridor's roof was the White Griffin, the ancient, ethereal advisor of past griffin rulers. He slowly turned his massive head in my direction and then his eyes. Josiah and I shifted and flew up to join him, bowing respectfully.

"He told me that he was pleased to meet me, and introduced himself. I had just enough time to share my name before the palace doors below creaked outward. The whole city was quiet. The row of soldiers facing one another unsheathed their swords and crossed them forward, forming a tunnel of blades. A procession of black-clad men stepped out, balancing a coffin on their shoulders."

I took in a sharp breath.

"It was a beautiful work of craftsmanship, perfect for a king like Brody had been. When the bearers passed into the city, we followed. Rexus climbed onto Josiah's back, and we three griffins took to the air to guard and honor the procession. It was a touching ceremony..." Peter quieted.

"What'd you do after the funeral?" I asked.

"I started a collage of the rulers that had governed this land in previous years and added it in one of the books," he said solemnly, then smiled and concluded. "After that, I spruced them up, sent them to Josiah, and we left to get you. Here we are."

We sat in silence. Once more, miraculous thoughts filled my head, dizzying me. It didn't seem like Peter knew much about the White Griffin. It was a bit confusing, the whole dream-reality thing, and I wondered how my body was doing and what it would be like when I woke up to it again. The nights got cold in Colorado, especially in winter. I didn't want to come to and find that I had frostbite.

"And don't worry about time here," Kayle said. "If there's something important going on in the dreamworld, time will slow down.

But if something important is happening in reality, time will speed up. It's one of the land's paradoxes."

"Huh?" I asked.

Mariah came to my rescue again and said, "If you're stuck in a battle, for example, time in the dreamworld will become condensed so you can finish the battle before you wake up. It might feel like you've been in the Land of Dreams for a week, but in reality, it's only been eight hours."

"And under normal circumstances, when you aren't comatose, if something pressing is calling you to reality, it may feel like you've been in the dreamworld for only a few hours, but you've actually been asleep for eight. A paradox." Kayle yawned massively. I saw that he was missing a couple teeth toward the back of his mouth. Not enough to be ugly, but he must've been in one heck of a fight. I watched as he moseyed over to a candle and started teasing the flame with his careful fingers. Of course, I'd hate to see the other guy.

Thinking about Kayle getting in fights made me wonder about his and Mariah's past lives again. Last time I had brought up that subject, Mariah had given me the cold shoulder. And I was too exhausted to ask anything more at the moment. Traveling and flying had really taken it out of me. And I knew that the others weren't feeling their best.

As if reading my mind, Peter sat up and said, "Let's hit the sack, kids. Our stay here might be long and certainly unpleasant. But first, let us eat."

Oh, yeah! Food! Just thinking about it made my stomach begin to growl in preparation. Mariah couldn't grow food any ol' time we were attacked with the munchies because it used up energy she wanted to conserve, so any meal was much appreciated.

Reaching into his pack, Peter extracted a small loaf of bread. It didn't look like the kind you'd find in a store, cut up into even slices and stuffed into a plastic bag. It more resembled something you'd find in a medieval bakery. It was deep brown, thick, and shaped like an oval.

Pulling a mini cutting tray out of the pack, and a knife from a pocket, Peter set down the bread and began slicing four thin pieces off the end. The sound of the crust crackling and the knife blade sawing back and forth in a poetic rhythm into the bread's soft center made my salivary glands perk up and start working overtime. I was afraid to look away, afraid the wondrous food would disappear.

Eventually, when Peter had wrapped the rest of the loaf in a green cloth and put it, the knife, and the tray back, he turned to face us with the slices in his hands and a grave expression.

"This bread will put us in a deep sleep, which will ward off nightmares—very important." He looked up at me as he passed Kayle a piece of the bread. "When you're stuck here like us, in comas, you're blessed and cursed with dreams within dreams. These dreams can go deep into memory—reveal parts of your subconscious that are strange and surreal. Or they can transform into beautiful landscapes reaching up from the ancient foundations of the dreamworld." He gave Mariah her piece, still gazing intently at me. "The nightmares, however, can destroy you, especially in a place like this, where evil breeds. I dearly hope you won't have to find out how. Eat it all, and sleep well."

I accepted my food gratefully and scarfed it down, trying to cling on to a measure of manners, but instead leaving tiny crumbs all over my sweatpants and almost gnawing off my own fingers.

Peter was already asleep. Mariah sleepily wished Kayle and I good night and gave her bed a once-over for critters before crawling beneath the covers. Kayle went around the room blowing out the candles. He flicked on his lighter long enough to situate himself in a cozy area on the floor, using his folded-up sweatshirt as a pillow. Then he turned it off and bathed the room fully in darkness.

I frowned grumpily and felt my way to an area that seemed less dusty than the rest, joining the others in a silent slumber.

One second I was sound asleep, the next wide awake...and eye to eye with a cockroach.

I cried out and clambered away, stubbing my fingers against the wall and falling over myself numerous times until I got to my feet. The large bug had been startled and scurried off into a hole in the corner wall.

Faint light filtered in through the stained-glass window, turning the room a dark bluish gray. I calmed myself down enough to realize that I didn't feel any bites from the roach's gnarly mandibles. It must've been looking for somewhere warm to camp out, attracted to my body heat. I shuddered involuntarily and focused on the more important matter. What had awakened me? Surely not the insect.

I tilted my head to one side, waiting for a sound. One came in the form of a slow clawing from the direction of the door.

I jumped, heart racing and sweat springing from my forehead. The quiet clawing came again, this time punctuated with a plaintive keen. I was frozen in place, my eyes struggling to take in as much light as possible to glean clues as to who was outside the room. Or what.

I dried my face on my T-shirt sleeve and took a step forward. The clawing came again, more frantic. The whining picked up a more urgent tone. Was it a dog? Maybe someone had been hurt and it was searching for someone to go rescue them!

Using the light from the window, I stumbled forward. My hands hit the rough wood of the door. I placed my palm flat on its surface and slid it down, feeling for the knob. My fingers brushed cold metal. I wrapped my hand around it, and—

"*No!*" Peter was suddenly there. He threw his weight at the door, preventing me from opening it. I cringed back, frowning uncertainly at him. The thing on the other side of the door growled angrily and clawed more fiercely.

Peter rushed over to his pack and began to rummage through it, mouth moving desperately, forming soundless words. Maybe a prayer? I wondered if something like that would work in this desolate place.

"What is it?" I asked in a strangled whisper.

Peter found what he was looking for: a shiny silver ball about the size of a marble. He clenched it tightly in his fist and rejoined me at the door, saying in a hushed voice, "A poor, cursed creature."

Outside, the clouds must have shifted, for a beam of moonlight filtered into our room, casting everything into better detail. I was hit by a revelation.

"It's a werewolf," I said, feeling a mixture of terror and pity.

"Yes," Peter confirmed. "And I strongly believe that it is the bartender."

I thought back to the man's appearance. His sharp teeth, his luminous eyes. "What does he want?" I asked faintly.

Peter was rolling the silver ball around in his hands and said, "You can never tell. Maybe food...or something to sate the evil spirits and poison filling his veins." The werewolf at that moment hurled himself at the door, snarling wildly, but the thick wood held even as the hinges creaked in protest. Kayle snorted where he lay and rolled over. "Or maybe," Peter continued, undaunted, "he's looking for love."

"That's sad," I murmured, looking down at the floor. I thought of Nikki, and my heart went out to the lost and lonely werewolf.

"Yes, it is," Peter agreed.

He kneeled and rolled the silver ball beneath the door; it made a low ringing sound as it moved. The wolf yelped, and we heard its heavy paw steps retreating down the hall. Whistling, Peter held his hand open on the ground. The ball rolled back inside and into his palm. He put it back in the pack, watching me.

"Werewolves have an aversion to silver," he said.

I nodded. "I remember reading that."

"He won't recollect anything in the morning," Peter said, and held his arm out. "Go to sleep, sonny..."

When I woke up the next morning, it was to white light glowing through the window, and with a sore back from the hard floor. Mariah's blonde-brown hair was immensely tangled, and as soon as she sat up, she began combing her fingers through it, giving me a bleary smile. Peter winced and popped his back, going over to the pack and rummaging through it. Kayle was staring up at the ceiling, lost in his own thoughts.

Peter murmured, "I suggest we bring up that recipe to someone today. The one that came with the key. May as well see where it leads."

I pulled the slip of paper out of my sweatpants pocket where I had transferred it and the key from my sweatshirt, and held it up to show I still had it. "Sounds good to me. The sooner we leave this place, the better." Perhaps I could get some time to myself today, explore the swamp, get some of the answers I sought. If any place had valuable information about Rankers, it had to be this dive.

"Agreed," Mariah chirped cheerfully, and went over to the window. A thin hook held it closed through a loop in the wall beside it. With a flick of the finger, she had unlatched it and pushed it open to a cloudy, pale fog that was settled low over the bog's now busy cobbled streets.

"I want to fly again," Mariah added softly, breathing in the semi-fresh air. I had to agree with her. Flying was something you didn't forget easily.

Peter had pulled out a pouch of clinking coins and attached it to the belt of his suspenders. He tossed Mariah a black blouse and loose leggings, and then Kayle a gray sweatshirt and faded dark-blue pants. He gave me some pants and a long-sleeved striped tunic.

Mariah got dressed first, emerging from the bathroom looking modestly radiant. She gave her old clothes to Peter, who vowed to get our garments to a washer and have them cleaned.

Two sharp raps resounded on the door, followed by three more, making us all jump.

"Here he is," Peter smiled. He opened the door to admit the second-in-command marine.

He looked completely different now than how he had looked yesterday in his MARPAT. He wore warm apparel, as we did: patchy trousers and a sweater. They made his vibrant light-brown eyes stand out. I heard him say, "We're ready, sir," before I shut myself in the bathroom to get dressed.

The clothes fit perfectly, to my gratification, and I re-entered the main room feeling fresh and ready.

Peter was asking the marine, "Are the rest of the men dressed casually?"

The marine grimaced and said, "Yes, sir, but the gladiators, Amazons, and knights feel vulnerable without their armor, and the samurai are completely offended at not having clothes befitting their culture. Is this really necessary?"

Peter put a hand on the younger guy's shoulder and said, "Afraid so, Sergeant. We can't walk around looking like a threat. We have to appear comfortable. Just like a band of traders on our way to a sell."

I snorted, and all heads turned my way.

"Oh, good morning, Prince," the marine greeted, bowing his head.

I dropped my folded, dirty clothes on our need-to-be-washed pile and said, "Hey, please just call me–"

But apparently the sergeant wasn't too into first-name terms. He turned to Peter and asked, "Is he ready?" before I could get my name out.

I looked from him to Peter and back again. "Ready? For what?"

Mariah answered, "Remember our plan? We have to make you look like a soldier 'cause no one saw you come in as a human."

And if there are any Rankers around I don't want them to recognize me, I thought, breaking into a cold sweat at the very thought.

Everyone was watching me.

I shrugged. "Okay."

CHAPTER SIXTEEN:
I Almost Get Stoned

Our big group of disguised warriors and griffin people tromped downstairs to the ground floor fifteen minutes later.

I felt and looked like a new person. The sergeant had ripped holes in the knees of my pants and frayed some areas along the hem of my shirt. Then he'd scruffed up my hair. I felt like one of the kids at school who spent evenings hunting or camping and were constantly going through clothes because of their rough-and-tumble lifestyle.

Peter had me tuck my coral necklace beneath the collar of my shirt, as it could arouse suspicions since I'd been wearing it as a griffin when we'd arrived. Also, one of the gladiators was taking a shift staying locked up in our room and making random noise so it would seem like a griffin was locked up inside.

Peter got the four of us a booth built into the wall. The squadron divvied themselves up and sat close by. I slid sideways onto the torn red cushioning of my side of the booth and folded my arms on the scratched wooden tabletop, facing Kayle. Kayle immediately plucked up a napkin from a small pile against the wall, unfolded it, and studied it curiously for stains (probably trying to decide whether or not to set it on fire).

It may sound completely bonkers to say so, but it was kind of cozy. We were situated in our own little boxy alcove. Facing each other over the table set with sheep's-wool napkins and empty tin tankards, we were bathed in warm light from the fat, half-melted candle set on a wide tray attached to the ceiling by chains.

Mariah slipped delicately in next to me, and Peter thumped himself beside Kayle, one leg sticking out from beneath the table.

A waiter with slicked-back hair and shadowy, baggy eyes traipsed over and passed out four menus. The menus were made of sheets of paper covered in scrawling, handwritten lime-green ink that seemed to sparkle and glitter and were fastened with a crude staple of dry twine. The script got harder and harder to read further on, as if the scribe's hand had gotten tired. I read some of the dishes:

Swamp Rat, bathed in a blend of slime root mushroom and lichen spice (traded all the way from the Fortress of Iron Teeth)

Bowl of Leeches, cooked to a fine roast and set in a soup of swamp froth

Fish and Swamp Mussels (recommended only if you have a very, very strong digestive system)

"Are we positive about eating this stuff?" I asked uncertainly.

Mariah, scanning her own menu with something akin to placidity on her face, replied without looking up, "I'm sorry, but I don't have the energy to grow up a huge meal for all of us; this swamp seems to drain my strength. And it would be too suspicious anyway, cleaning up after ourselves—there'd be some people bound to find out we were eating fresh, good food from somewhere. Leeks, tubers, a big juicy watermelon..." She dwindled off, gazing wistfully at the wall. I saw Kayle wipe some drool from his chin. Mariah shook herself and looked at me. "Plus, we don't want to use up any of the trail vittles we *do* have, do we?"

"If it means not having to fight for my life with one of these appetizers!" I exclaimed, jabbing my finger at one of the dishes and reading, "'Non-gutted pike with a side of either sour leeks or bullfrog.' Does that sound good to you?"

Mariah suddenly seemed to have swallowed a ripe batch of grapes whole.

"I don't know," Kayle said. "A little tartar sauce, ketchup..." I gave him a glare. I couldn't tell if he was joking or not.

The greasy waiter returned to take our orders, and the four of us decided on the only dish that sounded remotely normal: steak with a side of swamp escargot (I would not be eating that) and shredded and salted potatoes. When he had moved on, Peter leaned forward and murmured, "The plan is to split up and see if we can find what our little key opens–while we do that, we can question the civilians and see if they've had any news about Rankers or their allies."

"What about the recipe?" Kayle asked, voicing what I had been about to ask myself.

"We'll wait 'til the waiter returns," Peter said, "and then we'll ask him." I studied Peter, wondering if he had actually purposefully chosen this inn because he knew we'd get information. Perhaps the old guy had more of a plan than I'd originally thought. It made me feel a bit safer, more confident in our mission.

Our food was soon brought out to us on round wooden platters; it was difficult to keep from making a mess, eating greasy, slightly bloody steak on a flat disk with no rim. Our silverware consisted of heavy, metal, crudely fashioned forks that jarred painfully against our teeth if we bit down too hard. But none of us were picky. The food was decent, and we immediately dug in with the air of a famished pride of lions.

Before the waiter could slink off to another table, Peter caught his elbow gently. The man whipped about, eyes fierce, looking like he expected a rebuke. But Peter reached out to me for the gross recipe. I gave it to him, and Peter said, "Young man, could you possibly cook this up for us?"

The waiter pinched the parchment in his long fingers and held it close to his eyes. He turned a shade lighter and spoke hesitantly in a high, self-important voice, "I do not think you wish to try this stew, sir. You must understand it is a sort of work in progress. Strange men visit us from distant areas and parts of the land, and they bring with them ideas and theories new to us. We always accept new foods and drink for a cost, of course, but this one is different. This latest invention was brought to us by an eerie fellow. It gives the eater adrenaline and energy, but its side effects include fury and brief insanity. Those who dare to test it become addicted to its seductive taste." He looked around, as if checking for eavesdroppers, and his eyes fell briefly on the bartender where he hunched behind his bar scrubbing at a mug.

Lowering his voice, the waiter added, "The bartender hates it. When he drinks it, he becomes so fierce that he turns into... something else. And then no one can stop him." I believed I knew what that something else was and buried my fears in a mouthful of shredded and buttered potato slices.

I remembered reading about werewolves. How they could be the size of an SUV. How their fangs sometimes grew so long that they curved into scissoring tusks. How they feared silver and holy items, and how it was the poison in their saliva that carried on their... disease.

The waiter left, and Peter handed back the recipe, eyes distant and mouth pursed thoughtfully.

"Why would the Rankers leave an actual recipe as a clue? What kind of a clue is that?" I asked, grinding my teeth against a chunk of gristle.

"Your guess is as good as mine. I'll try and find out more," Peter said ruefully. "But if it turns the bartender into a monster, then what do you think it does to Rankers that drink it?"

We all exchanged serious looks over our plates, and left the question unanswered.

When we had finished eating, we all split up and went outside to find a place, an object, *anything* with a keyhole matching our tiny key–specifically places of business like a locksmith or blacksmith where someone could have commissioned the unique little key or an antique shop that may have sold it.

I went left down the unkempt street, its stones rutted by wagon wheels, its potholes full of dirty rainwater. The shops on either side of the street were dark and worn. Nothing looked very appealing. I passed a bookstore. Vials and jugs of different colored liquids bubbled on a rickety table out front. A patron stood over them trying to follow instructions from a thick, important-looking book. Nervous sweat slicked his forehead, and a scrawny tabby cat sitting tranquilly at his heels said, "You had better rectify this calamity posthaste, my good friend, or you'll be listening to me talk like this all day."

Smiling to myself, I moved on, scouring a market, a locksmith's, several other shops, and even peeking in the windows of a few dark houses, each new building bringing my hopes lower and lower.

None of these places accommodated something that my key could unlock—or if they did, we would either need a warrant to enter or a few weeks' worth of time to search everything. Then I came upon a carpentry shop.

It was the only friendly looking place I'd yet encountered. Mahogany tables with gracefully thin legs; chairs, soft from their recent shaving; and a wardrobe covered with images of flowers and trees all stood under the extended roof waiting to be bought. I was enticed forward by the skill, the craftsmanship that so many had forgotten in reality.

The door was open invitingly, and I stepped in. Furniture, wagon wheels, oxen yokes, a horse trough, a few baby cradles, and more were pegged up on walls or stacked on the floor, categorized by color and style. The objects became more beautiful, more intricately detailed, or painted brighter colors the deeper I delved into the quiet shop. Now I was surrounded by doors and chests. I ran my hand over the lid of one, tenderly feeling the specks of grain at its surface.

At the very end of the carpentry, pushed against the wall and surrounded by its own shavings, was a pale birch chest with a round gold lock keeping it closed. The keyhole was so promisingly tiny that I dropped to my knees almost in a trance, took out the key, and slid it in, jiggling it. But no, there was too much room.

I breathed out dejectedly, realizing I had been holding my breath. A cheery voice behind me made the hair stand on my neck, and I fell over on my backside.

"I ain't seen a chest for that thar key since the one I made for the bartender over at ol' Grub's Haven Inn." It was the carpenter himself.

He took in my heaped form on the floor, staring up at him wide-eyed, and chuckled. "Pretty easily spooked for a"—he looked at my scruffy countenance—"blacksmith's apprentice?"

I stood and brushed myself off. "Prin–Griff–*Warrior*," I corrected myself just in time and met the man's twinkling blue eyes with my own.

He was a tall, stocky guy with gray whiskers on his chin and a white shirt with the sleeves rolled up to his elbows. He stuck his hands in his pants pockets and briefly bowed his balding head. "Forgive me, then, young sir."

We stood staring at the unfinished chest, and then I asked, "What did you mean? About the chest?"

"Ah, may I see yer key?" The carpenter held out one hand. I reluctantly gave it to him, and he leaned closer to me, pointing at the key's teeth. They formed a heart shape.

"Hard ter make a key this way. The metal is difficult ter bend into a specific shape. I'd remember it anywhere." The carpenter returned it to me, and his face was sad. "The bartender's wife was killed by a werewolf. Then the beast turned on him... I made that chest as a wedding present to them. He keeps all of her belongings in it."

Bingo.

"He came in not too long ago, real upset, and told me ter make a copy of the key belonging to 'is chest, for some reason. I'm assuming he gave the copy ter you?"

I nodded, wondering what could make a werewolf distraught. "Oh, yeah. We go way back, him and I. We're friends." *Dial it back*, I chided myself.

The carpenter scratched his receding hairline in confusion. "Well, why you want the key's your business, but he had told me it was fer a fellow who'd be wearing a black cloak."

Cold fear washed over me, sending my nerve endings trembling. The bartender was in league with the Rankers? I looked at the chest, frowning, trying to get my adrenaline-pumped brain to slow down and think up a course of action. My fingers clenched into fists.

"Are you okay?" the kind carpenter asked, patting my back. "M'lord? Your eyes sort of looked, um...white, for a second there..."

"Y-yes," I stuttered, putting a hand to the side of my face and shielding my eyes. "I–I must go...tell them."

The carpenter reached out at me, but I backed away, apologizing. I tripped backward over an oak chest, picked myself up, and stumbled outside...right into the arms of an old lady.

She grabbed my shoulders firmly in her bony hands, talon-like nails digging into my skin. Her crooked yellow teeth gleamed, and her shadowy black eyes rolled. "Don't!" she shrieked at me. "Your eyes give you away!"

I thought back to when Nikki and I were in the park with the Rankers–how Garrett's buddy had said the same thing to me when my irises had glowed red in anger. I struggled to squirm out of her grip, but it was too strong, even for the extra drive my brain was sending through my muscles. I had to get away, had to tell the others.

The woman forced me to meet her bottomless pupils. She rambled on, her spittle flecking my face and shirt. "You can't let them see! Can't let them see the cloudy white or the red fire!"

"Get away!" I hissed, yanking to escape from her, but she shrieked, "Look away! *He* will see! He mustn't see!"

The carpenter rushed from his shop and shouted, "Hey there! Leave the warrior alone!" He tried to come to me but was held back by the crowd gathering around us. People of the village were emerging from the dark shadows and alleys, their eyes suspicious and flickering, their expressionless, sunken faces thirsty. Many grasped crude clubs or knives, and some of the younger kids were kneeling to pick up rocks.

Giving in to the woman's iron grasp, I held my hands up, palms out, and looked warily around at everyone. "Okay, guys, this isn't what it looks like. I mean you no harm. This woman just grabbed me and started shouting at me. Does she do this to people often?"

A guy a few years older than me growled, "Only if they're different." He held back his arm, aiming to throw a heavy rock at me. "And we don't like different." The guy tensed his muscles and braced his feet; I grimaced, waiting for the bone-crunching thud and the ensuing agony.

But a small, slender hand caught the man's wrist, and a young girl slipped around to frown up into his face. "Stay your hand! *Don't you know who this is?*"

The man's face was blank, his brain still trying to absorb the sudden change of events. I was both surprised and relieved.

It was Mariah.

She pushed through everyone to me, and grabbed my collar in one hand, pointing at my face with the other. "This is the great assassin of the Northwest Woods!"

There were sharp intakes of breath, and everyone took one big step back. The old lady clutching me released my shoulders and, scowling, merged with the other stiff bodies.

The man who'd been close to beaning me with his chunk of granite said perplexedly, "But, the carpenter said he's a warrior. Knights errant have no business here."

Mariah rolled her eyes upward and strode purposefully up to him, towing me by my collar. "'Warrior' is his codename, you odorous bucket of booze!"

The man stared, squinting down at us, half of the sentence not registering in his underdeveloped brain. "But," started another villager, "his eyes..."

Mariah's own eyes narrowed, and her voice dropped to a condescending hiss. "He has magic powers you aren't even capable of dreaming about. Imagine, if any of you had thrown a rock..."

A visible shudder rippled through the crowd at Mariah's trailed-off words. I looked behind me at the carpenter, whose whiskered face was a mask of confusion and fear. As imperceptibly as I could, I winked. He slowly smiled, winked back, waved, and vanished into his carpentry.

Mariah, cringing, turned to look at me and began pulling me away from the stunned bog folk. "Come on, Warrior, and forgive my interruption."

"You are forgiven," I said, playing my role nicely, but on our way past the guy that had been about to clobber me, I poked him in the chest and growled, "*You* can consider yourself lucky."

Mariah grabbed my hand. "Oh, come on!"

When we were away from the mob and back on the busy street, I whispered frantically to Mariah what I had gleaned from the carpenter: the bartender had the key made for a Ranker, who would leave it for their fresh troops to find. The bartender was apparently in possession of the *next* clues.

"That means there's a Ranker out there somewhere bound to notice real soon that no reinforcements are showing up at the bog and they'll show up to interrogate the bartender about their missing spare key–the bartender, their buddy, their ally."

Mariah didn't seem at all bothered.

"We intercepted the clue," she said. "Even if the Rankers find out, it'll take them a while to confront the bartender about it; they'll have to come up with another way to contact their allies, and we'll be long gone by then." I must not have looked convinced because Mariah smiled fondly at me.

She pulled me down next to her, crouching over a patch of young nettles sprouting from some upturned soil in the street. Making sure that our bodies shielded what we were doing from passing eyes, she poked her forefinger into the muddy dirt up to the first knuckle, closed her eyes, and murmured distractedly, "When life gives you melons..."

I watched, shocked, while the soil bubbled up and imploded on itself in tiny, quiet mounds. Then a tendril of green coiled and twisted up out of it like something alive. In the span of a few short seconds, a white bulb grew from the end of the shoot, first the size of a pebble but rapidly swelling to the size of my hand. Its color had turned from a ripe white to a healthy, shiny red.

Mariah extracted her finger from the ground, looking sleepy, then plucked the pumpkin-shaped melon and triumphantly held it up. I raised an eyebrow. She shrugged. "Lemons are gross." She held the fruit forward. "Want some?"

We kept walking, taking turns eating from either side of the melon. I wondered if that was Mariah's way of telling me we had everything covered. As if reading my mind, she said, "We'll tell Peter that the bartender is a Ranker ally and we'll have one of the soldiers tail him and pay attention to his communications. But we're griffins, Jonathan. Don't forget that even though we are frightened by nightmares, the Rankers fear griffins a lot more. No need to worry."

"*You're* a griffin," I said quietly. "I'm just..." but this time the words wouldn't come. The truth was, I didn't really know *what* I was anymore. Mariah just gave me a small, understanding smile.

We walked on in simple, easy silence. We came to the inn. I could hear loud, drunken voices from within. Sighing resignedly, I reached out to open the door, but Mariah tugged me back and to the side. She was avoiding my face, blushing lightly and fiddling with the hem of her blouse.

"What's up?" I asked, concerned.

She took a quick breath and said, "In France, where I'm from, for most of my life, I never had a television or a radio, or food that wasn't rotten or moldy. I've never seen any movies except through others' windows. I haven't slept in a real bed since I was ten years old."

My heart sank in pity. That was why she hadn't understood my movie references, she hadn't seen, let alone *heard*, of them.

Mariah lowered her head, face turning steadily scarlet, her fists clenched. "I can't remember what it was like before we were poor. My earliest memory is of my mother giving me her own food when I was hungry. My father was always off trying to find a job. He was the one who provided for us. He found us an abandoned house to live in and foraged for food, stealing from vendors' stalls if he had to. He was a good runner–the police could never catch him. He found us blankets and old rusty toys for me.

"He told me that we used to have a house and money, but when the economy suddenly sank, he lost his business and most everything else. I remember him always tucking my hair behind my ears and saying, 'We have each other, little *papillon*, ourselves and our spirits. We'll climb back to the top in no time.'" I smiled, touched by the special moment between father and daughter, and Mariah tried to return the smile, but her lips only twitched.

"I grew under their care. But I also came to see how different my life was compared to the other French children. I watched them come home from school in clean uniforms, talking with real friends. I was envious of them. Why was I poor, and they well-to-do? Why was my fate so different from theirs?

"One day as I was walking, alone, down a street, I stole a pie from a man. But a passerby saw me and cried out, 'Thief!' so I ran. I was not as quick as my father. The police followed me home."

I felt anxiety knot up in my gut. "What happened? Did they arrest you?"

Mariah shook her head. "They crashed through the door and cornered me. But my father pushed them away. While they were wrestling with him, he told me to run, and I did. My mother's screams are the last thing I remember about my poor family." She took a moment to just breathe and looked away from me, blinking quickly. I heard her sniffle. She cleared her throat, frowning down at the ground, and continued.

"On my own on the streets, I had to fend for myself for the first time. The nights grew more and more cold and dark just as I grew more thin and ill. One night, I caught a fever. I found a pile of blankets behind an apartment, curled up in them to rest, and woke up here."

She stopped talking, looking expectantly up into my eyes. I didn't know what to say. How did someone handle a situation like that? She had been here in this dreamworld for two years. Sick for two years. And I'd been complaining about being stuck here for a few *days*.

"So, you're ill?" I asked feebly.

Mariah nodded. "I think so. Very."

I bowed my head. "I am truly sorry. I guess I haven't been really considerate." I wanted to comfort her somehow, but the blunt way she had told her story made me wonder if she needed pity. It had sounded like she had accepted her life and what had happened, made peace with it.

"You're not a jerk." Mariah giggled. "Just scared."

Crazy emotions were chasing each other inside me. Before, I had felt a sort of acknowledgment toward Mariah, accepting the fact that she was there, that she was a nice, shy girl who could turn into a beautiful griffin. But now, I was feeling something else for her: respect. Respect for her courage and compassion.

"Can you forgive me?" I asked.

"Oh..." Mariah put her hands on her hips. "I guess so."

We shared a laugh and began to start back inside. "Hey," I started, "what about Kayle and Peter? How did they–?"

"Nope! That's all you're getting from me!" Mariah interrupted heartily, holding open the door for me to enter first.

I stepped sluggishly into the warm, dim inn, trying to ignore the raucous voices of drunken men. As Mariah followed me inside, scowling distastefully at a ragged, bearded old man collapsed on the floor beneath a window, I caught sight of someone outside.

It was a boy around my age. He looked familiar; too familiar to be there by coincidence, but I couldn't quite place why. He seemed to be blurry around the edges, but he was looking right at me from across the cobbled street.

I tilted my head to one side, nodded at him not unkindly but not too warmly, and shut the door.

CHAPTER SEVENTEEN:
MEANWHILE, BACK IN REALITY

AT ST. PAUL'S HOSPITAL

Tyson's eyes shot open, and he wriggled swiftly up into a sitting position. His leg had been detached from its suspension and lay plastered in a thick, heavy cast beneath his covers. Still, bruising aches echoed painfully in his bones as Ty moved.

His girlfriend, Lia, lying against him, jumped aside, rubbing her eyes. "Honey, are you okay? Should I call a nurse?" she asked sleepily.

"I saw Jonathan!" Tyson shouted, finally smiling.

From the couch by the window, Nikki sat up from her own slumber, hair brassy colored in the setting sun's light. "Jonathan?" she murmured plaintively.

Tyson immediately felt bad for waking her when Jonathan was actually nowhere in sight, but he couldn't help his excitement. "I was dreaming," he began, straining to remember. The two girls gathered close, eyes big and doubtful. "I was in a swampy place, but it was one of those dreams where you can barely see, like you're in a little cubicle of foggy glass. It was so realistic–I was on a street, and people walked past me on all sides. Then across the street and going into a big, old building, were Jon and some girl. Jon looked at me on his way in, but I don't think he recognized me. He just kind of flicked his head...and I woke up."

"Exactly." Nikki morosely patted Tyson's recently unbandaged, scarred arms. "It was only a dream." She stood from kneeling at his side and faced the window, the people on the streets below hurrying along, her lips trembling and her eyes filling with tears. "Jonathan's not...coming back." And then she clapped her hands over her face and broke into the sobs that Tyson and Lia had so often heard.

"Nikki, come on, how can you know that?" Lia asked. She put her arms around her friend and soothed her, a habit she was becoming increasingly good at.

Tyson was indignantly persistent. "It was so realistic–I could smell and feel and hear things! I swear to you both, it was, like, a vision!"

The girls continued to ignore him, faces dyed orangish pink in the dying sunlight. Nikki turned to face him, her tear-streaked cheeks red from crying. "If you believe what you saw was real, then what was Jonathan doing? Where was he?"

Tyson looked down into his hands, picking at his hospital bracelet. His stitched skin and muscles blistered dully under his pain medication. "I told you, I couldn't see that well, but it was dark and smelled funny, like peat, sort of, or compost. He was just eating some sort of fruit and went in a loud building with that girl."

Nikki's eyes flashed, her brows dipping down into such a fleeting frown, that Tyson wasn't sure he had seen it. "She wasn't...wearing a black robe, was she?"

"No," Tyson said, perplexed. "Why?"

Nikki shook her head in the way a person might to keep from sneezing, and tangled her fingers in her hair, more warm tears spilling from her bloodshot eyes. One fell onto Tyson's wrist, and he jumped in surprise, drying it off against his blanket. He felt bad and was beginning to think that perhaps he *had* only dreamed about his lost friend. How long had it been? A week, now?

Lia once more glued herself to Nikki's side, rubbing her back with one hand and gripping her shoulder with the other. The atmosphere threatened to escalate into a cry fest until the staticky intercom buzzed on.

Lia squeaked, and Nikki took in a sharp breath.

A voice, thick with an Indian accent and urgent with worry, issued from the speaker above the door. "We need all doctors, nurses, and able visitors to assist in evacuating patients from their quarters and out of the hospital."

After a weighty pause, during which the three friends gazed at one another blankly, with concern slowly seeping into their hearts like slow poison, Lia whimpered, "It's another disaster, it has to be." From outside the door came the frantic noises of running feet, high-pitched voices, and alarms.

"Rankers," Tyson heard Nikki say quietly.

"What's that sound?" Tyson scrunched up his face and tilted his head as if that would help him to identify the grumbling, shattering sounds steadily growing louder from the streets below.

A large truck, a snowplow built for shoving massive snowdrifts off of the Coloradan mountain roads, steadily approached from the far end of the main street that Tyson could just see if he sat up tall and strained his neck to the window. It was closely followed by a swarm of police cars with sirens yowling, smashing into, over, and through any vehicle in its way and picking up speed. Now it made sense why everyone was rushing around in the streets below, people abandoning their vehicles to the bedlam: they were fleeing.

A woman slammed open the door, startling everyone. Her hair was escaping her bun in frantic curls and snarls, and her eyes were perfectly round. She was pursued by Tyson's parents, who had both been out getting some afternoon coffee. The two shoved brusquely past her, and the nurse stumbled in with a wheelchair. Everyone was shouting at each other; it made Tyson's head spin.

"Come on!" Tyson's mother babbled, lowering the rail on one side of her son's bed.

"Mom, what's happening?" Tyson asked. On the streets below, people had started to abandon their vehicles and push their way into buildings, shrieking and glancing up the road.

The nurse threw her arm in an impatient arc behind her and yelled at Nikki and Lia, "Kids, get out!" In her rush, she accidentally hit Tyson's father in the chest, but he didn't seem to care. He was ripping aside the blankets, shooting furtive looks out the window.

"Sounds like someone's hijacked a truck and is aiming to crash it into the hospital. Law enforcement's been trying to communicate with the driver, but there's no response." Tyson picked up unspoken information from his father's silence: there was something more–a bigger threat than just a truck smashing into the hospital's parking garage or, by now, probably mostly vacated waiting room.

"Is there something wrong with it?" Tyson almost choked on his words just voicing them. His dad glanced at him as he started clearing Tyson's blankets away. "Is there a bomb or something?" Tyson asked even more quietly. His father didn't answer–silent confirmation.

The truck was getting closer. The police cars were squealing to a stop, too late to barricade the truck, too far back and stuck in the carnage left by the snowplow to continue the chase. Cops had stepped out behind the safety of their squad-car doors and were firing at the rampaging vehicle, perhaps desperately hoping to pop a tire, kill the driver, detonate whatever payload it was packing before it could reach the hospital.

Nikki and Lia, instead of heeding the nurse's order, flew over to help, locking eyes with their friend and talking to distract him from his pain and the mounting terror that they all shared.

The nurse slipped her hands gently but firmly under Tyson's thighs, using her foot to drag the rack holding his IV fluids and catheter over beside her. Tyson's father, with a care unbefitting his muscular frame, helped the nurse drag Tyson bodily into the wheelchair.

Tyson's mother brushed at her eyes, listening to her son groan in agony, watching tears slide from the corners of his own eyes as he clenched his teeth and gripped the sides of his gown. Nikki and Lia whimpered, pitying the deficient state their friend was in.

After managing to swallow his pain, Tyson cleared his throat, and gave Lia a half-brave thumbs-up. Lia choked out a laugh, heart swelling to the bursting point with admiration, and joined his side, looking expectantly at Nikki.

The van was near enough for Nikki to see the tiny rectangles that were the headlights. Everything happened at once.

Lia followed Tyson, his parents, and the nurse in a mad rush out into the hall, Tyson trying to see Nikki over his shoulder. "Come on!" he shouted. Nikki hurried to follow but looked around at the last second. They heard a terrible, distant smashing sound. The hospital trembled, and the windows rattled.

Nikki spun on one foot and sprinted out into the hall toward Tyson, dodging, ducking, dancing around the other fleeing bodies that were becoming a disorderly array of obstacles for their fellows trying to escape death. Tyson was helpless to do anything but watch her try to catch up, stuck in the mayhem behind him. When Nikki was about halfway down the hall, the world upended itself. The floor bucked with an explosion so loud it was felt more than heard–Tyson's father stumbled and fell, and Tyson coasted until he hit a wall, disoriented as the lights started to flicker and the building quaked–but he could only watch as another, smaller explosion almost directly beneath them sent Nikki flying toward a window that looked out on a parking lot...eight stories below.

Nikki shielded her face, Lia and Tyson shouted her name in anguished unity, but a boy came out of nowhere and sideswiped her. The two rolled heavily across the floor, skidding to a stop by the wall. She lay there, shuddering in the stranger's embrace, tingling with nerves and shock. Tyson wheeled over as fast as he could as the tremors began to subside, alarms went off, sprinklers turned on, and the odor of smoke and burning things started to reach them.

"Are you alright?" Tyson heard the boy ask Nikki. His voice wasn't accented, it was American, but it sounded old-fashioned–archaic. It made Tyson feel like he did when he was with Jonathan: safe. And by the look on Nikki's face, Tyson judged she felt the same.

But when Tyson got a closer look at his friend's rescuer, he saw that the hero was bizarrely different from Jonathan. His hair was bushy but tidy; the ends curled inwards toward his ears and forehead. His eyes were almost feminine, thickly lashed and a deep-blue color. His cheeks and nose were thinly sculpted, as if straight out of some sort of beautiful stone. He seemed to be their age if not a bit older.

The boy repeated his question, his strange, melodious voice slipping from between his blush-pink lips like a breeze of cool air. "Are you well?"

Nikki nodded, mesmerized at his odd way of speech. "I am now. Thanks to you."

The boy smiled, flashing pearly white teeth set in perfect place and harmony beside each other.

"Think not of it," he said.

CHAPTER EIGHTEEN:
BAR FIGHTS ARE INTENSE

So we entered the inn again, hit with the odors of beer and the food being cooked for the customers. A warrior approached me, bowing. I recognized him as one of the gladiators. He had an aquiline nose and curving lips that hinted at Mediterranean blood.

"Sir and lady," he said. "Peter requests your presence out back." He looked sidelong at me, and I got the feeling that he was hiding something about what Peter wanted, but I was too curious about the location of our summons to care much. Why weren't we meeting in our room upstairs in privacy?

The gladiator led us in a winding path around the rapidly filling seats and booths as dinner hour approached. A couple of the men who had gotten more than a few alcoholic drinks in them reached out for Mariah, only to have her snatch her hands away, eyes straight ahead and nostrils flaring. One guy pushed his chair back, separating Mariah and me from our guide, and grabbed at her.

Disgust flaring, I kicked the chair's legs hard enough to tip the man over, shoving Mariah behind me.

"No, Jon," she muttered. "Please, it's fine..."

The mindless babble permeating the room cut short.

The bartender looked up from where he was gnawing on a turkey leg atop a stool. His luminous eyes sized up the situation, and me, with a sort of interest. Unlike any other bartender, he didn't shoo us out or stop the violence but turned toward us to see better and resumed eating with a mocking smirk.

The man I had knocked over stumbled drunkenly to his feet, nearly tipping over his and his friends' table when he leaned against it to pull himself up. He fixed his bloodshot eyes blearily on me, swaying back and forth, and then leaned forward, grabbing my collar in his hands.

"You got a problem, kid?"

I didn't answer, biting the insides of my cheeks and looking down at the floor to hide my flaming-red eyes. The drunken man shook me like I was a disobedient dog, yanking my chin up toward him.

"Are you deaf, you addle-brained fool? Do you have a pro—"

The scarred blade of a dagger with a gold handle fashioned into a lion's head slid across the man's jugular. The hush in the room thickened with clouds of tension.

The gladiator leaned forward to whisper into the drunk's ear, "If you value your miserable life, you will release my charge."

The drunk's eyes slid down as far as they could in the direction of the knife. He slowly let me go. I straightened my clothes, glaring around at the wide eyes and open faces.

The gladiator backed away from the man and resumed leading us through a door in the back of the room and out into an overgrown garden away from the prying eyes. I watched the man stick his dagger into his boot where it had been concealed beside his leg in a hidden sheath.

"Thanks," I mumbled, watching my own feet tread the matted green grass.

I was surprised at the man's jovial tone. "No, thank *you,* Prince. Quite a coincidence you have proven your heart today. I didn't know that sort of fire was in you."

My suspicion returned full swoop, but I had an uncanny feeling that answers were coming soon.

I found myself becoming distractedly amazed by my surroundings. This eerie and unkempt garden held a haunting but mystifying beauty. The long grass and weeds had all but taken over the crumbled stone birdbaths and fountains decorated with chubby cherubim.

The playful sound of water no longer jingled a merry melody. No birds sang from the grand willows or maples or oaks. But there was a pulsating, invisible life force that suffused the air with its splendor.

A brick path wound in many directions about the various plants. A cat was curled up in the boughs of a tree, lazily watching clusters of butterflies flutter in the flowers.

Vibrant tulips, as yellow as the rising sun, were planted in rings around the bases of rose bushes with blooms scarlet red, hot pink, or a seductive blackish crimson.

Ivy covered the tree trunks, helping their thick hosts to completely obscure the back of the inn from view the deeper into the garden we traversed. Clover acted as a carpet in the places grass and brick had abandoned. Giggling to herself, Mariah knelt and plucked up a four-leaf shamrock, twiddling it in her fingers. I saw with amusement that she had stuck a purple-tinted morning glory behind one ear to hold back her lengthening bangs.

In a way, I thought the garden was prettier now than it might have been if it were actually tended to and cared for; it was wild and fierce and colorful. I strongly believed that that was what the garden had become after the death of the bartender's wife. Maybe she had been the one who had planted everything.

I realized that many of these flowers did not belong together. One required more sunlight than another, and another needed frequent rain. Some didn't even dwell in the same climate. It must have been because of what people dreamed. Over the years, people had created this with their imaginations.

It struck me then that something like this didn't exist in reality. I would never see this wonderment when I returned to consciousness. So I tried to lock it all up into my mind, a picture I would never forget. It was like a glimpse of heaven.

But then we came to the clearing, and I realized we were no longer alone.

The warriors that had been traveling with us reclined or sat in exhausted heaps on the ground, covered with films of sweat. I guessed that they had just finished sparring, seeing as how their various weapons lay on the ground beside them. Many of the men had removed their shirts, showing their herculean pectorals and abdominals, and wetted the fabric from water flasks, draping them over their faces or around their shoulders.

Kayle was conversing animatedly with a smiling army man, joking about something, patches of sweat darkening his gray sweatshirt. Mariah rushed over to them, sitting daintily on her knees, and gave Kayle the shamrock. Kayle's face lit up, and he closed his eyes, massaging the weed's tender leaves.

The soldier patted his back understandingly and I heard him say, "You miss it, don't you?"

"More than anything," Kayle said in return.

Peter stood in the center of the clearing; his sleeves rolled up to his elbows. Unlike the others, he didn't look like he'd sparred with anyone yet. He held a sword in one hand, out to the side. The blade was around eight hands long and spotless silver. The handguard above the hilt was fashioned to resemble the peeled-back petals of a red-orange tiger lily, and the leather and wire handle was a thick green-and-silver "stem."

"Thank you, Marcus," Peter said, addressing the gladiator.

The man nodded on his way past me toward a couple of his friends and said, "I do believe he's up to this, sir." He recounted what had taken place in the inn for all to hear, and I watched with indignation and stung pride as roguish smiles spread across everyone's faces.

Chuckling, Peter looked at me and chortled. "Brave and honorable, Jonathan, but if matters had gotten out of hand, Mariah would have been able to handle herself." I felt my insides squirm in embarrassment at my brash actions. It was true; Mariah was no weak little girl.

"Don't worry, I still appreciated it." Mariah beamed sweetly at me, and I tried to flash a convincing smile.

"But at least you're in the mood," Peter said. I was about to ask what mood when he tossed another sword at me, hilt first. I jumped back to avoid it, and it thumped to the ground, provoking mild laughter from those gathered. Guess who laughed hardest? I'll give you a hint: he's a maniac.

"Pick it up!" Kayle shouted, teeth bared in an unholy grin. "Or you're dead!"

"Um...I can shoot a gun. Could I have a gun instead?"

Peter replied, "No, for the following reasons: The sword is the weapon of knights, kings, heroes—the champions of storybook fables. So, naturally, it is the most common weapon in the Land of Dreams. And, just as you represent a legacy, so, too, is this sword a symbol of your lineage—of all who have ruled this land before you. The sword is only as good as its wielder. It will not do its job for you—you must be in complete control at all times, and using a sword teaches you patience, finesse, and grace. And a sword won't run out of bullets. It is important you know how to use one."

I considered objecting but realized I would only be hurting myself. Just like learning to fly, this was going to be a difficult lesson to experience, but if I were to make it in this Land of Dreams alive, to make it back to my friends and family and protect them from the Rankers, I would need to take advantage of training and practice.

I bent at the waist and wrapped my hand around the hilt. It was a good-looking weapon. The blade glimmered. The handguard was shaped like the curling claws of a griffin with each curve so realistically talon-like, I could almost believe they were real. The handle was a gripped steel, and bronze in color. There was a compartment in the bottom that I wouldn't have noticed if I hadn't brushed it with my fingers. I ignored that and focused on trying to pick the thing up.

Have you ever gone to pick up a soda can or the like, expecting it to be full, but your arm goes shooting up because the can is in fact empty? That was what lifting the sword was like—except the opposite.

I expected it to be light, like the plastic toy ones Ben had when we were kids, but it was not. I almost fell over, braced my legs and strained to lift it, nervous sweat popping out on my brow.

Wow! It was about as heavy as a pillowcase full of bricks. It wasn't that I was out of shape or anything, but I wouldn't be able to swing this thing around for long without overexerting myself.

As I struggled to point the sword's tip upward in a ready stance, my forefinger brushed the blade, and I quickly drew my hand back, but I wasn't injured.

Peter noted my astonishment. He pulled a small bottle full of something like oil from a pocket and shook it. "You're lucky the dwarves gave this to me," he said. "It's a tincture that can only be crafted a few days out of the year when the nectar of the brother's hand carnation is available for harvesting." He put it back in his pocket. "I put some on our blades while you were out. For a few hours, it will be impossible to hurt ourselves or our friends with these weapons."

I tried to say "cool," but was afraid that I'd throw up if I opened my mouth. Instead, I blanched and managed to monosyllabically squeak, "What?" a bit too late.

Peter smiled, expertly twirling his sword in a circle. "You've fought Garrett himself before, have you not?"

There were impressed looks from my audience, but in my own defense, I objected, "With my fists! Not this...can opener!"

Kayle's mouth was a large O. He leaned forward to catch my attention and asked with interest, "Who won?"

I avoided his penetrating red-brown eyes uncomfortably and groused, "He did, sort of. But he cheated. He stuck me with a knife while my back was turned." I twisted and showed him the faded red scar on my back where the blade had made its entrance.

Kayle's eyes flicked from my wound to my face and a crooked smile melted up his cheeks. "'Cheated,' did he?" He snickered. "Right..."

Peter came swinging wildly at me then. Unprepared, I dropped my sword, felt the blunt, hard edge of Peter's blade at my throat, and was looking into his bottomless gray eyes, half bowed back against the weight he was forcing on me. "Focus, Jonathan," he whispered calmly, like a teacher explaining a difficult concept to a lost child. "Remember our flying lesson–a foe will take advantage of any distractions." I nodded dumbly, and he drew back a few paces, resuming his ready stance. I staggered back into mine, inwardly groaning.

It all went downhill from there.

Peter was relentless. He taught me techniques and gave me pointers, all the while ruthlessly beating at my confidence and my sore arms. "Use your powers to your advantage," Peter panted, dancing around me and sometimes taking a break from speaking to beat at any part of my body. "You are young...strong, and filled with a fire that all men of your age possess. Plus, you're a griffin."

With that, and a clever grin, he vanished, sword and all. One moment I was looking warily up into his face, and the next at the wall of flowers across the clearing. With a jolt, I remembered Mariah telling me that Peter's griffin power was that of camouflage.

"Where am I?" His voice came from everywhere at once.

I jabbed diagonally out to one side and hit nothing but atmosphere. Something hard and cold bashed into my ribs, knocking the breath out of me.

Peter reappeared behind me, advising, "Trust your senses, not your gut. Keep a close watch for anything hinting at your enemy's whereabouts. Look for a disturbance in the air when I disappear." He dissolved again.

This time, I spotted what looked like vapor waves next to me, the kind you'd see over a road on a hot day. I stabbed vaguely at it. Peter dodged neatly, but came back into focus and congratulated me.

Just when I was beginning to become too tired to go on, Peter put his sword in the sheath at his belt and declared, "That's enough for today. You did well for your first time, Prince Jonathan."

I dropped my sword, arms and legs shuddering, believing his praise to be empty words. There was polite, scattered applause.

"Okay, men," Marine Sergeant Flaherty called. "Let's go get some chow!" Mumbling cheerfully to each other, those gathered hopped to their feet and wandered back down the flowered path to the inn. I was about to follow, but Peter softly called my name from behind me. I turned on my heel, a moan softly rolling in the back of my throat.

Peter was fondly caressing the sword I'd used to spar with, running his hands over the talon look-alikes in the hilt. My heart picked up its pace. This was it. We were alone together, and he had a sharp weapon in his hands; he was going to kill me right when I had no strength to fight back.

"You did well," he said again, and this time I believed he sincerely meant it.

I hung my head, embarrassed at my accusatory thoughts. "Thanks."

He looked up, brows rising in his effort to show me how honest he was being. "You show great promise. Here." He was offering me the sword, hilt first.

"For me?" I was shocked. Gingerly, I reached out and grasped it, letting its tip thump to the grass so that I wasn't once again carrying its whole weight.

"Yes," Peter confirmed. "And this." From the ground by the base of the flowers' stems and rough branches, he picked up a mahogany-colored sheath with a gold-plated tip. A clip on the back of it would hook on to my belt or around a belt loop.

"This sword," Peter said, "will never fail you. It was made by the land's most expert craftsmen: the dwarves. The very ones that made Mariah's necklace." He reached down and ran his hand over the sickle-shaped black handguards. "These belonged to the last king. It is a tradition among griffins that, when we die, we give something, namely a claw or a feather, to someone we loved or put the most trust in. The last things your predecessor did before he passed were entrust to me words of wisdom and comfort that are for my ears only, and to give his successor his claws in a symbol of trust and faith. It is an honorable custom."

A feeling I'd never felt before filled me with sadness and gratitude. I ran my fingers over the smooth, sharp talons. The talons that would curl protectively over my fist in combat, like the hand of a best friend. I wished I could have met the former king, if only to thank him.

I tried to sheath the weapon, but my burning arms shrieked in protest. "I don't know if I'll ever be able to use this." I chuckled, more than a little embarrassed.

Peter took the sword and turned it bottom up, so the compartment was exposed. "Well, this will help until you get the hang of it. If you press in these three talons, the compartment will open and–" He depressed the necessary talons, the little chamber popped open, and a switchblade handle shot out, partially ejected by a spring. I jumped. The rubber handle was set with three jewels on each side: a ruby, an emerald, and a sapphire. Peter pulled the blade out, and with a flick of the wrist, the knife extended to about half the length of the sword. The metal reflected the setting light like the tooth of some wicked creature.

Peter said, "In a hostage situation, if you don't want to risk pulling out your sword, you can use this baby with only a few simple movements."

"Wow," I said, inarticulate.

Peter replaced the dagger, put my sword in its sheath, and allowed me to clip it to my trousers with the dignity I had left. I expected the sword's weight to tug at my pants, but it didn't; it rested in firm poundage at my hip. He patted my shoulder, and we went down the path back toward the inn. I told him what I'd learned at the carpentry.

His eyes tightened, but other than that, he reacted in much the same way as Mariah had.

"If the werewolf had any concerns that the griffin we entered the bog with was the Griffin Prince, we would all be in Ranker hands right now. Our identities are secure. Still, I'll ask the Amazons to set up a watch tonight and keep an eye on him. Worst-case scenario, he *has* contacted a Ranker and we'll have to brace ourselves for a fight."

He looked at me, saw that I hadn't been entirely reassured, and added, "We're way ahead of the Rankers, son. They couldn't have known just how much of their plans King Brody uncovered before he died—that we've deterred their reinforcements. But, to be safe, we should probably hurry up and find that chest so we can get the next clues and leave." He didn't voice the inevitable, but I shuddered at what had to be done. Somehow, we had to get into the bartender's room.

Back inside the inn, we were abused by a wall of noise. Loud voices discussed the weather and other trivial happenings, or hiccupped and burped and drawled for more ale. The customers had really filed in.

Mariah, Kayle, Sergeant Flaherty, Marcus, and a samurai had saved us spots at a wraparound booth in a corner. Once we slid in to join them, and the samurai had finished discussing *iaido* with Marcus, Peter told them about what had happened at the carpentry. When he got to the enchanting part about who the key belonged to, everybody's expressions (except for Mariah's, who had already been told this story) turned from blank attentiveness to surprised interest.

"I propose we sneak into the bartender's quarters tomorrow night," Peter stated in a low whisper, "After the Amazons have some time to determine what the werewolf knows, if anything."

After the initial unexpectedness of this proclamation wore off, talk turned to other things until commotion at the candlelit bar turned heads.

Two middle-aged men were sitting on stools. One was livid, an ugly scowl on his bearded face. The other beside him was quailing, his balding head lowered and chubby face twitching. "Please, Nox, don't try it!" the man whimpered, pudgy hands grasping at the front of his friend's coat.

The grumpy guy, Nox, thundered, "I've had a helluvuh day, and I'm willing to try anything to help me forget it!" He twisted savagely to face the bartender, who was glaring back, and growled, "So I'll take that Bowl of Bemusement!"

Everyone gasped or cursed or laughed in disbelief. Us knowing ones exchanged looks. Was this guy ignorant of the broth's side effects?

The bartender jerked his head at one of his waiters who slipped around behind the counter and began to rummage beneath it for ingredients. Silent eyes watched him work. The bartender remained glued to his spot, as if not wanting to be touched by the foul concoction.

When finished, the waiter set the bowl and a spoon in front of Nox.

Ignoring his friend, Nox dug in. After a while, I started noticing changes coming over the man. He was twitching jerkily and tensing up. Soon, he started yelling at his surprised friend for staring at him, and then at the rest of the people in the bar. He became so abusive, teetering on the lip of violence, that the bartender had a couple of Dark Knights throw him out into the street.

Peter and I exchanged looks. Whatever the brew was, exactly, it did have a terrible effect on dream-creations, turning them vicious and violent. But why? What was the point? If it was a clue for the Ranker army, then why was the werewolf letting his customers drink it? I hoped the Amazons found out more that night. I'd hate to leave the swamp with questions unanswered, especially questions about the Rankers' plans.

CHAPTER NINETEEN:
A FATHER-SON TALK

Before bed, I went back outside and threaded my way through the untamed garden to get some more sword-practice in. I stood in the clearing from before, swiping and swinging my new sword, pushing through the complaining muscles in my arms and shoulders. At first I felt like an idiot, standing there trying to emulate the fluid movements Peter had taught me, trying to pivot and balance while ducking and dodging imaginary foes. I knew that I was clumsy and slow and that I was letting my guard slip. But football had been hard for me once, too. All I needed was practice, practice, and more practice.

As I moved through a series of blocks and counters, I considered the little I knew of the Ranker plans. They wanted me in the dreamworld to keep me out of their way. They had left clues behind to subtly guide their reinforcements to their mysterious base of operations. We had intercepted those clues in the hopes of finding their base and discovering their plans. Garrett had been watching me all these years—but he wasn't the only one. The gargoyle Ranker had been watching me too. Tormenting me with nightmares of my mother's death. Why? Why me? Did they really want to turn me into some kind of monster? To torture me until I became the tool that they had wanted King Brody to be? The...Dark Griffin?

I shuddered, letting my arms drop and the tip of my blade to scrape through the grass. While Peter and Mariah seemed to make the whole thing look easy, just a storybook case of good versus evil, griffin versus Ranker, I had reservations. Something in my gut told me that there was more to this whole Ranker thing than there seemed to be. I just didn't know what yet. My fingers tightened around the hilt of the sword. Once I found a Ranker, I'd do my best to find out.

A quiet, muffled sound came from the flowers nearby and I gave an almighty jump of alarm. Was it the werewolf? A Ranker? Nox from the bar, all crazy from the Bowl of Bemusement?

The sound came again, and I realized it came from the *other side* of the flowers, from another path. It sounded like someone was weeping, or muttering sullenly to themselves. My first instinct was to scurry back to the inn. This was a sheltering zone for nightmares, as Peter had said. I didn't want to push my luck and get eaten by a monster or something. But if the whimpers I heard belonged to a *dreamer* having a nightmare...then shouldn't I see if I could help them? If not because I was supposedly the protector of this place then at least because it was the right thing to do?

I snuck back up the path until it forked and then I stalked along between heavily laden lilac trees and dogwoods with fat, pink petals that stroked my face as I bent beneath their boughs. The deepening twilight was turning chilly and the air felt misty on my skin. I knew that this wasn't a place I wanted to linger in after night fell.

When I rounded the bend in the path, I came out into a cozy little brick courtyard ringed by stone benches. A tall statue of an angel stretched up in the center of the courtyard, its wings half-open, its hands spread as if calling down judgement, its face grim but beautiful. And there, on his knees at its feet, shaking his head and talking to himself, was–

"*Dad*?" My heart leaped and I was seized by two contrary impulses. Here was a person from the life I'd left, someone I knew, and I wanted to run to him and embrace him for his familiarity. But I also wanted to turn right around and abandon him to whatever cruel dreams tormented him. It was less than he deserved after all he'd done to me.

At my voice Dad looked up, and by the way his eyes roved around in my direction, I could tell that he couldn't see me. We may have been in the same bog, but his nightmare was affecting his perception.

"Jonathan?" he said desperately. He sounded so pitiful that my heart went out to him a little bit, but I still held my ground and watched him. After a moment, he stood up and said, "Are you there? Are you coming home?"

I shifted my weight, thinking. Dad wouldn't recognize this as real. To him, this was just a dream, and there was no guarantee that he would even hear or remember the things I said to him, no matter how I wished he would.

He gave another moan, a terrible, helpless sound like he suffered from a wound, and I said, "What is it, Dad? What do you want?"

"I'm sorry," he said. "I didn't ever mean to hurt you."

"Yes, you did," I retorted. "You went out of your *way* to hurt me."

Dad shook his head, huddling back against the statue, his eyes going round and frantic as if he saw himself surrounded by pacing wolves. I tried to calm myself down and mellow out my tone.

"No," he murmured, "No, I..." then he seemed to deflate and he sank back down onto his knees again, curled up like a child at the feet of the angel, gazing blindly out in my direction. "Yes. Ever since your mother died, I just...felt lost. Broken. I thought I was stronger. I thought I was doing okay when she was taken from me. I still had you, and I thought I could do it, be a father. But when I started drinking... all of the pain went away." He took a quivering breath. "And when I sobered up, I thought of how disappointed she would be, and I hated what I was doing... What I'd turned into."

There were tears in his eyes now. He said a few disjointed sentence fragments and I stood there listening, feeling as insubstantial as a down-feather. Dad had never been this honest with me as far back as I could remember. We'd never had this conversation before. I could only drink it all in, clinging to his pain and wanting it to be authentic.

"Then you started growing up, and I–I look at you and I see her. You have her laugh, her smile, her eyes. You have her bright-blue eyes." *Not all of the time,* I thought. "I blamed you for looking so much like her, being so much like her... As if you were purposely keeping the pain of her passing fresh...to remind me of it..."

"But I wasn't," I said coldly. "I was a kid who had just lost his mother, and I didn't understand why. You weren't there when I needed you most, when I needed a father, and now..." My anger built, threatened to pour over and bury my dad like an avalanche. He cringed as if waiting for the guillotine to fall and with a shock of surprise I realized that *I* was his nightmare; the words I wanted so badly to say, *I don't need you, I don't want you,* were the words that would break him, devastate him, horrify him.

So instead of saying the words I wanted to, I bottled my fury and tried to find the words I *needed* to say.

I stepped forward and squatted down so that Dad and I were at eye-level. Now he seemed to be able to see me, at least vaguely. He focused on my face and his mouth opened to give a choked gasp, or maybe it was a sob.

"What do you want to say to me?" I asked quietly.

Dad's eyes watered. "I don't know where you are. I don't want you to be dead because I need you to know that I love you. And if you just come back, I'll spend the rest of my life proving it. Please come back, Jonathan, please don't be dead."

Pity stirred in my chest. I half reached out, but I couldn't figure out why. Most of me wanted to wake him up from his nightmare, show him mercy and get him back to reality. But a very small, malicious little sliver wanted to watch him tremble in the throes of his conscience, to see him quail in fear as he had made me quail in fear so often growing up.

"I'll come back," I said after a long pause. "But not right now."

Dad's body started to fade so that he looked see-through, like a ghost. The settling evening pressed in upon me and I stood up. Time to retreat to the safety of the indoors.

"Come back, Jonathan," Dad said distractedly.

"Someday," I replied, turning to walk back along the brick path. I couldn't get out of there fast enough.

"Come back, Jonathan," I heard Dad murmur behind me, "Come home."

CHAPTER TWENTY:
MEANWHILE, IN THE HOUSE NEXT DOOR

A shadow-black raven was perched on the windowsill, watching the angry man stumble down the street. A claw made entirely of stone stroked the bird's breast. It felt like having a sharp rock scrubbed against it, but the raven knew better than to resist the touch.

To shame the gargoyle was to shake your tail feathers in the face of death.

The stone beast spoke in a low, gravelly voice. "I think the old man's starting to get ripe." The raven cawed agreeably. It had been a few days now since the gargoyle had claimed the house. The former resident had heard their knock, gone to admit them, and was dead from a blow to the head as soon as he had opened the front door. The gargoyle Ranker had thrown the corpse down into the basement, but he could smell the man getting gamey even on the top floor of the house where he crouched in the shadows beside an open window.

The gargoyle watched the bog-folk milling around the misty avenues of their pitiful village below him, their faces melancholy, mouths limp, eyes hollow. He sneered, absently scraping one of the spikes on his snout against the window frame, scoring a rent in the wood, as his mind wandered.

"There was once a time when we could have walked down the streets of this world and enjoyed the subjugation of the masses," the gargoyle muttered to his raven. "Once, we would have grown fat on the fear and respect shown us..." The raven burbled, pecking at the shavings left behind by the Ranker's spikes as if hoping to find bugs clinging to them, and the gargoyle showed his teeth.

The fear and cringing admiration of the people, dreamers and dream-creations alike, was no longer the Ranker's to enjoy—had not been for a great while. Not now that the griffins ran the show, not since King Brody the Gallant had destroyed some of their heaviest hitters and shown the entire dreamworld that the lion's share of power rested in the talons of powerful dreamers such as Brody had been.

Before he had killed the old man and taken his home, the gargoyle Ranker had been waiting for word of Garrett's allies arriving on the shores of Pebble Embark. When none was forthcoming, he had left his post in the Ranker fortress and gone to investigate. And the clue had been missing—which meant it had not called their allies to the dreamworld's golden shores from whatever nightmarish isles and seas they called home. Someone had taken it.

Garrett would be angry that he had abandoned his own duties to resolve the issue of their missing troops; he didn't want any of his Rankers getting directly involved in the trail of clues and risk being discovered by the griffins, not now, when Ranker blood was especially precious, when every Ranker would be needed for the final battle. But something had to be done, and he would be generously rewarded for capturing the thief.

But then, there had come word from the werewolf that a griffin had arrived in the swamp with a strange collection of men and women. The gargoyle had arrived as swiftly as he could and situated himself by the windows where he could watch the inn and the main street from the shadows. He had seen plenty of people entering and leaving the inn throughout the past few days, but no griffin, and he was beginning to think that it had been a false alarm—someone's dream creation, or a hippogriff or some other animal that the idiot-bartender had confused for a griffin.

But now...

The Ranker perked up. A window opened toward the very top of the inn, and a young man leaned out, carrying some bread and looking around at the darkening bog. The gargoyle leaned forward. How interesting. He had seen this boy wandering the streets earlier with a young woman and had glimpsed him meandering about the gardens in the back of the inn. The gargoyle hadn't recognized him then, in patchy clothes and with dirty skin and messy hair. But now that he'd washed up, the Ranker knew him instantly.

"So this is where you've been hiding," he growled, his black eyes glittering. "*You're* the thief..." The implications of a griffin, no, the Griffin *Prince*, having intercepted the Ranker clues were severe. It would mean a lot of work for Garrett, and the gargoyle, by extension, as one of Garrett's lieutenants. They would have to move quickly, place new clues, work under the radar to collect their allies under the griffins' beaks and also try to prevent the griffins from finding the rest of the clues.

The *right* thing to do would be to leave instantly and report to Garrett. They could capture the boy, or at least begin manipulating him, right here in the depths of this forsaken swamp. And yet...

The raven examined the boy with a beady eye and flapped its wings impatiently. It wanted the bread that Jonathan was holding.

Thinking, the gargoyle bared his canines in a sneer and said, "Wait for your chance."

He would pay the prince a visit that night. After all, he had a special place in his heart for Jonathan He'klarr...

CHAPTER TWENTY-ONE:
WEREWOLVES AND GARGOYLES

I stood at the window, letting the murky night cool my face. I was wearing my pajamas, glad to be free of the filthy clothes I had donned during the day.

"What a crazy day, eh?" Kayle yawned from his spot on the floor.

"Note to self," Mariah teased, "don't have the Bowl of Bemusement."

"No kidding!" I smiled, enjoying her optimism. I opened my mouth to take a bite of bread and then stopped and half turned. "I saw my dad a bit ago."

"Really?" Mariah paused on her way to the bed and Kayle rolled onto his side to look over at me.

"Yeah. We...had a talk."

Something in the tone of my voice must have told the pair of them a lot more about my relationship with my dad than I had meant it to, because Kayle said, "Ah... Not a nice talk, then?"

"No, it was okay," I said, rolling my shoulders as if to shrug off their attention. "It's just...Dad and I don't get along really well and it was...awkward to say the least, I guess." I thought of the sound of his sobs, hearing him beg me to come home, that he was sorry, and old bitterness oozed from my heart like an infected wound.

"You're likely to meet other people you know too the longer you're here," Mariah said reassuringly. I glanced up just in time to see her switch an uncomfortable look with Kayle and could tell that they were taken aback at the prickly relationship I had with my father, at the fact that their new prince had "issues."

But Mariah's words made me remember the vague, wispy form I'd seen across the street as we'd entered the inn before my sword-training with Peter. I perked up a bit.

"Actually, I did see somebody else today. I, uh, I think I knew him, too."

Mariah crawled into bed and smoothed the covers over her lap. "Who was he?"

I leaned against the side of the open window. "I don't know. He was sort of fuzzy in the face. It could have been anyone."

"You said 'him,' so it looked like a guy?"

"Yeah, kind of tall and skinny...like my friend Tyson..."

Peter stepped out of the bathroom then, wearing a flannel nightdress. It was very old-fashioned, and I only held my laughter out of respect for him.

"Well then," he said jovially, having been eavesdropping, "It probably was!"

I smiled. Seeing my friends again would be wonderful. I stared at my sword for a while where it was propped up by our traveling pack. I had a lot to tell them. Would they even believe me? Or, like my father and Mariah's mother, would they just be stuck in the dream, oblivious to the truth of what they were seeing?

"Is Nox still wandering around out there?" Peter asked as he folded his bedsheets back.

I leaned back out the window and scrutinized the street; it was too painful to think of anything I had left behind.

"No, he's long gone," I said, striving to see into the shadows.

A whispery whoosh brushed past my ear, and sharp, strong little claws yanked my bread from my hands. A raven craned its head back to croak at me as it soared high into the air. It got a beak-full of my food before dropping it to the street where it was ravenously pounced upon by a few scrawny alley dogs.

"Great," I scoffed. I withdrew abruptly into the room and latched the window shut. Mariah and Kayle went pale, and Peter frowned deeply.

"Sorry," I apologized, though I didn't really think that what had happened was my fault. "Do we have any more bread?"

"Nope," Peter said. "That was the last of it."

"*Last?*" I cried, waiting for an explanation while my insides fluttered nervously.

Peter sat on his bed and shrugged. "I figured we'd be leaving tomorrow night immediately after we found that bartender's chest. The sailors had run out of bread for tonight, so I gave them the rest of ours."

I slumped in despair. "Well, then, what am I going to do?"

Peter locked eyes with Kayle. "Stay close to him. He's going to have a rough night."

At first, I fought to stay awake. But the day's trials had taken their toll on me, and my eyelids slipped shut. My breathing slowed, and I decided to rely on Kayle. Kayle could keep me safe. Everything was fine...

And then the nightmare started.

I was in a familiar alleyway, sitting against a dumpster. When I opened my eyes, I saw a slick, brick wall moist with rainwater. Groaning, I pushed to my feet, glaring at the same flickering streetlight by the road that I had seen so often before.

Using its erratic light, I moved forward inch by inch, mentally steadying myself for the viewing of my mother's death, unable to do anything about it but wake up crying like a baby.

This time, however, even as I stood still in the darkness when the light flickered out, cold hands reached for me. Arms sprang from the walls and when the light bathed everything in a dull, yellow luminescence, I saw that they were covered in billowing black Ranker sleeves.

I fought to pull away, terror making me crazy, clouding the logical part of my brain. And just when my last dregs of resistance were snapped, and I went to my knees in despair, a gentle musical voice floated faintly by my ears. It was speaking fast, blending in and out of intelligible sound, but the Ranker hands reluctantly recoiled, slipping back into the walls.

Every time the words sounded, the streetlamp burned brightly, and I hurried onward. The words followed me, and I recognized them to be a foreign language. The strange phrases were repeating themselves on an endless loop. The voice became so clear for a few seconds that I could pick up some words: *"Impím ort, a Dhia, é a chosaint le linn na tubaiste seo..."*

Shaking my head slowly, I looked down the street to where the carjacker had once again cornered my mother. In slow motion, I ran forward, striving against the forces that made my body move so slowly.

The words went on, a comforting backdrop: "...*bí i do loinnir dá threorú chugat féin.*" They gave me strength and confidence. I pushed forward furiously, renewed with determination.

I blinked, extended one leg to run forward, and was suddenly a griffin! Finally! Fate was on my side! I spread my cavernous wings and tail fan, unsheathed my hind claws, and opened my razor beak, *so* ready to maul. My slitted eyes flashed red. I emitted a triumphant warning shriek.

Letting the words of the phantom speaker thunder in my ear tufts, "*Cumhdaigh é ar na deamhain ghránna atá siúlach anseo,*" I bunched my wild animal sinews and pounced.

In one fluid movement, the carjacker spun, a billowing night-dark Ranker cape flowing about, and smacked me back with an iron arm. I yelped and was wrenched backward by the blow, sliding on the wet street on my back. I kicked at the air with my hind paws and rolled over, splaying my talons in preparation to grab and claw.

The beast grabbed my mother's upper arm and dragged her forward with him. Her eyes were terrified, and she stared pleadingly down at me, whimpering.

When the Ranker walked, his hidden feet made a grating sound on the asphalt, like boulders grinding together. The triangular tip of a thin tail poked from beneath the cape. My mother clawed at the monster's arm, riding back his sleeve and breaking her nails on his slate-gray cement "skin." With a flourish, the Ranker shrugged back his hood, and I went cold beneath my pelt, my crown feathers fluffing up as if to make me look bigger.

The words *"go n-éagfaidh siad i do láthair,"* echoed in my ears.

The Ranker was the same one that had visited me the last time I'd had this dream. The same one that had spoken those ominous rhymes: "the Prince of Dreams must break his ties..."

"You," I gasped out.

The shark-like gargoyle cocked his head, grinning. He had two pointed bat ears on top of his horned skull. His empty, expressionless eyes gleamed, and his sharp teeth gnashed excitedly. "You know, I thought Garrett was crazy when he sent me into your nightmare back in reality."

My skin prickled with a sudden, creeping chill. His voice was the exact same as the man's who had attacked Nikki and I in the park. His eyes narrowed and he went on.

"How could you be the one to inherit the throne? I never met him, but I knew of your predecessor." The gargoyle pawed the ground once with one back foot, making a sound like chalk coughing on a blackboard. "*He* was a king. Yes, I humbly admit to some admiration for his skills, for the threat he posed."

Now he leaned forward, his tail lashing to strike his legs. "But you're...paltry by comparison. A desperate hope that you will grow horns and be the ram that protects his flock–not the sacrificial lamb to bleed out on our altar."

He chuckled tauntingly, coming to a stop a few feet from me. "Look at you. A scrap of feathers and flesh. It's almost insulting to think that you are the one standing in our way. You know, things are falling apart back 'home.' Your fellow humans haven't seen the worst of their problems yet. But they will. When you're gone."

I let my gaze wander over to my mother and linger on her scared face. "Let her go," I ordered, putting as much malice into my voice as I could.

The gargoyle seemed surprised to see that he was clutching a woman in one hand, as if he'd forgotten about her. "You've been sticking your nose in where it doesn't belong. Crafty little griffin you are, to find our clues and interpret them. But now it's time to start over." He lifted his free claw out and moved it in a vague circle over the road.

The background voice grew briefly louder and more intense. *"Cosain é!"*

The Ranker cringed and snarled, "Cursed prayers." He straightened up and tried again, motioning with his claw. A hole appeared out of nowhere between us, growing wider and deeper. He shifted his grip on my mother to her neck and dangled her out over the pit. She screamed pitifully, feet kicking.

"*No!*" I stepped forward. I couldn't reach her.

The Ranker bellowed, "You think yourself brave, little griffin? I know the truth. I have seen your fear in the face of another, when I once looked through the eyes of a murderous man."

I stared at him, half-mad with panic for my mother's life. "What? What do you mean? Are you talking about the one who created you?"

The Ranker sneered. "The one who gave me life, yes, and power enough that when he died, I still lived. Now..." He shook my mother so that she gave a strangled cry. "Tell me where the key is!"

Rage and hate made my eyes burn red. "And prove you right?" I snapped, hackles rising. *Prove that I'm a wimp? A coward? Weak?*

The gargoyle let go of Mom so that she fell a bit and then caught her. I growled helplessly. "Time's running short," he warned.

"If I tell you," I calculated, "you'll kill us both anyway."

The Ranker shrugged. "My arm's getting tired."

I argued inwardly with myself. If I told him, the fate of mankind was thrust into his claws. If not, I would have to watch my mom die. She was only a figment of my imagination, though, right? She had already died long ago...hadn't she? My mind was fogging up, and I was finding it harder to think.

The foreign words were wavering in volume, louder then softer.

"You lie!" I cried.

The Ranker growled in a bored voice, "Ten..."

I sat down, though it took all of my willpower not to spring to my mother's aid. "She isn't real."

"Nine..."

"And you will never win against me."

He scowled. "Eight..."

A piercing probe entered my mind and pushed at my logic. I fought it but could feel myself slipping into a state of peace. Would it hurt if I gave him some answers?

Even the background voice was fainter... *"Impím ort..."*

"Seven..." the gargoyle continued.

"No..." I murmured faintly. I fell to my elbows and knees weakly, human again. With the departure of my griffin form, a chunk of my resistance seemed to have abated too.

"*...a Dhia...*"

"Six..."

"*...é a chosaint le...*"

"Five..."

"*...linn na tubaiste seo...*"

"Four..."

I looked up. "Wait..."

"Three..."

"Wait! The key is—"

"*COSAIN É!*"

The gargoyle reeled back, dropping my mother on the road where she turned into a croaking raven, and covered his ears with a high, keening cry. The nightmare burst into a shimmering window of color and inverted images, and then I jolted to my body in the inn where I was gasping on the floor.

Peter and Mariah knelt at my side, eyes worried, and Kayle was leaning back on his heels as if recently collapsed. He stretched his arms out behind him to prop himself up, and I saw that sweat coated his hair and face.

"Was that you?" I asked feebly, still breathing hard. I started trembling. The nightmare lingered powerfully, just barely tempered by the soothing mystery words I had heard.

Kayle managed to nod. "You started talking in your sleep, saying 'mother' and 'key.' That flashed the warning lights."

I struggled to a sitting position and accepted a flask of water from Mariah, who draped a damp cloth around my neck. I smiled at her, and she smiled tentatively back. Wiping some excess water droplets from my chin with the back of my hand, I asked Kayle, "What were you saying?" I needed time to collect myself, to settle my nerves.

He turned his maroon eyes to me, debating how much to tell me. I took note of how his posture had tensed.

Finally Kayle replied tartly, "It was a prayer. They require intense focus, but Rankers despise them. I always used to repeat it when I was...when I was younger."

I thought back to the language he had used. "It wasn't in English. Was it, what's that Irish language called...Gaelic?"

Kayle inclined his chin and nodded. His face had closed up, and I doubted I was going to get any more out of him, but now wasn't the time to prod him about his past.

Peter and Mariah both asked a question at the same time.

"Did you tell him anything?"

"What did you see?"

I wasn't going to tell them about the alley or my mom, but I said, "I saw a gargoyle-looking Ranker."

Peter tightened his lips grimly. "The one that's had its eyes on you for a while?"

I nodded, feeling sick. A fierce, protective glint flickered in Peter's pale eyes.

"Shadow type. One of the toughest. Did you give anything away?"

"No," I spoke sheepishly. "But…"

"What?" Mariah whispered.

I looked at the stained-glass window, remembering the raven that had so conveniently been there to steal my bread. "But I think he's here."

"Are you sure?" Peter asked roughly.

I thought of the raven, shivered, and nodded firmly. Everything turned into a flurry of movement. Kayle and Mariah started packing up and getting dressed. Peter had washed my clothes, so I put my jeans and sweatshirt on over my pj's, throwing on my coral necklace as well. After a moment's hesitation, I strapped on my sword.

Peter stepped from the bathroom wearing his suspenders. He said brusquely, "We must move now!"

Kayle shouldered the pack and stepped aside as Peter led us into the hall. He gave the code-knock against Sergeant Flaherty's room door, and the marine emerged tousle-haired and blinking like an owl.

"Sir?" He frowned in confusion. "Is something wrong?"

Peter almost didn't wait for the question mark at the end of the sergeant's sentence before saying, "Long story short, a gargoyle Ranker has picked up our trail. It's a race as to who gets to the chest first. Find the Amazons watching the werewolf's room and have them report back to me. Quickly!"

Flaherty saluted and raced downstairs in catlike silence on the tips of his be-socked feet. While we waited for his return, Mariah awoke the rest of the squadron, briefing them on what was happening and helping them pack. I'd never seen so much going on with so little sound. By the time the sergeant returned with a pair of tall, dark-haired women in tow, everyone was nearly prepared for a hasty exit.

One of the women, her eyes deep-set and predatory, whispered to Peter, "His room is on the bottom floor to the left of the bar. It's the only room down there."

The other woman, her hair wound into a tight braid that dangled the length of her spine, added, "He's been silent all night. Our sisters have not reported any signs or sounds of movement."

Peter fondly thumped the woman's back and said, "Good work." He turned to me with an *I'm not asking, I'm telling* countenance.

"Jon, bring the key and open the chest."

"*I'm* going?" I almost shrilled. I was surprised—I'd assumed that they would want me somewhere safe and protected—like the king in a game of chess. But to be honest with myself, despite my sudden explosion of anxiety, I was a little eager to prove myself—to get something done, find out what I could, if anything, on my own so that I could bring it back home with me and use my knowledge to protect my loved ones, and say a fond *screw you* to the gargoyle Ranker in the process. I found myself thinking wryly about how I had to get more accustomed to life-and-death situations.

Peter scowled and scolded, "Everyone else is needed! Just sneak in. If you are threatened, it's more than likely that your necklace will release your power!"

He practically chased me down the stairs, and I slipped down, muttering darkly, "'More than likely.' What a bunch of..."

I pulled the key out of my jeans pocket and ran my fingers around it, realizing with some disgust at myself that they were shaking with fear.

In all of my time here, I had not seen any other inhabitants of the inn. I knew there *were* some, for, at night, I heard them stumbling up to their rooms to get lost in drunken slumber. The Ranker could be behind any one of those doors, listening for my footsteps. The thought made a shiver zip up from my feet to my head, raising the hair on the back of my neck.

In an effort to look behind me, I tripped over a patchy section of the hall rug and stumbled forward loudly. After a few stomps, I righted myself, eyes squeezed shut, biting my lip...waiting...

When no heads peeked from around the hall doors, I rushed the rest of the way down into the common area. It was strange to see it pitch dark and deserted with the chairs all up on the tables and the mugs stacked up behind the bar.

The bartender's room was around the bar opposite from me. I approached the door cautiously. It was painted a thick layer of black. The coat gleamed brightly from the blue-tinted moonlight beaming in through the stained-glass windows. The golden knob had become tarnished from the numerous times it had been turned by a dirty hand.

I skirted a table and pressed my ear to the cold wood, my fingertips grazing the frame. No sound.

I wrapped my hand around the knob, turned it squeakily, and pushed. It slid open against the floor along a well-worn trail of dust.

I was surprised to see that the walls within were *painted*–a deeper shade of beige. The ceiling, slanting together to form a triangular point, was steepled five feet above me. It was different from the main room behind me that had a flat ceiling and was more like the upper story I dwelled on. I held my coral necklace clamped in one hand–it made me feel comforted.

I came into a short hallway. As I traveled slowly down its length, I squinted hard at some pictures hanging up on the walls. They were tucked behind ornate frames and painted with dark, blotched colors. I saw a stern gray-haired man with long sideburns forming a bushy mustache beneath his nose. He could have been the bartender's grandfather. A plump, ruddy, smiley woman could have been his mother.

Glass crunched under my shoe. I stepped back and looked down. There was another picture, broken and dirty. Claw marks ravaged the wall right beneath the spot it had been hung, as if some beast had found it excessively intriguing. But carefully fingering away the sprinkled bits of destroyed framing, I came to a different conclusion.

This painting was of a stunningly pretty girl. Her eyes were warm and expressive, her lips turned up in a smile. Her sharp and elegant face, framed by strands of brown hair escaping her bun, hinted at European blood if there was such a thing here. It had to be the bartender's deceased wife.

Saddened, I crept on.

The sitting room was floored by a tapestry-like tasseled rug sewn with twisting patterns that had become faded. Bookshelves stood around the walls, their tomes dusty and unread. An oil lantern was positioned by a large red-velvet chair that faced a fireplace. Only one window illuminated the setting.

Standing just inside the room brought to my mind many bemusing and haunting thoughts. Maybe the bartender, on the lonesome nights when he took on the form of a wolf, would curl up in that high-backed chair and stare into the fire, or open the window and climb out to roam his lost beloved's garden, or trot over to her broken picture to ponder on all that could, and would, have been.

Sighing, I found another smaller door just beyond a bookcase and pushed it open, instinctively drawing to one side in case something should leap out. It didn't even cross my mind to wonder why no one appeared to be home. When nothing jumped out of the room, I rounded the wall into it, my sword bumping against my thigh as if to remind me it was there. I had my forefinger flittering around the hand guard, just waiting to spring the switchblade.

I was in the bedroom. The bed itself was surrounded by four violet curtains, tattered and dirty. The pillows had been gutted and their goose-down feathers were strewn all over the unkempt comforter. The window on the wall opposite me, on the other side of the bed, was open to the black night. A cold breeze made the curtains around the bed dance.

I was about to let myself feel the first stabs of frustration when the moon burst from the cloud cover and shone through the window. It flashed on something I could only see a sliver of from where I stood. It looked like wood.

I moved toward it and saw the chest. Inflating with success, I fell to my knees and brought out the key.

This chest was about the same size as the one I'd seen in the carpentry, but it was engraved and touched up with chipping paint. I ran my fingers over the peeling pictures of a dove, a rose, ringing bells, and two hands (one dainty and thin, the other large and strong) striving to touch.

The lock was small and bending in some places, so it took some effort to fit in the key. I hoped none of my friends snuck up behind me. I was wound up enough to give myself heart failure.

I forced the key to turn, worried it would snap, but instead I heard the satisfying *clunk* of the lock turning. I lifted the chest's lid, the moon shining its light on the contents.

Jewelry, and lots of it, reflected the moon in thousands of different-colored facets and planes. There were necklaces, earrings, and bracelets. I saw one hair tie made of pure pearls and diamonds. These couldn't be clues. Carefully, I removed the jewelry and set it aside in a weighty pile. A quilt, green and white with a flower pattern, was next. I took it out, spread it across my legs, and gave it a hasty pat-down, in case an object had been sewn into the lining. No luck. I fished out a few lacy baby outfits and an unopened bottle of wine before I came to an interesting box.

The box was hand-carved oak and studded with rubies so that none of the wood showed through. When the box was opened, I was struck by a sweet perfume that reminded me of the air after a fresh rain, recently cut fruit, and spices all at the same time. The smells wafted up from a coil of midnight-colored flowers resting in the box's silk interior. Lifting out the chain, I found out the blooms formed a necklace–like a Hawaiian lei. Attached to the lei by a thin strip of interlocking metal links was something like a silver ninja star, its ragged disk of teeth waiting for blood.

I tucked the lei into my sweater pocket, arranging the star so that it wouldn't cut into me, and tipped the box upside down in case I'd missed anything. Something clinked to the floor, bounced once, and flickered gold.

It was a wedding ring.

"Mmm," I murmured sadly, and nudged it with my toe into the rest of the abandoned jewelry.

The moon was covered by a sudden swath of clouds, and I was shrouded in menacingly quiet darkness that pressed against me like an evil force whispering threats in my ear. Not moving an inch, I waited for the lights to come back on, so to say.

When they did, and the moon obediently poked into the room, I turned. Face-to-face with the bartender.

"Prince, eh?" He gave me a wicked, lopsided grin, fangs dripping.

I was hit over the head from behind with what felt like a rock.

A bruising ache washed through my body from my skull, closely followed by a wave of numbness. My muscles slackened, my legs gave, and I entered a deep slumber where I knew absolutely nothing and had no dreams.

CHAPTER TWENTY-TWO:
MEANWHILE, BACK IN REALITY

ON TYSON'S FRONT PORCH

Getting Tyson home had been quite the ordeal. The hospital had been thrown into chaos by the attack and the staff had had a time of it relocating patients, making sure the power still worked, and assisting emergency personnel in tending to those who'd been injured or killed in the explosion.

Tyson had opted to go home early–his discharge had been coming up soon anyway–and his parents had helped him to get settled in his room. They were inside now, giving him his medication. He was putting on a brave face, but Nikki had been watching him closely on the ride home. His skin had become ashen, his jaw muscles tensed as if he were gritting his teeth against a whimper of pain, and his eyes were weary and hollow.

Nikki sat in the rocking chair on the porch, watching the horrible events from the hospital on repeat in her mind's eye. She dissected the weightlessness she'd felt as she'd been thrown toward her death, picking at the shock that'd rang through her upon realizing that she was about to die, as if fascinated by the sensations.

Her hero, Donovan, sat silently on the porch swing adjacent to her, watching her muse. She looked up at him, and he gave her a supportive little smile, one that she tried to return. He'd latched himself to her and her friends as if he wanted to keep an eye on her, and she found the sentiment admirable. It was exactly the kind of thing Jonathan would do. In the rare times they'd had a chance to talk, Donovan had told her that he was from England and that his grandmother, whom he'd been visiting in the hospital, had died in the attack. He seemed to find comfort in being close to others his own age, and Nikki wasn't going to turn him away. He was charming and helpful, and though she couldn't really say why, he seemed to fill a gap in her heart, in their circle of friends, like he was a plug that had shown up just in time to try and dam up their misery in the face of losing Jonathan.

Tyson's front door opened and Vince and Lia came out, speaking mutedly. Lia plopped into a chair beside Nikki and after a moment of hesitation, Vince took the only other remaining seat beside Donovan on the swing, giving him an awkward but courteous nod of the head.

"How's he doing?" Nikki asked Lia.

Lia appeared completely drained. Her hair was knotted and frizzy and dark circles shrouded her eyes. She shook her head, eyes wincing.

"He's in a lot of pain, but he's getting better." She leaned forward over her knees, resting her head in her hands and gazing forlornly down at a stain on the porch. "What is happening? Why is everything so...insane all of a sudden?"

"Whatever 'it' is, it is happening all over the world," Donovan said gently. He looked from Vince to Nikki, as if seeking their support or confirmation. "People have always been insane. Violent. But this is something else entirely."

"Mm," Vince grunted, nodding, "Like someone turned the crazy up and then broke the dial. But it all seems so organized; like it's happening methodically, step by step. There are plenty of terrorist groups claiming responsibility for everything, but no one's been caught and arrested. I think it's all talk."

Lia suddenly looked up at Nikki. "What did you call them, Nikki?"

Nikki looked at her blankly.

Lia combed some blonde strands out of her eyes and said, "At the hospital you said something about, um...Rankers, right?"

Nikki thought back. Everything leading up to the explosion was shrouded in a fog of fear and misery. She wrenched at her thoughts, trying to focus and penetrate that fog to remember what it was she had known, if anything. Hadn't it been something Jonathan had said? But it felt like months now since she'd seen Jonathan.

Her eyes stung with tears. What with all of the chaos now taking hold of their world, the police would have to prioritize their cases and she doubted that finding a missing teenager would be high on their list next to preventing further terrorist attacks or aiding victims of the violence. Something in her heart told her that it would be a long while before she saw Jonathan again, if she saw him at all.

Donovan stood up and moved to put a hand on her back. "It is okay," he said soothingly.

"I don't remember," Nikki croaked. She looked up and saw that Vince and Lia were looking at each other oddly, as if Donovan's presence bothered them. She felt a spurt of frustration with them— Donovan had saved her life, couldn't they at least give him a chance? But then Lia's phone buzzed and she pulled it from her pocket and read the screen.

"Kitty and Ben are coming over," she said. "They want to see Ty."

Donovan looked nervous, as if meeting more new people made him shy. He glanced at his car in the driveway and seemed about to suggest that he should leave, but before he could Nikki smiled wanly at him and said, "I'll introduce you when they get here."

Donovan's curving lips lifted in a meek smile and he bobbed his head and said, "I will not argue."

"Good," Nikki said.

She wasn't sure what Ben and Kitty would make of Donovan, but she told herself that she didn't care. Donovan made her feel safe, important, and cared for, just as Jonathan once had. And she was not about to let that go without a fight.

CHAPTER TWENTY-THREE:
I'm An Unlucky Boi

I was drifting peaceably, dreaming about Nikki, when something shook me so violently, I awoke.

My good ol' Ranker buddy had a hold of my hair and was jiggling my head around to wake me up. I had a splintering headache. It didn't help that I could barely breathe. The bartender had just tied the knot on the ropes that bound me to a chair.

The gargoyle's hood was down, revealing his stony snout and shark-like teeth. He held a sort of five-pronged trident that was made so that when it was plunged into a victim, it would have to be twisted to be pulled back out. The raven was balancing on its master's shoulder, occasionally flapping its wings.

I was in the main room of the bar, right in the center spot. All of the tables and chairs had been pushed to the sides to allow my captors room to pace.

The lei I had so rightfully obtained was now around the Ranker's neck, and the sight of the flowers resting against his chest would have made me laugh if I had thought it would've gotten me somewhere. But no, here I was. Tied to a chair. La-de-da.

"Intercepting our clues," he said slowly, scornfully. "That's your plan?"

The familiarity of his voice stung me. Seeing the monster that had haunted my nightmares so frequently of late brought a quiver of fear to my stomach.

The Ranker was enjoying what looked like a Bowl of Bemusement. I wondered if it affected him the same way it did normal people, or if it made him more powerful. I was leaning toward the latter. The monster set his half-full bowl down on the ground next to me and ran a snakelike tongue around his jowls. His small eyes were scarlet, his lipless mouth arranged into an ecstatic smirk. It felt wrong to see a human expression being used by a monster.

I nodded at the bowl. My voice was still a little slurry, and I tried to get my aching brain to stop ringing, but I asked, "What do the clues mean? If you're guiding people toward a rendezvous point or something, then what's with the soup? Is it in case they need a pick-me-up?"

The werewolf's glowing eyes narrowed. He glanced at the Ranker, then away. I took note of his reaction, then frowned up at the gargoyle when he said, "A means to an end. It would have given our troops additional strength–"

"–And it was corrupting dreamers for you, too," I added, "People having nightmares who were trying to escape their pain. Or dream creations. You were creating more bodies to throw into the war."

"The more, the merrier," the Ranker said brightly.

"Where are my friends?" I asked, my voice quivering.

The Ranker, and the bartender hunched behind me, shared a laugh. Swishing his robe, the gargoyle cried, "They are gone, Jonathan. They've left you."

My heart sank. I tried to counter his retort with reasoning. "No, they...they wouldn't leave me because–"

"What?" The Ranker simpered, putting on a voice as if he were talking to a baby. "Because you're their prince?"

"No!" I snapped, face burning.

The gargoyle grabbed my chin in one cold claw and looked observantly down into my face. "You haven't learned courage yet," he said. "Fear, yes. Anger is there as well. But I don't see bravery." He released me with a flick of his wrist, jerking my head.

"Oh, yeah?" I retorted. My conscience was warning me to keep my cool, but I had hardly gotten any restful sleep and was a tad grumpy. "How's Garrett doing? I think I remember kickin' his ass!"

The bartender sucked in a breath. The raven cawed. The Ranker halted in his tracks.

Having seen that I'd hit a sore spot, I rushed mindlessly on. "The chicken-shit had to go and stick a knife in my back. So don't stand there and tell me *I* have no courage!"

"*Shut up!*" The Ranker whirled and struck me in the cheek with the back of his claw. It felt like someone had thrown a rock at my temple. My vision blurred, my head wailed in protest, and I threatened to pass out again. The Ranker had his fists balled in rage. His tail danced like a lashing serpent.

"You know nothing," he snarled. "There are different kinds of courage. The sort *you* lack requires relying on faith alone. You're still afraid to die."

I didn't deny his statement but moved my tongue around the inside of my mouth, searching for loose teeth, and said quizzically, "Faith? You mean, like, praying?" I thought back to the powerful effect that had had on the gargoyle in my nightmare and added, "'Cause I could do that if you want me too."

The stone beast chuckled scathingly. "To whom? You don't even know your God. Go on and try. Your words would be empty. Where will you go when you die? How will you face your end?"

"I haven't ever had time to think about it," I lied, trying to keep him talking so that he wouldn't move on to the inevitable: using that nasty-looking weapon of his.

The gargoyle tightened his grip on his trident with a satanic grin and said, "Nor will you ever have any."

"You must have been a great kid to have in class," I jabbed sarcastically, hiding my terror, as usual, behind a sassy facade. I began to pull at my bindings more frantically.

I knew almost without a doubt that Peter and the others were around here somewhere close by, but it would be nice of them to show themselves *before* I got poked full of holes. I was quite accustomed to pain: football, snowboarding, and of course those infrequent beatings I would get from Dad had all helped to up my pain threshold. Don't get me wrong, I *so* wasn't looking forward to being skewered, but I would try and take it with as much dignity and courage as possible.

The gargoyle hefted his trident like a javelin and aimed it at my torso. I looked away and grimaced...waiting...

"Wait!" a voice barked. Surprised, I watched the bartender cross around in front of me. The gargoyle halted his trident by force of will. The points just barely tapped the werewolf's chest, tilting him back.

Withdrawing, the Ranker quivered furiously. His raven took flight and landed on a stool, croaking irritably. Horned head lowered, the Ranker growled, "How dare you stay my killing stroke! You have defied the command of Garrett and, in doing so, our Liege Master—king of death, nightmares, and power. The prince must be killed!"

I felt the knot chafing my wrists begin to loosen. I leaned to the side to watch what the Ranker was doing around the werewolf, and at the same time caught movement out the stained-glass window in the wall slightly ahead and to the left of me. That's where everyone was... It seemed I wasn't alone after all.

The bartender defended his actions. "I thought Garrett wanted to kill the boy himself."

The gargoyle squirmed uncomfortably and muttered, "It's not really his call, it's the—"

"Liege Master's, I know," the bartender interrupted. "But he's appointed Garrett to take his place and to do that, he needs Jonathan alive."

"Not necessarily," the gargoyle said in a dangerous low voice. "He may just need the boy's blood."

The werewolf fidgeted on the spot, his eyes searching the room, and he finally said, in an uncomfortable sort of voice, "I don't want blood shed unnecessarily on my floor."

I was genuinely shocked. Did this guy actually have a conscience? The Ranker chuckled darkly, his thick shoulders shaking with mirth. "Unnecessary blood? This is the beast that entered your inn as a griffin. That shamed you by lying and wandering the streets disguised as a warrior. That slipped past your Dark Knight sentry that

I so kindly posted at this forsaken bog's entrance to stop these very people from entering. He was rummaging through your wife's old chest, sword fighting in her garden." He laughed again.

The raven had hopped over to its master's bowl and began slurping from it, keeping a beady eye on me and jabbing its beak at my pant leg when I shifted to get leverage on the bindings.

With each accusation the Ranker made against me, the bartender's head hung lower and lower. The gargoyle finished, "You *like* blood. You're a werewolf." And for emphasis, he drifted over to the moonlight falling in through the window.

The bartender hugged himself and said, "It's taking all I have not to shift forms right now. Luckily the moon has begun to wane."

"*Yes, you see?*" cried the Ranker, pointing at me triumphantly. "It is people like him that bring this curse upon you and your kind. Their mindlessly intrusive attempts at heroics only backfire upon the countless thousands they fight to protect. If it weren't for that stupid young villager who found a scrawny malnourished 'wolf' wandering the swamps and treated it back to health in secret, out of the kindness of his sentimental heart, your wife would still live, you would be happily wed, and the boy who went out of his way to care for a poor creature would not be dead at its teeth. That is how all kindness is repaid. And was there vengeance on the animal? No! The beast escaped and left another in its place."

The bartender recoiled and looked over his shoulder at me, hurt and anger in his glowing green eyes. But suspicion had slowly crept into my mind...the gargoyle was manipulating the werewolf, using his sorrow and anguish against him. Peter had said that that's how Rankers worked—breaking people's spirits by going after the ones they loved. Like little lightbulbs flickering on, my thoughts all started to connect until, for the first time, I thought I understood the Rankers' tactics—and how they had managed to corrupt the bartender.

"Oh, come on!" I said gently, giving the poor man a pitying look. "Why is 'gullible' written on the ceiling?"

I waited for one of them to glance up, and when neither did, I stretched out my legs pompously, ready to divulge my knowledge.

"I have read in a reliable book, written by a wise scholar, that werewolves are not, in fact, swamp-dwelling creatures. They are natural to woods and deciduous forests where prey is plentiful and they can remain hidden. If anything, it sounds to me like that sick old werewolf was *brought* here on purpose and meant to be found and taken in. I'll bet my sword"—which I noticed was over against the wall—"that this gargoyle brought it here, meaning for it to kill your wife, though possibly not infect you, so that you would be mentally and emotionally weak enough to do whatever he wanted for whatever false promises he made you."

The Ranker was giving me looks of fury and loathing. Obviously, I wasn't too far off the mark, if at all. I felt bad picking on the bartender like that, but he needed this—closure. Justice. It was nice to play a part in giving him that. Especially when the creep who had ruined his life was standing right there in front of him, glowering at me.

"You...you have a point..." the bartender said meditatively. He eyed the gargoyle, showing his sharp teeth in a wild scowl, and started a fresh argument with him. I lost all focus on the conversation: I had an idea. The gargoyle was ready to go Conan the Barbarian on me with his trident, and I needed a big distraction.

I scooched my chair little by little to the left, away from the Bowl of Bemusement. The raven belched and looked up from the meal it was enjoying to watch the werewolf poke the Ranker bravely in the chest a few times while bellowing in his face. I teetered side to side, building up momentum, the chair legs loudly clunking on the floor. But the Ranker had begun to shout back and was beyond hearing me. The raven was flapping, bloated with soup, around the bartender, harassing his tangled hair with its talons. I rocked hard to the right and fell over with a tremendous thud.

I had moved far enough to the side so that my face smashed right into the rest of the stew. The foul liquid ran up my nose and in my eyes, burning. I took a mouthful and held it, though it stung my tongue like peppers. Already it was quickening my heart rate and racing my blood. If I swallowed, it would turn me into the same crazy lunatic that was kicked out of the bar last evening.

My actions had finally caught attention, and the Ranker shoved past the bartender and rudely lifted the chair back on its feet. The werewolf pushed in beside the gargoyle so that both of their angry faces took up my vision.

The Ranker scowled. "Don't think you can–" He broke off, obviously wondering why my cheeks were puffed out.

I flicked my eyebrows up and down at him, turned to the bartender, and spat my mouthful into his face. The werewolf cried out, his hands flying to his eyes. His voice deepened into a harsh roar–like a noise from a nightmare. Long, wavy black fur sprouted weed-like from his pores, bursting from the fabric of his clothes. A bushy tail came from the seat of his pants, his jaws lengthened, his head hair shrank back and became a grizzly mane about his chest and neck. By the time the bartender had finished transforming, he was the size of a bear with strength rippling in the muscles of his legs and sides.

I had read that if someone stared at a werewolf, the eye contact would aggravate it and push it into attacking. So, I looked away. But, uh-oh...the Ranker didn't. He was gaping at the monster before him with shock and alarm. Snarling, the wolf leaped at the gargoyle, slamming him into the bar. The lei was forced off the Ranker's neck, landing on the floor. The raven flew around their heads, cawing repeatedly.

With a burst of splintered wood, Peter swooped through the doorway in griffin form. He spread his wings to brake and, with precise aim, sliced the ropes tying my wrists with a large talon. I shouldered the bonds off over my head, massaging my arms.

The werewolf yelped and backed into a corner. A jagged cut ran from his chest to his back from the bloodied tips of the Ranker's trident. The gargoyle regained his balance, perched hunched over on the bar just like the gothic stone sentinel that he was. His red eyes zeroed in on me standing free beside my empty chair, and then landed on Peter.

Peter's huge, brown-feathered body was low as if to pounce, and he shrieked challengingly. The gargoyle bared his teeth and hissed. Pushing off the bar, he bowled Peter over. The two somersaulted into a wall, where Peter shattered one of the windows with his wing, and the two began fighting for death grips in a shower of colorful glass shards.

I grabbed my sword, strapped it on, and put the lei back in my pocket.

The werewolf whimpered, watching the primal violence of the conflict now tearing up his bar. He licked at his long, bloody wound, then limped out into the street, where sounds of struggle were beginning to wake up the bog dwellers. People started screaming. Guns were fired. (I guessed from the squadron since the villagers didn't have enough gun-powder to shoot off their pinkie toes.) Fire started mysteriously writhing to life from random places, lighting up the streets in yellow and red light.

People were running by, children tucked under their parent's arms or torn away by the rampaging crowds. Kayle flew by, his burly griffin form as dark as the night. He gave a harsh eagle cry and corrected the path of one wandering child with a scoop forward from his wing. Mariah was diving to strike with her talons at an amassing group of armor-clad Dark Knights. Two were tangled up in knots of thorny vines that Mariah was sprouting up with her power. The squadron was spread out and hidden behind houses and barrels of water, readying their weapons and signaling commands to each other.

The raven came out of nowhere.

It burst into my face with a formidable caw and a beat of its feathers. One of its hooked little talons grazed my eyelid, but not hard enough to draw blood. I turned away, shielding my eyes with an upraised arm. The raven wrapped its feet around my limb and began to peck viciously at any part of me I allowed it to reach.

Desperate, I clenched my other hand around the hand-guard of my sword, blindly feeling for the switchblade handle. Once I'd grasped it, I flung it open, pinned the raven against the wall with the arm it had perched on, and stabbed deep into its chest. The bird emitted a horrible high-pitched croak, flapped its wings feebly, and fell dead to the floor with a dull thump.

I hastily shook the droplets of blood from my knife, drying each side of it on the legs of my jeans. I put it back in its compartment and this time drew my sword.

It crashed to the floor, totally bursting my bubble. So much for cool and in control.

I had never killed a thing in my life, except for maybe the occasional bug or two, or the grouse I'd hunted from a distance. And now I had just sliced open a bird up close and personal and wiped its blood on my clothes! Pretty soon, I'd be catching fish with my teeth or something, like a complete barbarian.

To compensate for my atrocious crime of actually murdering a bird, I said to its lifeless body, "That's for impersonating my mom."

The gargoyle seemed to be slowly gaining the upper hand. His trident had cut several places on Peter's body, and the old griffin was wheezing for air.

I raised my arms and snuck forward, aiming to slash straight down into the Ranker's spine, but without even looking, the gargoyle kicked back and knocked me to the floor with an aching chest. I put my hand on my sternum, feeling for damage, and then retreated to one side to rethink my plans.

Two Dark Knights slipped in, holding a weighted net between them. When the Ranker had cornered Peter, the two swung it over him, and he got tangled in the corded ropes. Almost as soon as he was trapped, Peter started biting at his restraints, snapping holes that were stretching increasingly wider the harder he pushed out with his pinned wings. The Dark Knights stood with swords out and ready should Peter escape.

The gargoyle swept out his cloak (dark and cliché) and spun to me. I tried to raise my sword; the task had become doubly difficult with my bruised chest muscles.

"Now we will see just how brave you are, little griffin," the Ranker hissed. His voice was almost rendered unintelligible by the hatred twisting his words. "Will you weep and beg as you did so many times in your nightmares?"

"You don't know me," I spat.

The Ranker charged, aiming to thrust his trident up into my guts, but I caught it on the edge of my sword and managed to redirect it past me. I shuffled around him, alert, my muscles tensed and my nerves jingling with energy.

"I only know what I have witnessed," he replied. There was something oily and clever in his voice now. "My creator spent long years carefully crafting me, committing the atrocities that would feed me, nurture me. Eventually I became strong enough to take a form, to act independently of him and begin creating my own nightmares in the minds of humans. But I could not have known the significance of his final act. His final murder."

The Ranker's eyes danced. "We knew who she was, of course, my fellow Rankers and me. *Your* kind may be ignorant to the constant battle waging among humans, the battle between Ranker and Griffin, but not us, the creations of darkness. When my creator snuffed so bright a light as hers, oh, how we celebrated." He licked his lips as if relishing a delicious meal.

I stared at him. And in one heartbeat, I understood.

"You killed my mother," I breathed.

"No," he said, "Your mother was killed by a *man*."

I took him in; the height of him, the lifeless eyes, the stony skin and shark-like smile and in those features, if I tried, I could pick out the features of a human. A man. The man who had murdered my mother.

I could feel the blood leave my face and I stumbled on the spot, having to quickly lock my legs and brace my feet before I sank to the floor.

"Yes, now you understand," the gargoyle whispered.

I *did* understand, much better now. Until now I had seen the conflict with the Rankers as nothing more than that–a storybook battle between good and evil, against monsters that fed on wickedness. But that was only half-right. The Rankers were terrible, sure, and their influence was broad. But when it came down to it, they were just creations. The *true* power, the real evil, lay with their creators. With dreamers. With humans. And that realization, that the bulk of the threat in the Ranker war came not from an outside source but from within every man, woman, and child, from the darkness they *allowed* to develop inside them, chilled me to my core.

"They killed your creator," I said weakly, trying to kick my brain back into gear. But my entire body felt like lead now.

He shrugged. "And we lost a valuable tool. But I had become independent from him, and could continue my own work in the minds of your kind. We hadn't anticipated Esther's son becoming the next *prince*," he said this snidely. "We suspected as much, when rumors began to spread that the White Griffin had chosen another, and your name started to cross lips, but we couldn't know for sure. But with Esther's light being so bright, I suppose it doesn't come as too much of a surprise. Talk about coincidence, eh?

"So," he raised the trident and gave it a shake as if to remind me that it was there. "Now you know. Do you truly feel brave, little prince?"

"Jonathan, look out!" Peter barked. I whipped my head around to see one of the Dark Knights striding toward me with his weapon lifted.

But it was at that moment that Kayle decided to drop in.

He shot in through the hole Peter had made; only, Kayle was on fire. Like, literally.

His eyes were molten yellow orbs; smoke billowed from his beak in black clouds. Tongues of furnace-hot heat wafted from his flickering body. "Good morning, sunshine!" he screamed at the gargoyle in a distorted, crackling voice.

For some reason, his words stirred something in me, and my coral necklace turned warm at my neck.

Kayle landed, but his paws didn't set anything on fire unless he wanted them to. He jerked out with his beak and caught a mouthful of the Ranker's cloak. The material made a ripping sound as it was stretched.

I, meanwhile, was about to remove my necklace should it grow too hot to endure. But instead of burning up, tendrils of its warmth spread up my neck, into my face, and behind my eyeballs into my brain. It was like a door had been opened: I knew how to control my ability to shift.

Concentrating on that knowledge, I hastily turned into a griffin, taking a brief moment to stretch my powerful new muscles and get reacquainted with how to move. My weapons were gone, but I no longer needed them. My daggers were my talons, sickle-shaped and needle-sharp. My sword was my beak, hooked like an eagle's and a foot long.

Kayle saw that I was strong enough to kick some gargoyle butt and darted away to attack the knights guarding Peter.

The Ranker gripped his trident and circled me. I turned with him, keeping him in my sights. And then another strange thing happened: he told me what he was going to do right before he did it.

The Ranker puffed in a labored voice, "I'll go for his eyes."

I stepped to one side just as the prongs of his trident appeared where my face had been moments before. He stumbled, off-balance by my dodge, and I slashed out with my talons, ripping five gashes in the hem of his robe. I gritted my beak when I felt unyielding stone under my claws.

How could I kill something made of rock?

"I'll come around at his back!" the Ranker declared. He arched his spine and twisted, gracefully gouging down with his weapon. I snapped my wings wide, buffeting the monster back and knocking the trident from his hands. I took the weapon up in my mouth and bit down hard. The metal screeched and bent into an upside-down U shape. I dropped it to the floor where it rang hollowly, virtually useless.

Now we had to fight tooth and claw. We locked together like feral beasts, pain so frequent it was like a third being hovering around us. For some time, we fought and struggled, the sky outside melding into the off-white that was the color of the average sunny swamp sky.

I took a blow to the throat and gagged, trying to find air with mounting terror. Finally, I was able to breathe, but that had been a close one. I could so easily turn and run...or fly, but then not only would I be leaving behind my new friends but also my new responsibility as the prince that everyone said I was—the duty handed down from griffin child to griffin child to try and end the war with the Rankers and save the world. If I turned tail now, countless millions would die. Tyson, Father, Nikki... With my girlfriend's name came a burst of energy.

I waited for the gargoyle's next monologue. This time, there came two sentences at the same time. But one was louder than the other. I thought it sounded like he said, "Can he understand me?" in a hushed and scared voice, and then, "The neck!" in a tone that echoed with finality.

He reached out with his hand, preparing to crush my jugular, but I ducked and pounced into his knees—just like when I tackled someone in football when I was playing defense.

With a breathtaking flash, the sun appeared for the first time since I'd arrived through the thick clouds covering the bog. Its beautiful golden touch reached in the tavern doorway and threw dazzlingly bright colors and shapes through the stained-glass windows.

Peter squinted his eyes at the light, but Kayle, no longer on fire, smiled full-on into the glow, his maroon irises turned a honey red.

I had pushed the gargoyle into the light from the doorway, and he flinched as if bitten. "*Nooooooo!*" he bellowed, as if trying to fight back some mighty, progressing foe. I was waiting for him to move away into the shadows, but then realized that he couldn't—his feet were frozen to the floor. Actually, not exactly frozen but turned into inanimate granite.

Little by little, the Ranker became rigid, first his legs, then his torso, then his arms. He twisted his head to me, glaring with his red eyes. "Garrett...will..." He struggled to finish his last sentence, but his eyes glazed over and turned into slits of black obsidian, his mouth open in an eternal roar.

I shivered. Even though he had become a statue, I could still feel a sort of evil emanating from him—an immortal anger and spite.

With the sound of a small mountain crumbling, the Ranker broke up into a pile of rubble, dust ejecting up in a cloud turned gold in the sunlight.

And that was how I killed my first Ranker.

CHAPTER TWENTY-FOUR:
MEANWHILE, BACK IN REALITY

AT JONATHAN'S HOUSE

Ethan He'klarr hadn't shaved in days. The clothes he wore were wrinkled, his baggy eyes dry.

Jonathan's father had come to accept that his son was dead. But he knew that if his mind lingered on that thought, he would go crazy with guilt and remorse, and some sore part of him would surge up and force him to keep fighting.

He didn't want to fight; he was sick and tired of hope–and he was drained of faith.

On the news, signs of terror and possible war made common headlines. His son's friends had survived that truck crashing into the hospital because of the heroics of a nice, strange young man. But so many others had died. And that was just the beginning. There were minor bombings all over Europe, and no one knew who was causing them. South America was suffering floods and storms. Africa, droughts. The US was wracked with crime.

Ethan welcomed the trouble. Anything to ease his suffering–or end it. Some small part of him could not help but believe that all of this was his fault. He had spent his whole life pushing Jonathan away. Maybe, if he'd been there, if he'd been more involved, if he'd had more conversations with his son, then he would've learned something about his life and the people he was interacting with; something that he could've told the police that would have helped them to track him down or find his attacker.

Ethan grimaced, thinking of the blood the police had found at the scene, and the last time he'd seen Jonathan, when he'd hit him across the face. He lifted one hand and rested it across his eyes as if to keep the tears in. What was left? What did he have to live for? He had lost the last, most precious thing in his life.

It was then, when his mind nibbled bitterly on that thought, that a vanilla-scented perfume slipped beneath his nose, and he closed his eyes, resting his head back against his chair.

Esther...

His wife's voice seemed to sound by his ear, but when he turned his head, Esther wasn't there. Maybe he was going mad. Maybe he was dreaming. But Ethan forced himself to relax and listened.

His wife's voice came again. "Darling...our son is safe and well."

Ethan's heart raced. "But, where is he? Has he left because of me?"

Esther's gentle tone carried a ring of sympathy. "He is not far, love. You will see him again. Have faith. Be strong, be patient, and wait..."

And then her voice and the scent of her perfume were gone. Ethan sighed longingly–sinking back into his vegetative state. But he felt, with some amusement, an indescribable feeling of hope blossom in his heart. He may have exhausted all of his limited resources in attempting to find his son, he may have done all that he could for the time being, but this was by no means the end.

AT TYSON'S HOUSE

Tyson's bedroom had been turned into a mini-hospital. He was getting better, day by day—could achieve a great speed on his wheelchair and could breathe without obstruction. His IV was no longer needed, only bed rest, fluids, and food he could keep down.

Posters of snowboarders, skateboarders, and some of his favorite movies were plastered all over the place haphazardly. A partially empty bookcase, his bed, a nightstand with a lamp, and a closet full of clothes, snowboard, and miscellaneous collectibles were normally the only other things showing that his bedroom was actually dwelled in. But today, six people sat in chairs brought in from the kitchen around his bed, wide awake despite the fact that it was almost four in the morning.

Vince was twiddling his thumbs—a new nervous habit—and tapping his shoes. Lia was slowly caressing Tyson's hand with her own. Ben and Kitty were close together, Kitty staring up at the light, Ben looking hard at the boy Nikki was sitting beside.

There was something so weird about the new kid. His voice, looks, habits, the way he moved even. It was almost...royal...as if he were a duke. He wasn't mean, but he was also *too* nice and polite. It made Ben sick.

"This is Donovan," Nikki said to Ben and Kitty, touching Donovan's arm. "He just came from England last week and was in the hospital to visit his grandmother. He saved my life." She smiled at her hero gently. There were mumbles of gratitude, and Donovan dipped his head, his eyes briefly veiled.

Ben was very good at reading people and interrogating them without their knowledge. Not a person on the planet could avoid answering a question he asked. In an indifferent tone of voice, Ben queried, "How is she? Your grandmother?"

Donovan's head slowly tilted toward him. He blinked. "She has passed. The explosion obliterated her room." He looked minimally sad, turning down one corner of his mouth and averting his gaze.

Vince understood what was happening and watched the spectacle without trying to seem too wary. When they'd first met, back before Ben had honed his skill, Ben's probing questions had earned him a punch in the jaw from Vince before Jonathan had explained that he was just trying to be friendly and get to know him. Now it was Vince's turn to be ready if Donovan got too uptight.

Ben tilted his head, looking genuinely curious. "If you're from England, where's your accent?"

Kitty drew away from him, shocked at how brash he was being. "Ben!"

A frown glimmered across Donovan's face, but he concealed it just as quickly behind a mask of polite grace. "It is alright," he consoled Kitty without looking at her.

Ben's eyes hadn't even moved from Donovan's face. Donovan seemed to have figured out what he was doing, so he decided to call it quits for the time being–after he got his answer.

Donovan spoke curtly, but not enough for anyone but Ben to notice: "I was born in Connecticut. I studied in England for a year and a half. Psychology and the arts."

Kitty jumped in with a question of her own. "What's it like over there?"

"Terrible," Donovan murmured, and Ben noticed with puzzlement that, once again, Donovan was not looking at Kitty as he spoke to her, but gazing at the floor by her chair legs or the wall just beside her head. "Men and women are terrified and childless. Public places are in ruins. No one knows what to do or who to blame." Sad mumbles droned through the room.

"We have to do something," Lia declared morosely, resting her forehead in the palm of her hand. "Talk to someone, go somewhere. We can't just sit here and wait for..." She didn't finish her sentence, shaking her head at the floor.

Everyone but Donovan, who knew nothing about how close the friends were, surreptitiously looked at Tyson. It was a known fact that Ty was second-in-command whenever Jonathan was gone.

The young man straightened up as best he could and made sure to look into every eye when he spoke. "There's a town meeting soon. We'll go and see what's on everyone's minds and make a few suggestions of our own."

"I hope it's good news." Vince sighed.

Ben read the room, absorbing his friends' sorrow. He was sad, too. In all of his admittedly sheltered life, he had never thought that one of his best friends would go missing, or that another of his friends would almost die in a plane crash. He peeked at Donovan, who was watching him back with an unreadable expression—something almost...calculating in his deep blue eyes.

Ben's heart thudded in his chest as an uncanny, foreboding feeling crept along his back. Whatever was happening, this wasn't the end. Something told him that it was going to get a lot worse. But if there was anything he'd learned in fire cadets about traumatic injuries, it was that the smallest wound was sometimes the most lethal, and what seemed to be the most harmless symptom was sometimes masking a more malicious disease. Carefully, so that none of his friends would see, Ben gave Donovan the kind of smile that said, *I'm onto you.* Donovan blinked at him and looked away.

Leaning back, tangling his fingers with Kitty's, Ben took comfort in the fact that, in a world where nothing made sense anymore, he had stumbled upon one certain truth: there was something wrong with Donovan. And Ben was going to find out exactly what it was.

CHAPTER TWENTY-FIVE:
VICTORIOUS

The two Dark Knights that had been watching Peter were lying over by the wall, their armor ravaged by Kayle's talons.

"Are you alright?" Peter asked me. He acted almost reverent. I recognized his lowered tail and half-open wings to be signs of submission—had read as much in Peter's book on griffins.

"I'm fine," I said, shaking myself and watching a few of my feathers float to the floor. "Are you two?"

Kayle looked at Peter, and when the older griffin nodded, he did too, adding, "And even better, we can finally leave this place."

We stepped outside. Kayle let Peter lean against him, both moving at a slow, exhausted shuffle. I sagged against the buckled doorframe, surveying the damage that had been done. Dead Dark Knights littered the street. Sword slashes and pockmarks from daggers marred the sides of shops and still-leaking barrels of water.

As my adrenaline leaked away, true, bone-deep exhaustion settled in. I pondered all that I'd learned. I'd just terminated the Ranker that had killed my mom—but that wasn't right. I had killed the Ranker of the *man* who had murdered my mom. Rankers were just the manifestations of the shadows that already existed in the human heart. I wasn't here to do battle against monsters, I was here to fight the human condition.

I spent some time wandering up and down the street, trying to shake off the rest of my post-battle jitters and counting our losses. There were wounded—knife grazes, bumps, and bruises, and one of the Amazons had a fractured arm. But the only truly dangerous casualty on our side was one young army man who had most of his forearm cut off. Already, Mariah was growing it back, her jeweled collar gleaming.

The sky was a pristine blue, the air fresh and young. Villagers were cracking their doors, peeking outside. Some were returning from the depths of the bog where they had run to escape the fight. Their eyes were big and glassy, and they avoided our gazes. A few of the more polite inhabitants were touching their hands to their foreheads in a sort of salute. I guess we weren't the only ones who hadn't liked the Dark Knights.

Something dark moved in the corner of my vision–a shadow within a shadow. I looked over alertly. It was the bartender, still a shaggy black wolf. He was cautiously padding over, limping on his injured leg. I let him come close enough to where we stood eye to eye, him a little taller than me in my griffin form. He tilted his head to one side and wagged his tail a little. There was joy in his eyes–he was finally at peace. I smiled at him, and he barked in a friendly manner, letting his tongue hang out and beginning to pant.

"You're welcome." I chuckled. "No one will ever trouble you again." He wagged his tail jauntily and loped off in the direction of his wife's garden.

"Excuse me," I heard a familiar voice say. "Do you know where the assassin is?"

Entertained, I watched the carpenter move from the confused samurai he had just confronted to the gladiator Marcus. He repeated his question.

"No..." Marcus replied, scratching his head. The carpenter moved on and blanched, one hand on his chest. He had just seen griffin-Mariah, who was growing another fruit of some sort to eat. His eyes wandered to the rest of us, his mouth open in awe.

I faced him, making him jump.

"Call me Jonathan," I said.

The man stared at me for a few long seconds, his brow furrowing with anger. Crossing his arms, he growled, "What's going on? Why are you really here? I trust it wasn't only to rid us of the blasphemous Dark Knights?" I studied my talons, feeling guilty. A moment went by while the carpenter waited for me to speak.

"Who are you really?" he pressed. Peter walked by on his way to talk to Sergeant Flaherty. As he passed, he clipped my beak with his wing–giving me the okay to explain.

I moved toward the carpenter, who stepped back in fear, but I sat down a few feet from him and said softly, "I am here...to help defeat the Rankers."

The carpenter didn't have the same reaction I'd had when I had been whacked over the head with almost those same words. I braced myself for sarcasm or skepticism. ("Well, if you're here to save the world, then I'm gonna go carpenter-up my coffin.") Instead, he literally wriggled, and a joyful expression appeared on his face.

"Are you...the next prince?" he asked hopefully.

I almost whimpered, having come to hate that word, but cleared my throat and said, "Yes."

The carpenter laughed. "I had heard rumors, but I never thought..." Practically jumping, he walked a circle around me, babbling good-naturedly about how kingly I looked. Gesturing at the others, he remarked, "You must be the ones sent out by the White Griffin!"

Kayle extracted his head from a barrel he was drinking from and said, "That we be."

Some of the villagers had gathered in a ring around us, and their voices mingled into unintelligible chatter as they discussed the good news among themselves. Even the old woman who had confronted me outside the carpenter's shop was smiling.

The carpenter was pacing now, frowning with determination and pumping his arms. "I have waited for so long. I want to help. Take me with you!" A clamor of agreement went up from the villagers, who began to press in closer to try and make their individual voices heard.

Peter called for quiet and shouted, "It is a dear sight to me, all you who are so eager to assist us, but in all honesty, you would only encumber us."

Indignant, uproarious voices rose up in a tidal wave of sound, each person trying to justify themselves.

"I can run faster than anyone here!" one young woman called.

A boy shouted, "I can fell a bumblebee with my slingshot if the need called for it!"

The cacophony got louder and louder–I pinned my ears back, still feeling edgy from the battle. I stood up and opened my wings, and the voices turned off as a unit. Peter clacked his long beak contemplatively and said shrewdly, "Alright. Any can come along if they are ready to take the risks. You have been ruled tyrannically by a few Dark Knights for a couple of weeks. Those creatures are cunning, thieving, and openly malicious. But you cannot begin to understand those who employ them: the Rankers.

"If you defy a Ranker, they will first go after your family. Most often, they use their easy, most painless tactic: they burn your family's house down while they're barricaded inside." A few people blanched. Peter stood up and started pacing, looking into each and every face. "Next, after a few days have passed, during which they will allow you time to grieve, so that the true bitterness of your loss sinks in like salt in an open wound, they'll go after your friends. They'll probably torture them slowly, and leave them just alive enough so that when you find them, you can share a final farewell." Peter, immense, stolid, majestic in his dark plumage and bristling fur, sat again and bowed his head so that he was gazing at everyone through the ridge of his eagle's brow. "Finally, they will kill you after torturing you until you go insane or unless you join them. I won't go into details, but if you are willing to travel to dangerous and long-distanced places, possibly only to die the most excruciating of deaths, you are welcome to come."

Even before Peter had finished speaking, people were wandering off, trying to do so unnoticed. Some shouted that they would travel to the capital themselves, though I didn't put much faith in their promises. The picture Peter had painted was not a nice one. I had half a mind to walk off myself.

Family and friends? Did that mean that mine were in danger? Eventually, only the carpenter still stood with us.

Mariah's brows raised, impressed, over her mango. Kayle and the marine sergeant were laughing in half disbelief, half admiration.

The carpenter seemed smug as he proclaimed, "I stand by what I said before. I wish to help. I've nothing to lose."

Peter shook his grizzled head sadly. "You'd be surprised at how much you *do* have to lose whenever the end comes. But I was serious about what I said before: you can't come with us." The carpenter looked crestfallen. Watching him studiously with his silver eyes, Peter relented. "But the White Griffin may find some use for you at the capital."

The carpenter brightened, the sun shining warmly on his flushed face. "This is wonderful news! I can use my craftsmanship to make weapons, and I have a few ideas that could revolutionize our armor and fortresses!"

Peter strode forward and sat back on his haunches, raising one long claw to tap each of the carpenter's shoulders. "Then go forth, and may you be blessed for your willingness to sacrifice yourself for the greater good. What is your name?"

"J-Joshua, sir," the carpenter stammered.

In what seemed like some sort of an initiation or welcoming, everyone repeated, "Joshua." I hurriedly added my voice, excited for the friendly man.

Peter whistled toward the gap in the bog fence, and the trilling pitch echoed into the marsh. He was calling for a mysterious creature known as the eso-grohd. We all heard its hoof beats before we saw it, a fact none too surprising as the eso-grohd could only be seen by those whom it allowed to see. From straight ahead in the gloom approached a tall, thin creature. When it came into the light, Joshua made a small mewling sound of bewilderment.

Eso-grohds came in many colors. This one was a pale violet with a white mane and fringe at the end of its long tail. Its stilt-like legs ended in deer hooves, but its body and face resembled a greyhound's with a tapered muzzle and wide, erect ears. Instead of canines, the creature had flat, horsey molars used to grind up the vegetation native to its habitat.

Once it reached us, the eso-grohd bucked its neck to flick away its silky forelock and pranced sideways playfully. Peter bowed to the creature, who returned the gesture in kind, and said, "This animal will take you safely to your destination. You can trust him with your life—once you ride him, he will become your faithful friend and steed until your bond is broken by death. But forgive me; I must make sure he is still on our side."

Peter sniffed the air; his head protruded forward toward the tolerant eso-grohd. An eso-grohd normally didn't have a bad bone in its body. It was wholly pure, just like its cousin the unicorn. But once an eso-grohd had been tainted by evil or Dark Magick, it would do the dark bidding of whatever possessed it. One of the four ways to check if one was good or not was to see if it smelled like fresh rain recently fallen on blooming flowers. If it did, it was good to go. But if it reeked of carrion or other such nastiness, had eyes like a crocodile, solid hooves instead of cloven, and unsightly patches instead of speckles in its fur, you'd better turn and beat feet.

"All clear," Peter said. "Collect whatever wares you need from your shop and the eso-grohd will do the rest."

I bowed to the creature and gestured up at its back with a talon. "Hop on."

I gave Joshua a boost up on his new mount. He slowly, anxiously reached down toward me, and I stretched up my wing so that my longest pinion touched his fingers.

"I hope...we meet again, Prince," the carpenter murmured.

"Count on it." I smiled. Joshua kicked gently at the eso-grohd's flanks and was off galloping down the street toward his carpentry.

After that, we grouped together, cast one more glance around us at the Melancholy Bog's only town, and trekked solemnly out between the tree-trunk fence posts, now guarded by a cheery villager.

Peter turned our path around the fence, following its border until it cornered sharply north at a ninety-degree angle. Still griffins, our talons were once more eventually coated in slime and mud, but we were too happy that we were leaving to care.

Soon we found a path of hard-packed earth and gladly followed its narrow trail. The warriors were in their uniforms, having cast away their disguises. Smiles were on every face. To our right was a marsh of acid-hot bubbling ooze. To our left, a continuation of the rocky cliff side, now close enough to the ocean waters that we could hear the crashing breakers that I had learned to fly above.

Mariah had just returned from flying herself. On the wing, she was graceful and acrobatic in the way she rode the air currents and flitted into arcing turns. She was so fast–like a starling–that my gaze had still been fixed on where she had been before I found out where she had banked to.

One of the Amazons tentatively brought up our new clues, the disk and the lei, asking me for my thoughts as to what they meant. I was surprised that she wanted my opinion–and the others near her were giving me their rapt attention as well, as if expecting something wise to fall out of my mouth.

"Well, the flowers appear tropical," I mused, thinking of the dark, fragile blooms. "Wherever we end up, I think it'll at least be warm." A few of the warriors chuckled at that, and I asked Peter, who was walking ahead of me, what he thought the clues meant, but he said that we'd discuss that evening around the fire.

After that, the only sounds became our thudding steps and breathing. In the relative silence, my mind wandered. I had *helped* those people. They had *needed* me. It was like the feeling I'd gotten on the mountain after I'd saved Carl–that sense that I was capable of...more. The pride trying to blossom in my chest and fill me with warmth warred with my desire to return home as soon as I could, forget about all of these people, and help my loved ones. What if I *was* here for a reason?

What if I *could* make a difference?

I looked at the stumpy trees and their pale, flaky bark, and gazed up into the sky and its infinite realm, naked of clouds, letting my senses flood me with the pleasantness of the afternoon. I deserved a bit of a reprieve. This was a moment to just bask in victory.

A breeze seemed to whisper past my ear until I realized that it had not touched me, not riffled my fur or feathers. It came again as soon as my attention focused on that understanding, and this time I found out that, in fact, I was picking up conversation.

Automatically, my pointed ears swiveled back over my shoulders, and words became transparently clear from Kayle and Mariah, who were following near behind me.

"He's bold, I'll give him that," Kayle was musing grumpily. "Jonathan talks too much, and he's a smart-ass, but he's got spirit. Still, he has a long way to go before he's anything near King Brody's caliber."

"Jonathan did well today," Mariah chirped matter-of-factly. "He truly has the heart of a griffin–but he's impulsive, brash. My father would say he is an *imbécile*... But a *nice imbécile*."

"Hey!" I cried, whirling to face them; the squadron stopped marching, bemused. Mariah and Kayle were both surprised.

"Oh, don't act all innocent!" I snapped. "I heard you talking!"

"What are you talking about?" Kayle growled shortly. Mariah was frowning in a wounded way at me, shifting her weight from one talon to the other.

"I know you have your reasons for loathing my very existence, but that doesn't give you or Mariah the right to mock me! I was trying my best back there, and sure, I may not be as beasty commando as you guys, but I found the clue, didn't I? Twice! The second time after almost getting skewered by that gargoyle Ranker!" Everything tumbled out in short breaths. My sides heaved, my hackles a raised ridge on my spine.

Mariah sounded pitifully close to tears when she stammered, "We d-didn't...*say* anything, Jonathan..."

I was about to get even angrier until I saw that some of the soldiers behind them were nodding in agreement.

Peter shouldered me and said with concern, "They *didn't* speak, Jonathan."

I looked from one face to the next, wondering why they were lying, when Mariah gasped loudly and squealed, "Jonathan! You've found your power! You can read minds!"

Murmurs of awe burbled through the gathered. I was stunned into silence. Was it true? I suddenly remembered back to when I had been battling the Ranker, how I had known his every move before he had put it into action. How, right before he had died, I had heard two things at the same time, one of them being a fearful question: *Can he understand me?* And now that I thought of it, his mouth had not moved to form words as I had heard them.

"Here, what am I thinking?" Mariah asked excitedly. She laid her head on her talons with her rump in the air, like a puppy inviting someone to play, and screwed up her face. I listened, just as I would have in a verbal conversation, but...deeper, focusing on her only and shutting away everything else except her and my mind, striving to touch hers.

Snapping into focus, I heard her think, "Can you hear me?" I jumped a bit.

"You thought, 'can you hear me,' right?"

Mariah beamed. "Yeah!"

Kayle asked impishly, "What about me?"

I listened, hesitant, and then glared at him and repeated, "You said I can fight about as well as your grandmother's goldfish." Snorts of badly disguised snickers came from the soldiers shaking with mirth.

"Ooooh," Kayle said with indifference, faking being impressed. "Spot on."

Peter gave me a mini-noogie with the joint of his cream-colored wing, scrubbing loose a few of my head feathers. He laughed and teased, "Great, we'll never hear the end of it!" That provoked everyone into a fit of laughter, and I stood there fuming with irritation, wishing they could hear *my* thoughts...

That evening, just as the setting sun was throwing vivid colors into the sky from where it was sinking into the ocean, we left the Reekwood Swamp. Our dirt path slanted up-hill and became a sinuous carpet of pine needles and dried resin. More than one of us whooped, exultant at the change in scenery.

Peter stopped us when it became too dark for the squadron to see and pulled us aside into the trees. One of the sailors started a fire while Mariah rummaged in a bag for vittles, using some of her power to grow a basketful of squash and exotic fruits. It was to be a celebratory feast. Peter was confident that Garrett didn't yet know that one of his own was dead and assured us that the Rankers wouldn't be able to pick up our trail for a long while.

As the food was being cooked, and gentle laughter and content conversation sprinkled the air, I slipped away to watch the sunset from the cliffside.

Stars, so numerous that they looked like specks of sugar poured onto a black silken blanket, formed constellations known and unknown. Violet, indigo, scarlet, orange, and pale-pink clouds ringed the sun, seeming to set with it and leaving the sky above me open and cool.

I breathed in the smell of salt water and herbal pine needles, and tipped headfirst over the cliff. I opened my wings and felt the wind collect under them, boosting me up.

Despite the near-death experience and my confrontation with the gargoyle-Ranker of my mom's killer, today had been a wonderful day. I'd learned how to transform, how to use my power, defeated said-Ranker, and helped save a town from destruction. It felt good. It felt humbling.

The wind was rougher closer to the water. It sounded like a screaming crowd. The winds sent up from the tireless waves were warm as they mixed with the night's atmosphere. I abandoned all care and dove to just a few feet above the swells, dragging one talon through the surf.

From the depths right below me, a gray-yellow back emerged as sudden as lightning. Startled, I pulled up, flaring my tail fan, backpedaling my wings. I threatened to sink down, but with a few agitated flaps, I had reached a safe height.

Assuming the worst, I opened my mind, searching for the creature's thoughts. When I connected, I didn't hear words of malice or lust or evil; in fact, I didn't hear any words at all. Instead, I gathered... emotions. Simple, blunt feelings. There was joy for the water, love for the few other beings it swam with, and a curiosity and playfulness toward the big creature above it.

The animal and its friends circled back, and my sharp ears picked up clicks and tinny whistles. Locking on to their sleek backs below me, I finally discovered what they were, feeling embarrassed that I'd panicked: dolphins. Simple bottlenose dolphins.

One raised its head from the water, chattering with its cone-like, tooth-filled muzzle, and I heard it inviting me with its uncomplicated mind. *Come frisk with us, lion-bird*, it seemed to say, sending me mental images of the wild, beautiful, unpredictability of its ocean home: Water flat as glass beneath a hot sun, and tumultuous and steely like a living monster, churning under forks of lightning. The amazing creatures it had seen below and above the surface of its ocean home. Hidden ruins of ancient metropolises, the bones of ancient dreams, tucked away in undersea caverns. *Ride the swells and see what it means to be a dolphin.*

Excited, I shrieked piercingly and dove, soaring just above them, watching their stream-lined forms glitter in the setting sun. One shot from the water, spraying me with droplets, and then arced back beneath the ocean. They flew themselves, it seemed, through the water.

We frolicked together until the moon, on its way to thinning into a crescent, rose into the sky and turned the ocean black. Someone called my name from atop the cliff some ways behind me, and I shrieked a farewell to the dolphins, peeling back and up into the sky. They chirped their own goodbyes and disappeared into the depths of their land.

Peter was waiting for me on the ledge. I swung my body forward and landed, muscles weak from not touching earth. I breathlessly recanted what had taken place, licking the salt from my beak and straightening a few feathers on my wings so I could close them without discomfort. Peter wore a lofty half-smile, and when I'd finished, said, "It's experiences like those that make being here worthwhile. Come, food's ready."

As soon as everybody had dished up, all of us taking huge helpings, Peter turned the conversation toward the clues I had obtained.

We were all in human form, since it was easier and less uncouth to eat our bread and salted meat with teeth and fingers. And, Peter informed me, griffins ate more, so we'd be less of a strain on resources if we dined as humans. I reached into my sweatshirt pocket, mouth full, and held up the lei and ninja star on one finger. Wiping my mouth on my sleeve, I leaned across Marcus and handed Peter the items.

He set aside his plate and observed the lei's flowers first. He smelled them, nodding appreciatively. He fingered the soft indigo petals that had not yet turned dead and limp, and counted the long red stamen sprouting from the blooms' black centers. Peter's hands moved to the metal disk, reflecting the firelight almost painfully in its shiny surface.

I watched him for a while, then, impatient, I asked, "What's it mean? Where are we going next?"

Passing the clues around, Peter gave his conclusion. "These things came from the Tahtltiki's beach."

We all released our bated breath, glad that we weren't to be heading to another swamp. The Tahtltiki territory extended from the coast up into a lush jungle–I remembered from my reading that almost every plant native to the area had some good or bad purpose. Because of the various springs and rivers threading from the melting mountain snows to the ocean, everything flourished. It would be a lovely contrast to the bog.

"The razor disk was made by the Tahtltiki warriors from the minerals they mine in their caves. They are used to bring down the ferocious jungle dogs that dwell in their territory. The women make the leis and send them to all major cities of the land, which, in return, send food and building materials. Depending on what sort of flower is used for the lei, the lei has a different purpose or meaning. These dark blooms are a symbol of death. Someone of importance must have passed."

Mariah spoke up, eyes misty with thought. "They love to sing and have dances."

"They're very festive in custom, apparel, and manner of living." Peter nodded. "The rest we'll find out when we get there."

"Why would the Rankers want to go there? It's not a place of nightmares?" Kayle mused aloud.

"To hurt us," I said. Everyone looked at me, as surprised as I was by the confidence in my tone. "To hurt *me*. It's two birds with one stone: they get their reinforcements and, on the way, take out some of my allies and supporters."

"That's what *would* have happened," Peter said. "But not now that *we* have the clues."

"That's right," one of the marines said.

"Garrett's going to be pissed when he finds out what we did," I said to Peter. Even though I meant it seriously, a grin pulled up one corner of my mouth. We had dealt Garrett a crippling blow. I would relish that for weeks. A few of the soldiers, even Kayle, chuckled.

"He won't find out for a while. The only one who pieced together what had happened was the gargoyle Ranker, and only after the werewolf summoned him to the swamp. Now that you've defeated the gargoyle and healed the swamp, it's unlikely that Garrett will even know that we have his clues until it's too late."

"I hope you're right," I said. Something else was eating at me, something that the Ranker had said, but I couldn't remember it at the moment. I forced myself to relax and, for the moment at least, enjoy our hard-won victory.

CHAPTER TWENTY-SIX:
BONDING TIME WITH KAYLE

I was one of the last to fall asleep. My head rested in my hands, and I stared through the tree canopy at the stars, lying on my back and feeling infinitesimally small. My scalp had begun to prickle and itch more lately, unaccustomed to the scruffy length of my hair. I could feel how disheveled it was becoming with my fingers. I wondered what Nikki would think of it.

Homesick and lonesome, still struggling to remember what the Ranker had said that was nagging at me so much, I rolled to one side, the pine-needle-packed ground awkward against the alignment of my spine and hip. In truth, I was probably the loneliest guy there. The squadron all knew each other, as did Peter, Kayle, and Mariah. I still had stubborn questions that wouldn't go unanswered and had to take on my new responsibilities and knowledge with a mute acceptance. No one was there to have empathy with me, to sit down with me and just listen to what I had to say. Tomorrow I would have to start getting to know everyone better, especially if my very life was to be held, at times, in their hands. I needed to have friends—not just allies. I imagined myself as a fluffy bunny cupped in Kayle's palms and then him crushing me with a dark smile.

The dying fire at my feet crackled, and sparks burst upward on a path of smoke. Peeking down, I saw Kayle poking at the fire's ashes with a stick, stirring them around blankly. *Speak of the devil...I may as well start with him.* I had something I wanted to tell him anyway. Kayle nudged a bag out of his way with his foot and sat down. He stared into the flames, teasing them, and took a deep breath through his nose.

Clearing my throat, I sat up slowly as if just awakened, and stretched. Kayle shifted his gaze to me, blinked languorously, and resumed his scrutiny of the fire.

I approached him in the same manner one might approach a stallion that they're afraid will kick. He was acting totally oblivious to me, even as I sat down beside him. I watched the stick slowly get licked up by flame, its tip consumed by the satiny curtains of orange and yellow.

Reaching out one hand, Kayle made intricate motions, almost as if trying to pop his knuckles or stretch out sore joints. But in the current of fire above his stick, there appeared a break in the ceaseless pattern of swaying flames. The unearthly reddish light flickered, died. Smaller tongues briefly blazed to life, only to be followed by another form.

Eventually, Kayle had formed a griffin head above the burning stick, facing us. With one opening and closing of his thumb and forefinger, the griffin spread wide its beak, and shut it again. Dissolving this picture, Kayle started on another, this one becoming a shamrock. The four petals looked as if burning.

"Whoa, that's cool!" I whispered reverently. Kayle shrugged and curled his hand back around the stick with the other. Studying him out of the corner of my vision, I spoke awkwardly, hating feeling like the underdog. "I, um, I actually think I have you to thank for me finding out how to morph the right way and use my power today."

"Oh, really?" Kayle murmured mildly.

Clenching my fists and taking a breath, I went on.

"When you burst into the inn, and you were on fire, you said, 'Good morning, sunshine,' remember?"

"Barely," Kayle said.

I shuffled a bit and continued in a lower voice. "My mom used to tell me that in the mornings. It's one of the last things I remember her saying before...she..."

Kayle interrupted me, and I was surprised to see sympathy in his eyes, which were finally focused on me.

"Aye. I know. Peter told us all about you and your...mother." He briefly looked away, as if finding the subject awkward.

I tried to act like I wasn't uncomfortable.

"Yeah, so...thanks."

"You're very welcome, Jonathan," Kayle replied seriously.

Not waiting until my courage gave out, I blurted, "Why do you hate me, Kayle? What have I ever done to you?"

Kayle actually laughed a real laugh: the sound was faltering, short, as if it weren't made often.

"I don't hate you. I just like things quick and efficient. When you came, it's like we had to start all over again, had to school a wee, naïve babby." His face turned hard. "It's just the way I am."

"What do you mean?" I pressed.

Kayle hunched forward, closer to the fire. The flames were mirrored in his vacant, glassy eyes, dancing madly.

"I was born into a wealthy family a few leagues from Belfast. We had maids, stewards, an ancient butler... They all loved me and my parents and my older brother, Shane. One of the maids, Cynthia, was always caught sneaking Shane new treats from the kitchen. She was an excellent cook. And once, I saw the pair of them carving their initials into an old tree on the grounds. They loved each other. Dad sort of frowned upon Shane for falling for a maid, but the more my father saw of Cynthia, the more he gave in. No one could dislike her for long. At first, I hated her for stealing Shane from me, but as I learned to entertain myself, I came to sort of like being alone."

Kayle lay back, using the bag beside him as a pillow. I couldn't relax; I had a feeling that something bad was going to happen in Kayle's narrative. He was speaking too simply, too...past tense for a happy ending.

I turned around to face him better, curling my legs into a criss-cross and leaning forward. He spoke again, and I shut my eyes, envisioning his words.

"Our manor was big enough to get lost in. So big that Mother, for the first long years of my life, restricted me to my bedroom and the lower floors—so that she knew where I was at all times. We had expensive furniture, only the finest pure-bred Connemara ponies, and acres of beautiful, rolling green fields. No matter how hard she tried, Mother couldn't keep us from exploring the grounds. It was there I spent most of my time trying to find a banshee or a leprechaun.

"For my eighth birthday, Mother bought me a piano, imported straight from India with bright-white ivory keys. It was one of her attempts to culture me. But my brother and I were wild children. It was in our blood to climb trees, chase foxes, and wrestle in the dirt."

I grinned, but Kayle took a deep breath, shivered, and went on, face contorted into a mask of disgust and anger.

"When I was twelve, an anti-Irish British mob came. They always had their marches in town. If anyone Irish was caught outside, they'd have their arses kicked to near death and then be dumped on the side of the street for the family to find later. But on this one day, when my brother was in America looking for a university to go to so he could make connections, get a job in life that would support Cynthia and him, the British came through the fields past *our* house.

"It was evening, and I was out on the lane trying to find a lizard to bring home. I heard many loud footsteps coming my way, and around the bend came a group of men. They were halted by a guy in front, who was smiling down at me.

"'Wot we got 'ere chaps? A li'l lucky boy?' I hadn't done anything to them, didn't know who they were, but they quickly surrounded me and began to beat me. I was shoved to the ground and got kicked in the face, and the next thing I knew, I was opening my eyes to a starry night, lying bruised, bleeding...half-alive in the ditch right beside a dead rabbit. I had foolish revenge on my mind, and followed the lane to my house, only to see that it was on fire and ringed by the same mob."

"No," I gasped. Kayle didn't respond–didn't even look at me.

"Screaming in fear, worried for my family, I tore at the men, pelting them with rocks. One of them, he was plastered, simply picked me up and tossed me into the fire too."

I recoiled, but Kayle didn't acknowledge it and went on unemotionally.

"I didn't feel anything; there was no pain. But I saw pictures, colors, the fire dancing around me and licking up past me into the exposed sky. Smoke filled me; timber crashed around my fallen body, but I couldn't move.

"I beheld the sight of a pure-white griffin. A pillar of fire came from his beak and flew right at me. I looked away, ready to feel it hit my face, but it never did. I opened my eyes to my destroyed home and discovered that life had returned to my legs. The fire had gone out. I climbed outside over timbers and ash and ran as fast as I could toward the city, choosing not to think about the vision I'd had. It had to have been brought on by the fumes of the smoke, right? It's what I told myself."

"And you weren't hurt at all?" I asked, incredulous.

Kayle shook his head. "Not a burn on me."

"What did you do in the city? Did you alert the police?"

"Oh, I meant to. I reached the city in the late morn, exhausted, mad with grief, and followed a crowd down the main street where they were gathering to watch a parade. But you know what? The parade was led by a bunch of bloody Britons! The same sort that had killed my family with fire. I had the bloodlust. I tried to get to them so that I could rip them apart with my own two hands, but a group of people beat me to it. I was stunned, frozen in place, watching them.

"Someone shouted, *'Erin go bragh!'* and then the British were pelted with bottles and stones that had the names of people written on them. As soon as the coppers came, the pack had vanished. But so had I.

"I had followed them down an alley, told them I wanted to join, but many were dubious. They said I was too young and soft, that I couldn't understand what they were fighting for. But a woman stepped out of the crowd and convinced them that I did. It was Cynthia. She was the only one beside me to have escaped the burning of my house."

"What about your family? Your fortune?" I couldn't imagine what it had to have been like for Kayle, leaving behind the ashes of what had been a wonderful life to run and gun with an embittered, violent fringe group.

"It was all smoke, Jon," Kayle said. He didn't sound angry–just tired. "Smoke and char. There was nothing there for me anymore, no bodies to bury, nothing for me to reclaim."

"But you had to have at least an inheritance or something–"

"I didn't give a shite about money. What I cared about was causing the same pain I'd felt. My world had burned–and I just wanted to see the rest of it burn too."

I studied him quietly for a moment, feeling for the first time like I really, truly understood him. We had more in common than I could have ever imagined.

"So...did Cynthia take you in?" I probed.

"They all did. I grew up under their care. An orphan adopted into a strange new family of sorts. When I needed food or shelter, I found an Irish family that supported our cause and stayed the night in return for the promise to 'keep up the good work.'" He added in a mumble, "Whatever that was.

"One day, Cynthia told me of a planned raid on a new British police station downtown. I met the rest of the gang, and we joined together, setting fire to the place and breaking the windows. Little did we know that the police had snuck out a back way and began firing at us.

"One had Cynthia in his sights and was ready to pull the trigger, but I shoved her away, told her to run. The bullet intended for her hit me instead. I felt it slice between two of my upper ribs, punch through something inside me, and exit out my chest. I remember a shock wave of pain, my legs giving out. I remember staring at the blood on my hands, and I couldn't believe that it was mine. The noise died. My sight winked away. The last thing I saw was the fire eating up the police station, clawing at the sky. And I woke up here.

"At first, I didn't believe what I was told. Just as you didn't. I saw myself as a nobody, with no great purpose or destiny. I was perfectly fine with doing what I had surely been intended to do and dying. But I met Mariah, and, uh, she knocked some sense into me." Kayle looked over at Mariah's sleeping form and smiled softly. My own heart was aching as if run through with a sword.

"Gosh, Kayle...I had no idea..." I started meekly. "You had–*have*–every right to–"

"I don't *hate* anybody. Not really anymore. Except the darkness in people's hearts. The Rankers. They're the ones that started everything, that really ruined my life," Kayle said.

"I agree." I nodded gravely, thinking of Garrett and feeling fury course through me. "Thanks for telling me your story."

At first, Kayle moved as if he might pat my back, but he stopped and only half-heartedly put on a moody scowl.

"Ah, you would have read my mind eventually anyway."

I grinned, feeling happier than I had in a long while. "How long did it take you to master your ability?"

"Well, at first all I could manage was a few fireballs," Kayle replied. He gave a casual snap of his fingers and the fire sparked. "Then, with practice, I could start making–"

I sat bolt upright with a sharp gasp, making Kayle jump and roll up onto his knees with fluid, silent grace. "What?" he gasped, looking wildly around us.

"Master," I said. The conversation the werewolf and the gargoyle had had came flooding back into my brain. "Master. Master–Liege Master! Who is the Liege Master?" I spun on the spot to stare at Kayle. I must have looked crazy because he leaned away from me, his mouth working but nothing coming out.

One of the Samurai nearby grumbled and sat up, rubbing his eyes. Others had started to stir awake, muttering about the racket I was making.

"Peter!" I said, half-crawling half-running over to where he had rolled onto his back, massaging his face. "Peter, listen, the Ranker! He said something to the werewolf about a Liege Master!"

"What?" Mariah croaked nearby, one of her eyes barely squinted open. "What are you talking about, Jonathan?"

"They have a damn master!" I cried, striking the ground with a fist. A bird sleeping in a nearby tree gave an alarmed caw and flapped off, startled by my shout. Silence fell heavily around us. I took a breath, scouring my memory.

"The Ranker wanted to kill me...but the werewolf said that would go against the Liege Master's plan."

Peter frowned down at his legs. The fire shone off of his silver eyes and there was something sharp about them, as if he were searching through his memories, too.

After a long minute, he said, slowly and carefully, "King Brody discovered very little about the so-called Liege Master before he died. All of our information indicates that it's an idol or god that the Rankers worship."

"I thought *Garrett* was their leader?" I asked.

"He *is*." Peter held one hand up toward me as if to calm me down. "The Rankers have only ever attacked under the command of a series of generals. King Brody, in all of his years fighting them, never saw hide nor hair of any kind of Ranker king or master. There's never been one in our centuries of combat battling nightmares."

"But it has a plan," I said, an edge to my voice. "Their Liege Master has a plan, they said."

"And we are disrupting it," Peter said, "Right now, by taking their clues. Even if this...'Liege Master' is calling the shots, it's Garrett who is carrying out his plans, and it's Garrett we need to destroy. Our God is more powerful than theirs, and our prince too, once he's been trained up a bit more. You'll see. We have the upper hand. We're doing okay, Jonathan." He tapped my arm with his fist reassuringly, but now the wheels were turning in my brain. There was something more...one more connection I needed to make.

"Prince," I said. I felt the eyes of the squadron fixed on me. Kayle's eyes were intense and hawk-like, as if some of my intuitive fear had passed over to him.

"What is it, son?" Peter urged.

"'He's appointed Garrett to take his place,'" I repeated. "That's what the werewolf said..." I had assumed at the time that the werewolf had meant the Liege Master's place, or that Garrett had taken his place in some kind of position in readiness for the next phase of the Rankers' plans. But now that I thought about it, the inflection had been all wrong.

He's appointed Garrett to take his place. The werewolf had been trying to prevent the gargoyle from killing me because it would interfere with the Liege Master's plans for Garrett to take...

"That's it," I said. It felt like I'd been punched in the gut—my voice came out in a weak wheeze.

"What?" Peter leaned forward and some of the soldiers nearby gathered closer with concern as my eyes flickered white with fear and shock.

"That's why Garrett's been watching me, that's what his plans are. He's going to take *my* place." I looked up at Peter, locking eyes with him and seeing the truth dawn in his mind too. "Garrett is going to try and take my place as King of the Land of Dreams."

Epilogue

LEAGUES DISTANT, IN A HOUSE IN A TREE

The old man gazed up at the gigantic wheel suspended on the wall of his hut. The sun was just rising, peeking in through the windows, illuminating the thick wooden wall behind him and the painted scrawls upon it. When daylight had illuminated enough of the wheel for him to identify the minuscule details carved into it by ancient, long-dead hands, he frowned and leaned closer, ready to study the fine marks.

He saw a broken crown resting in a pool of blood–but a bright, shining one suspended in the air above it. Seven shadows surrounded by seven flaming torches. Yes, the old prophecy–it had broken with King Brody, its mysterious verses dying with him.

The old man glanced at the image of the floating crown again. Or had it? Had the old prophecy, the one discovered years upon years before and lost to memory until the arrival and ascension of King Brody, actually been referring to someone else? Eagerly, hungrily, the man shuffled closer, reaching up to touch one of the sections of the wheel but stopping himself a few inches from the heavily lined painted and carved bark. What else was there? What was to come? How did the future read?

He saw a crimson fang, a grave, a golden feather, a fiery sword, sigils and symbols that he didn't understand, more and more the longer he looked.

No!

Sharply, the man pulled his eyes away. No, he could not look further—it was not his business, and reading the powerful prophecies of the future could do worse than destroy him as it had so many other foolish seers. He heard the young Tahtltiki chieftain stirring above him as the boy awakened in a room on an upper floor of the hut and he sighed gratefully.

Other duties called...and he had much preparing to do before the arrival of Great Prince Jonathan.

ABOUT THE AUTHOR

Alesa Corrin first realized she wanted to be a writer when she was in middle school. The stress, peer pressure, her mother's battle with cancer, and an impending major back surgery in the eighth grade drove her desperately to seek a distraction. Writing became an escape for her, and she soon found that she wanted to create that escape for others, creating realms of adventure through her stories.

To Corrin, writing is not merely a means of taking others through a looking-glass into a fantastic world of heroes, villains, joy, and beauty, but a mirror through which we can examine ourselves and discover our own shortcomings and strengths. She hopes that her readers are carried away on a grand adventure, driven to reflect on their own identities and, ultimately, that her book gives readers hope, empathy, and compassion for the souls around them.

Jonathan the Griffin Prince

Made in United States
Troutdale, OR
02/17/2024

17520140R10206